Hersband

Copyright © 2006 Christina Batista
All rights reserved.
ISBN: 1-4196-5105-6
ISBN-13: 978-1419651052
Library of Congress Control Number: 2006909255

Visit www.booksurge.com to order additional copies.

CHRISTINA BATISTA

HERSBAND

2006

Hersband

CHAPTER ONE

Brooklyn Hospital, March 24, 1961, 10:20 am, the obstetrician proudly announced, "It's a girl!" Dena Vargas had entered this lovely world. Dena was the youngest of three. Her brother, Mike, was older by nine years, and her sister, Nancy, was older by two. Dena's mother, Dolores, thanked God for her healthy baby girl. Her father, Timo, on the other hand, had been praying for a son. But guess what? That's exactly what he got!

The Vargases were a typical Latino family. Timo had been born and raised in Brooklyn. His father, whom he had never known, was from Cuba, and his mother was from Curaçao. Timo was a short, handsome man with wavy jet-black hair, black eyes, and a brown complexion, and he was built like a Marine, thick. Actually, he *was* a Marine. His arms were three sizes bigger than those of the average man.

Dolores was an attractive, shy woman with a brown complexion and hair not as straight as most. You know, the kind of Puerto Rican who still needed a permanent. And her eyes...her eyes were ocean green, a feature that blended nicely with her complexion. Dolores had not come to America until she was seven. Her mother, Rosa, had come to New York and given birth to Dolores, then sent her back to Puerto Rico until she and her husband, Gregory, could save enough money to send for her, seven years later.

Mike, Dena's brother, with his light complexion, curly hair, and light brown eyes, favored his mother's side. Nancy, on the other hand, favored her father's side. Slightly darker than Mike and Dena, with black eyes and straight hair, she looked more Native American than Puerto Rican. Beautiful in her own way, Dena was a combination plate, with light skin, curly hair, thick eyebrows and eyelashes, and oh, green eyes.

Dena had all those nice qualities and the face to match. She had the kind of beauty you could not help but be impolite about. You could not take your eyes off her until you had absorbed all of her beauty. When Dolores' friends or neighbors came by the house, they would always comment on how cute Nancy and Dena were. But they were so different in their own ways, and had totally opposite characters. Nancy was so ladylike in her sunflower dress, sitting quietly on the sofa, playing with her dolls. Dena, on the other hand, would be in a pair of ripped jeans, her hair only partially combed, lying on the floor, playing with a toy truck. What a difference!

Dolores would always explain to her friends how she tried to get Dena to put on a dress, but to no avail. Regardless, the neighbors would always try to squeeze Dena's cheeks. But Dena did not have a clue about her beauty and did not want to know how cute she was. "Boys aren't cute," she always thought. She never wanted to wear a dress, have her hair combed, or have her face washed if she could help it. Give Dena a pair of Wrangler jeans, a striped tee shirt, and sneakers, and she was content.

The Albany Projects in the Bedford Stuyvesant neighborhood in Brooklyn was a safe and decent place to play and grow up in during the 1960s. Nancy and Dena had an average childhood. When Nancy was five years old and Dena was three,

Nancy went to pre-kindergarten right across the street. Dolores always felt so terrible because she would have to awaken Dena on cold, blustery mornings and get her dressed so they could escort Nancy to her school, just to bring her right back and put her back in bed.

One morning, when Dena had a slight temperature, Dolores decided to let Dena sleep and run across the street to Nancy's school, drop her off, and come right back.

But as soon as Dolores locked the front door, Dena awoke. An eerie feeling came over her and she called for her mother. No answer. She looked up and down the hallway and realized she was alone in the apartment. She decided to go look for her mother.

She went to find her clothes. Dressing herself, she put her shoes on the wrong feet and buttoned her coat unevenly. Dena then unlocked the door and left the apartment. She made it down to the first floor lobby and was headed for the main door when a man approached her and said, "Little girl, where's your mommy?"

Dena started to cry, saying, "I don't know. I am looking for her."

The man took her hand and said, "Let's go find your mommy." But the stranger started to walk Dena in the opposite direction, back toward the elevators. "What is your name, little girl?" the stranger asked.

"I want my mommy!" Dena cried out. "Do you know where she is?"

"Yes," the man replied. "Do you like candy? I have—"

At that moment Dolores entered the lobby and recognized Dena's winter coat from behind and shouted, "Oh my God, that's my daughter!"

At the same time, Dena yelled, "Mommy!" and ran toward her.

The stranger handed her over willingly, saying, "I heard a child crying and saw her wandering in the lobby. I was wondering where her parents were. I was going to call the police."

Dolores blessed and thanked the man, and said to herself, "From this time on, Dena, rain, sleet, or snow, you are coming with us."

Dolores always felt that Dena had an angel watching over her, and maybe it was true. One summer when Dena was around five years old, her parents, Nancy, and their cousin, Ellen, went to Red Hook Pool in downtown Brooklyn. Ellen was a teenager and always came over to help Dolores with the girls, doing everything from brushing their hair to babysitting. It seemed Ellen enjoyed helping out, like she was preparing herself for motherhood. While Timo, Dolores, and Ellen sat by the poolside, Nancy and Dena played in the water.

Dena stood by the pool, watching Nancy splashing from afar, and decided to sneak up and surprise her. When she jumped in from the other side of the pool, she started to sink, all the way to the bottom, not realizing that she had jumped into the seven-foot section. At five years old, Dena did not know how to swim yet. From a distance she could see the chrome ladder leading to life, so she waved her open hands and kicked her feet with all her might for as long as she could, but that just made her sink faster. After what seemed like an eternity, she was exhausted and stopped, just as someone grabbed her little body from behind and pulled her up to the surface. It was her dad, Timo, her hero, who had now given her life twice. Afterwards, Timo taught Nancy and Dena how to swim.

One morning, Nancy and Dena were getting ready for

elementary school. Timo and Dolores worked extra jobs and hours to send their kids to Catholic school. Dena woke up that cold winter morning thinking about the long walk she and Nancy had to travel just to get to school, at least seven blocks, when she threw her head back down on the pillow and went back to sleep. Dolores came back into the girls' bedroom and woke Dena up again. She lifted her head to see Nancy almost dressed. Nancy had always liked school. "At least one of us does," Dena thought. Dolores did not have time to make the girls lunches, so she gave them both a quarter and told them to buy themselves a pizza and a soda.

"Boy," Dena thought out loud, "what a treat. Thank you, Mom," she said as she jumped out of bed. For Dena, it was definitely worth going to school to get pizza and soda.

Dena was shy and quiet in the first grade at Saint Matthews. But by the second grade, you could not get her to shut up, or keep her out of trouble. You see, in Catholic school back in the day, all your classmates were the same from the first grade on until you graduated high school, so Dena only needed one year to get to know her fellow classmates. Dena really didn't care much for school, except for at the beginning of the term when all her books, her book bag, and pencils were new, and then at the end of the term. But in between, no. However, she did like gym, playing in the schoolyard at lunchtime, and being on the track team.

In New York City, Saint Matthews and Holy Rosary were the top competitors in sports. Both schools would take turns, year after year, being number one. Never cared for one another because of it. Dena was the starter of a four-girl baton relay race team and loved it. Dena and her teammates were all very close and they always watched out for one another. She respected and loved her coaches, Mr. Jones and Mr. Wilson. She took it personally when one of her teammates was jumped in the park bathroom and hurt pretty bad by some of the girls from Holy Rosary School. Mr. Jones begged the team not to retaliate. He just encouraged the team to do their best on the track field. "That will be payback enough," he added. He also told the team to go to the bathroom in groups from then on.

Dena's team had one of the best records in Catholic school history. Dena was the second fastest of the four team runners. Cherrie was the fastest. So Coach Jones put Dena as the starter of the race to get a good jump on the race. This way, just in case Dena or one of the other girls fumbled or dropped the baton, Cherrie, being the fastest, would have a chance to catch up to the other runners or even pass them and win the race, which is what happened many times. Coach Jones knew what he was doing.

Dena was sad when they announced that Saint Matthews would be closing due to lack of funding. She would not have the chance to graduate from the eighth grade, because she was only in the sixth grade, but Nancy would. "Oh well," she said to herself, "let's go to this last class trip in style." It was the biggest class trip Saint Matthews had ever had, for all the students from the first grade to the eighth grade. It was a fun but sad class trip, knowing this was going to be the last.

"Maybe we'll never see each other again," one student remarked.

Another student from the eighth grade replied, "Then we all better say our goodbyes now, just in case." Every chance Nancy and Dena had, they hugged their fellow classmates, crying, and saying, "May peace be with you."

Throughout childhood Dena remained a tomboy, playing

football, baseball, and any other sports involving boys. She fell in love with her sixth-grade teacher. Not all teachers in Catholic school were nuns; some were regular, conventionally trained teachers. In general, while all the other girls were in love with the Jackson Five and the Osmond Brothers, Dena was in love with Emma Peel from the television adventure series, "The Avengers," Diane Carroll from "Julia," and Laurie from "The Partridge Family," and she admired and wanted to be just like the cartoon character, Speed Racer, and Major Don West from "Lost in Space." Dena thought Major West was so cool in his silver space suit and black high-top boots. He always wanted to kick the aliens' and Dr. Zachary Smith's ass.

But Dena never felt she was a true tomboy until she received her first set of stitches—ten stitches on the forehead, inside and out. Dolores had always told Nancy and Dena, "No playing in the house. The furniture is not going to rearrange itself because you kids are playing in the house." As Dolores was rushing Dena to the emergency room, she said, "Maybe now you girls will listen to me."

After receiving her stitches, Dena told herself, "Now I'm a real tomboy."

One Christmas while all the other kids received their new Apollo bicycles, Dena got her Christmas wish: a hard-to-find, unique Chopper bicycle. Dena had managed to get all C's that winter in exchange for the bicycle. It was candy apple red. Everyone wanted one. The price was out of reach for most parents. She could have traded her Chopper bike for three Apollo bicycles.

One afternoon when Dena wasn't doing so well in school academically, she arrived home from school to find her bicycle missing. She begged her parents for information on the whereabouts of her favorite pastime until her father, Timo, said, "I took it outside and left it there."

"Why couldn't you just bring it to work or something until my grades improved?" Dena demanded while running outside the house to try to retrieve it. Dena stayed outside for hours trying to locate her Chopper bicycle. She cried when she realized her bike was gone. She asked herself how her father could be so cruel. She swore that if she could help it, she would never have anyone buy her a gift again, just so they could take it away.

Aside from Dena not doing well in school, Timo had a real problem with her playing with boys. Dena would explain to Timo, "Dad, when I play punch ball or even softball, it's hard to find any girls that play those sports. So I have to play with boys. Why can't I play sports with boys?"

Timo would respond by saying, "Because I said so, that's why. I'm the father here."

Dena would disregard his rule and play with boys anyway. The only problem was sometimes she would lose track of time and Timo would come home from work and catch her. He would stand there and call over to her to "come here!" Dena would have to quit playing, get her stuff, and go upstairs with her father. Timo would punish her by not letting her go back outside, even on a hot summer day. Dena would beg Timo and Dolores to please let her go back outside, which they would, but not until hours later. After a while, no one wanted to play with her, no matter how good she was—and Dena was good, better than most of the boys—because they were afraid of losing her in mid-game.

After Saint Matthews closed, Dena went from school to

school; first to Saint Gabriel, then P.S. 218. As Dena grew older, she spent most of her time on the handball and basketball courts, and following behind Nancy and her teenage crowd. Dena wanted to learn. The teenage crowd spoke about some very interesting topics. They covered all the bases.

Dena would just sit on the bench with them or slowly walk behind them, listening carefully. Nancy and her friends would always scream at her to get lost and hang out with her own friends. She would respond by saying, "I'm not following you. I'm just walking in the same direction." They finally got tired of yelling at Dena and just accepted her being around, at least outdoors. Whenever they went into someone's house, however, they would close the door before she entered.

By hanging out with an older crowd, by the time Dena was around thirteen, she had seen just about all of the hit movies the seventies had to offer. Forty-Second Street back in the day had mainly all X-rated movie theaters, but one or two theaters had the latest hit movies. Dena saw "Claudine," "Johnny Tough," "The Monkey Hustle," "Coffee," "The Mack," and Dena's favorite, "Truck Turner." She fell in love with Truck Turner's girlfriend in the movie, Annazette Chase. Most all these movies were rated R because of profanity, a breast exposed here or there. But that's what teenagers lived for, at least teenagers who were seventeen and eighteen; though not Dena, who was just thirteen.

Nancy's crew would all get together and go to the movies as a group, about eight or nine of them. Forty-Second Street was not a decent place for a teenage girl. All the teenage boys would look out for the girls in the group, even Dena. When the crew got to the movie theater, the ticket seller would not see adolescents, just a group of kids and dollar signs. He would not ask them for identification, just shout "Two dollars!" Someone would always purchase Dena's ticket, because even though she was thirteen, she looked about ten. In this way, she even saw the uncut version of "Caligula." How else was she going learn about the birds and the bees?

In junior high school Dena kept the fact that she was gay hidden, just admiring women from afar, fantasizing a lot, and waiting for that special day and that special woman. She had close friends who she thought had an idea about her being gay. But they never asked, and that was cool. Dena would never forget the first time she kissed a girl. One day a friend of hers named Rae came to her house with this cute little kitten. She fell in love with the kitten and asked if she could have it. Rae, seeing how happy she was with the kitten, gave it to her. Dena held the kitten in the air and said to Rae, "Thank you so much. I'm going to name him Diego."

"There's other ways to thank me, you know," Rae suggested.

Dena looked at her and said, "Oh, yeah? How?"

Rae just pointed to her lips and said, "You could thank me here."

Dena was totally shocked, because her friends were just her friends, and she would never disrespect her friends. Dena licked her lips and walked over to Rae and gave her a nice long kiss on her lips, and that was it. It wasn't much of a kiss, but to Dena it was spectacular.

Kelso was a tomboy like Dena. She was a cute little replica of Dena with curly hair and sparkling eyes. They were starting to become best friends. But this did not last for long. One afternoon, Dena and Kelso decided to borrow two cigarettes from Kelso's mother. Dena and Kelso went in the closet and closed the door. After about one minute, Kelso's brother quickly opened the door and shouted, "Got you!" He was always trying to catch them at anything. He was such a tattletale. They knew they were busted, and begged Jeff not to tell, but Jeff told his mother anyway.

Hours later while Dena was sitting in the living room watching television, the doorbell rang. It was Kelso's mother asking to speak to Dena's parents. Dena thought to herself, "Kelso's brother is a snitch. I'm not going to be friends with him anymore." When she tried to leave the living room, Timo ordered her not to move, knowing damn well this concerned her.

Kelso's mom went on about "You two lesbians don't know what it's like to be gay. Wait until you come across a real lesbian."

Dena thought to herself, "I can't wait." She wondered if she should correct Kelso's mother and tell her that they had just been smoking cigarettes, not fucking. Then she thought, "Which is worse? They're both bad in their eyes." So she decided to let her finish her lecture and go on thinking she and Kelso were lovers. "It sounds better," Dena thought.

After Kelso's mother finished her speech, she left the apartment. Dena thought she was in for another lecture from Timo and Dolores. Instead, they just shook their heads and sent Dena to her room. Kelso and Dena were kept apart from each other after that. Dena felt it was wrong of them to keep her and Kelso apart, but what could she do? Shortly after that incident, Kelso and her family moved to Long Island.

CHAPTER TWO

At about the same time, Dena's father and mother began having problems. Then Mike, who did not get along with his father, joined the Navy right after high school and moved out. Then, to top things off, something even worse happened. One morning, after Dolores and Timo had already left for work and Nancy and Dena were getting ready for school, Nancy told Dena, "I'm not going to school today. I'm going to a hooky party."

"Can I come?" Dena asked.

"You're too young," Nancy quickly replied. "You can't hang with the big boys."

Still, Dena asked Nancy the who, what, and where question.

"It's in the next building." Nancy informed her. "Shawn is giving it."

Dena knew Nancy had a crush on Shawn, so she told her to be careful as she watched her head out the door. Then she continued getting ready for school. She looked at the clock. She had plenty of time to get ready for school, so she took her time. About forty-five minutes later, she heard the front door open. Dena peeked into the corridor to see who was entering the apartment. It was Nancy.

"Did you forget something, or did you change your mind and decide to do the right thing and take your ass to school?" Dena laughed. Then she noticed there was something wrong with Nancy. She was talking out loud like she was having a conversation, but not with Dena. Dena put both hands on Nancy's shoulders and grabbed her and shook her, thinking she was playing. Then she looked straight into her eyes and said, "Nancy, what's wrong?"

Nancy looked right through her as if she wasn't even there and started screaming senseless words. Dena got scared and asked her if she had taken any drugs at the hooky party. Again to no avail. She could not control Nancy. She looked for her parents' work numbers, but could not find them anywhere. She tried to get Nancy to lie down, but that didn't work. She ran water over her head in the shower, but nothing worked. So she grabbed her and took her to Dolores' workplace, which was closer than Timo's. Still, it was a long train ride away.

Dena told her mother the truth, and her mother called Timo and asked him to come and pick them all up. "I'll explain to you later," Dolores told Timo. Dolores and Dena explained to Timo the story of what had happened to Nancy on the way to the hospital. Dena was so scared she was crying.

At the hospital, they registered Nancy and sat waiting for hours before they actually saw a doctor. Dena sat at one end of the waiting room watching Timo walking in circles. Dolores sat with Nancy, holding her and comforting her while she rocked back and forth in her chair and talked to herself. The doctor looked serious when he said he had decided to keep Nancy overnight for observation. The family could not believe their ears. They just thought she would be medicated or sedated, then sent home. Instead, Nancy was admitted to the psychiatric ward at Kings County Hospital.

On the drive home from the hospital everyone was silent without Nancy there. No one could believe what had happened. For the first time in Dena's life she witnessed her father openly crying. Dolores broke the silence and said, "We have to pray, and put everything in God's hands." Dena kept quiet, thinking about the two men who had escorted Nancy away, in their white double-breasted hospital uniforms. It had looked like a scene from the fucking "Twilight Zone." Damn, Nancy must have been so scared. The scene played over and over in Dena's head that night until, finally, she cried herself to sleep.

Dena and Dolores went to see Nancy at least two or three times a week after that. Besides school and a part-time job, Dena made it her business to go see Nancy. She hated Nancy's new living conditions in Kings County Hospital. It was like a dungeon. Locks on every door. You had to wait for a turn-key just to go to the bathroom. The hospital was exceptionally clean except for the windows. They were covered with filthy screens. You would never know it if it was a clear, sunny day outside. It broke Dena's heart to see Nancy locked up in a ward with crazy women. "Nancy doesn't belong here," she thought to herself. "She will get better and get the fuck out of here."

Sometimes Dolores and Dena would visit Nancy and she would be alert and talking and asking for cigarettes, saying she was feeling better and asking, "When am I going to get out of here?" And other times they would find her in a straitjacket with a sheet tied through the metal loops on the jacket and restrained to a stretcher, drooling from the medication, light years away.

Nancy told her parents she had cut school and, yes, she had gone to a hooky party. But she claimed someone had put a mickey in her drink. She would never voluntarily take any drugs. She had to say something, because the doctors had found LSD and angel dust in her system. Dena thought Nancy might have taken the drugs herself, not realizing what she was inhaling, and that was a good excuse to tell Timo and Dolores so she would not get in any trouble.

Shortly after Nancy got sick, Timo announced he was leaving his family. "Perfect fucking timing," Dena thought. Dena knew that her parents were having problems. There was hardly any conversation in the household. Not much at the dinner table either. Timo was staying out later and later on weekends, and weekdays too. He was doing a lot of things by himself. The only time her parents seemed to get together was when Timo drove Dolores to the hospital to visit Nancy. They had become distant. But she had never thought her father would actually leave. But he did, and Dolores and Dena were on their own.

In high school, Dena started cutting class. She couldn't believe what they were teaching her. It was stuff she had already learned in Catholic school, in the fifth grade. Besides, she barely had any clothes to wear to school and didn't always have lunch money or bus fare. She had only been issued a half-fare bus pass by the school district. Figure that shit out. Sometimes Dolores could not give Dena enough money for lunch and bus fare. They were struggling.

There came a time when Dena really needed a pair of shoes for school. She swallowed her pride and called her father, who was already living with another woman. Dena had not met Timo's new girlfriend yet, but Dolores knew of her. Dolores explained to Dena, "I know her. She was from the same downtown Brooklyn neighborhood where I grew up, but she was not a part of our crew, the Johnson Street girls."

Dena had never wanted to ask Timo for anything after the bicycle incident, but she had to. He gave her a lecture about the shoes and about how she only called him when she needed something. Then he gave her the money. By all rights, since she was only sixteen, he should have been paying child support for the next three years, which he was not. And he was bitching about twenty dollars for a pair of school shoes.

More than the financial hardship, Dena was bitter toward

Timo for the way he had hurt her mother. She felt he had abandoned her mother and her. She had no rap for him for years. Dolores loved Timo, and was still in love with him after so many years. She was so devastated she began losing weight, couldn't sleep, and cried a lot. Dena did her best to comfort her mother. Dolores had lost her oldest daughter and her husband in the same year.

Dena at sixteen was doing what every average teenager was doing: hanging out at block parties and park jams, and smoking a little weed every now and again. She was always a little paranoid about getting high and having a nervous breakdown like her sister Nancy, so she stuck with weed and a pink champale. She was always offered more, but likewise always refused it.

One day, Dolores found out Dena was failing in high school and had been ordered not to come back. Actually, the way the principal worded it was, "Dena is finishing the tenth grade, and she is getting held back. If she continues here, it will take her five more years to graduate, give or take. She's a very smart girl, and she's better off taking the equivalency diploma test and getting her diploma by the time she is supposed to graduate." Then, the principal said, "It's a shame too." Dolores asked why. The principal replied, "Because the school was considering her for a basketball scholarship."

At the time Dena did not realize the importance of a scholarship or college. She left high school and started taking a high school equivalency course. Dolores must have mentioned the news to Timo, because one week later Dena came home from school to find Timo sitting in the living room. She thought to herself, "This can't be good." Then again, Timo often came around to discuss Nancy and drop off paperwork, divorce paperwork, that is. Sometimes he would drive Dolores and Dena to visit Nancy.

However, Dena had a bad gut feeling about Timo being there this time, and her gut feeling was right. Her first instinct was to go straight to her room, but she decided to make herself a sandwich and sit in the living room to hear what Timo had to say. Well, Timo did not waste any time.

"Your mother and I have decided to put you in a home," he announced. Dena's heart dropped to her stomach, but she remained cool and continued to eat her sandwich to show her father that no matter what he said, she was not bothered by it one bit. But in truth her head was spinning—dormitory beds, fighting, maybe gay girls. A smile came over her face as her father waited for a response.

Dena looked at her mother and asked, "Do you agree to this, Mom? Or did Daddy talk you into this like he does everything else? Don't you see what he's doing? If I leave, you will be all alone, and that's what he wants. Mom, I'm sixteen years old. Do you think I can survive two years in jail? Because that's what it is, Mom, jail. I will never be the same afterwards. I promise the both of you, if I do go away, don't bother to visit me, because when I get out, I will never see the two of you ever again. Mark my words." And with that, she got up and went to her room.

Two weeks later, Dena and Dolores went to family court. Timo did not even have the guts to go. It was a long wait to be seen by the judge. Four hours after court started, hungry, ass hurting from the hard-ass wooden benches, Dena heard her name called. Dolores and Dena stood side by side in front of the judge. She felt like a criminal. "And for what?" she thought. "For switching schools, a little weed every now and then? Well, then ninety-eight percent of teenagers should be dragged into court." Dena looked nervously around the courtroom.

The judge questioned Dolores. "Why is she here?"

Dolores said, "My husband and I decided to put her away. She's out of control."

The judge looked at Dena and must have seen the fear in her eyes and asked, "How old are you?"

"Sixteen, sir," Dena said

The judge looked at Dolores and said, "The age limit for a minor to be placed in a home is sixteen. She's too old to be put in a home. Next case."

She looked up at God and said, "Thank you," and thought to herself, "Too old? That's a first," and smiled.

It took Dena some time to forgive her mother for not sticking up for her, but Dolores was all she had, and she did provide a roof over her head. So she did not hold a grudge against her for long. But Timo...Timo was another story. It would be years before Dena gradually forgave her father. Eventually, she realized she still loved and needed him and worked on being friends again. Dena thought about leaving school altogether and working full-time off the books at the supermarket. She was thinking about what some of her friends had told her about how a high school diploma was just a piece of paper. But then she also realized, so is money, and she surely had to have that. So she decided to stay in school and get her GED.

CHAPTER THREE

When Dena was eighteen, she began hanging out with her new male friend, Hank. Dena and Hank were like brothers. Hank was book smart, and Dena thought he was the baddest deejay in Brooklyn. They shared the same interests: souped-up cars, mixing music, sports, and eventually sex. Dena wanted to experience sex with a man because she might like it, and she wanted to compare being with a man to being with a woman one day. So for a year, Hank and Dena were lovers. She knew it would be much better with a woman, sexually. Just the mere thought of being with a woman made Dena feel butterflies in her stomach—the approach, asking a woman to dance, holding her close, looking into her eyes. "Damn," She thought, "just thinking about kissing a woman makes me feel special." Dena would become so excited, she would just have to experience the rest live.

She had many friends and close family members. She had a beautiful cousin named Hilda. Hilda had the most beautiful brown complexion Dena had ever seen. She had sharply defined features and had inherited her mother's straight hair, which she always kept shoulder length. Dena admired her for being so cool and outgoing and living her life to the fullest. Hilda had her own apartment, her own car, nice clothes, and fifty times more friends than Dena had. Dena wanted to be just like her, but in a gay way. Hilda and Dena would talk on the telephone and see each other from time to time. Dena had to know what was going on in Hilda's life. On March 24, 1981, when she turned twenty, Dena was single again and she made a promise to herself for her new decade: I'm ready for a girlfriend, and I will have one.

In October 1981, Dena called Hilda on a Thursday just to see what she was doing for the weekend. Even though Hilda was straight, Hilda and Dena had a lot of fun together. Dena was five years younger than Hilda, but Hilda didn't mind the age difference and Hilda and Dena hung out. Dena knew Hilda had a lot of girlfriends, and they were cuties. Maybe one or two of them were gay. She was always welcome at Hilda's house to spend the night, and most of the time she did.

One day Hilda told Dena she was having a house party that Saturday and asked her if she wanted to come. Dena quickly agreed and asked if she could spend the night so she wouldn't have to take the train home so late at night. Hilda agreed and said, "But…" Dena waited for Hilda to finish her sentence, and just when she was about to say, "But what?" Hilda said, "It's not the kind of party you're used to."

"Well, what kind of party is it?" Dena asked,

"It's a gay party," Hilda responded. "Only women will be there."

Hilda was saying something else when Dena dropped the telephone and raised her hands to the sky. "Hilda, I'll see you Saturday!" Dena yelled.

Dena called her friend, Zebra, explained the situation to her, and asked her if she wanted to come to the party. "I'm not into women, but it's cool if you are," Zebra told her. "I would like to go for the music, and something to do. I'll pick up a nickel bag. Do you want to go in half on that with me?"

"Sure," Dena said, "I'll pick you up at your house around nine p.m."

Dena notified Dolores of her plans and asked her if it was okay if she spent the night at Hilda's house.

"Okay, have a good time," Dolores said, "And if I need you, I know where to reach you."

Dena gave her mother a kiss, and Dolores said again, "Have a good time."

Zebra's sister let Dena in. "I'll be ready in a minute," Zebra yelled from the back room.

Dena thought that Zebra's younger sister was a little pain in the ass. She would always call Dena a green-eyed redbone and threaten to kick Dena's ass. Dena just ignored her and said, "I don't have time for this shit," and yelled at Zebra to hurry up.

Zebra and Dena started walking toward the Avenue to catch the B10 bus. Zebra lit a joint and said to her, "Luckily we only have to catch one bus. It's cold out here tonight."

"Yeah," Dena agreed as she looked up at the clear sky and stars and said, "The bus leaves us off right in front of her building."

Zebra knew Dena really didn't care much for weed, at least not as much as she did. She also knew to pass the joint to her just in case. Dena grabbed the joint and took a couple of drags to relax herself. She did not tell Zebra how excited she was or that she would not leave this party without a telephone number, even if she had to lie across the exit door.

Zebra and Dena arrived early, around 10:30, to see if Hilda needed any help. Of course she did, so they helped out with whatever needed to be done. Hilda already had a few other friends helping out. Dena's antenna had already gone up, because these women were gorgeous. Dena found Hilda in the kitchen and pulled her to the side. She had never gotten the chance to tell Hilda how she felt about the party. "I've been waiting to meet a gay woman all my life," she began. "Thank you so much for inviting me to your party and giving me a chance. You know, I'm going to be pulling you to the side all night and asking you questions about the women here." She swallowed, then asked, "Are you gay, Hilda?" Dena had never suspected Hilda of being gay. She thought maybe Hilda was giving the party for some of her closest friends, because she was cool like that and had a really nice place.

Hilda looked at Dena and said, "Ever since I broke up with my last boyfriend, which was about two years ago, I've been gay."

Dena was shocked, not because she was gay but because she had hidden it from her for so long. She could have started her gay life two years ago. "Oh, well," she thought, "let's party." But before they did, Dena inquired about this cutie-pie named Sandy, the cutest of the helpers. She was beautiful, straight, shoulder-length hair, brown eyes, and a melting smile. HOT!!! Hilda laughed aloud and said she had slept with her already, plus that she liked women with money because she liked getting high. Dena thought, "Shit." One rule Dena made to herself was never date within the circle of friends. And starting Monday, she had to get a better job.

Little by little the girly girls came in one by one, two by two, all bundled up because of the cold. They went to the back room, took off their coats, and out came beauty queen after beauty queen. Zebra wasn't kidding when she had said she did not want any part of the women's party. She stayed in the deejay room and smoked weed all night. She only came out from time to time to go to the kitchen to get herself a drink or to use the bathroom. Dena thought, "If it's cool with her, it's cool with me."

Dena was sitting on the windowsill observing for the first time women dancing together, some holding each other very close. Some women were drunk and horny, and seemed to be connected by their pants zippers. She sat watching the cuties dancing by themselves and watching women watching her. Dena felt femme. She went to the bathroom to take a look at herself. Her hair—well, butch or femme, Dena's hair was Dena's hair. But she felt femme in her clothes. She wanted a femme and did not want to attract an aggressive woman. "Oh well, nothing I can do about it tonight. But believe me, I will change my style."

Then she went back to the living room, got another Absolut and cranberry, woofed that down, and went to dance. She wasn't shy at all. She had wanted this her whole life, and here it was, short, tall, thick, slim, mmm, mmm. Dena made up her mind that she liked two out of the crowd. "Okay, where's Hilda?" She needed a run down. Hilda was dancing, so she stood to the side and was waiting patiently when this aggressor approached her and asked her to dance. Dena kindly said, "No, thank you," while she flirted with one of the two women who looked like sisters.

As soon as Hilda finished dancing, Dena grabbed her by her arm and said, "Got a second?"

Hilda said, "Thank you, girl, I needed a break. I can't sit down for one song." As soon as Hilda said that, here came another woman asking her to dance.

"Hilda," she said, "you promised."

Dena jumped in and said to the woman, "Just a minute, sweetie, she's just going to get some more ice," as Hilda and Dena walked to the kitchen.

"Damn, girl, I want to be just like you. Hilda, who are those two fine women with the long hair? Are they sisters?"

"Yes, they are. Their names are Mamay and Miko. They're twins." Then Hilda said, "Miko was asking about you." Just as Dena's eyes lit up, Hilda said she had told Miko to leave Dena alone. Dena defensively asked why. "She's a jailbird," Hilda explained. "You don't need that kind of shit."

Dena said, "I guess you're right. We could never have a good relationship with her going back and forth to jail. Damn, she's fine. What about her sister, Mamay?"

"Nah, she looks femme, but she is really aggressive. She only dates femme women, and even though you look a little femme tonight, I know you're still a boy." They both laughed as someone pulled Hilda out of the kitchen and onto the dance floor.

Dena went to check on Zebra and bring her a drink, save her the embarrassment. Then she went back to the living room, looked at her timepiece, and said, "Man, it's two-thirty. Got to work fast. Going to ask Miko to dance. It's only a dance." But before she approached her, she saw the most beautiful woman walk through the front door. Talk about making an entrance. Must be club hopping. Dena was in love. She knew she had to act fast. It was getting late. She stood by an open window because she had started to sweat and to plan her move. Dena laughed. That October chill cooled her hot ass off quickly.

The woman did not waste any time getting to the dance floor. Dena tried to peep her—her body, her clothes, her dance partner. She looked very feminine. Nice body, huge ass to be so small at the waist, but she was dancing with a femme. "Doesn't matter," she said, "most of the women here are feminine. Maybe she didn't have a choice." The woman now noticed Dena. Maybe she had felt her staring. Whatever the reason, she sized Dena up, then caught her eye and smiled at her. Dena noticed a woman repeatedly go up to her while she was dancing and whisper something in her ear then walk away. "What's that about?" Dena thought. "Maybe a friend."

When the record changed, the woman stopped dancing and started to walk toward her. Dena got ready.

"Hi, my name is Marcy. What's yours?"

"Dena."

"Where you from, Dena?"

"Brooklyn."

"Not much of a talker, are you?" Marcy asked.

Dena said, "Where you from, you want to dance?" all in one sentence. Talk about being nervous. While Dena and Marcy danced, she noticed how beautiful Marcy was. "Wow, if I could be with her, I would never want another lover," Dena thought. After the dance, Dena felt so high. She went to check on Zebra. When she entered the bedroom, Zebra pointed to her and told the deejay, "That's her."

Dena was wondering what was going on when the deejay asked her, "Do you spin?" Before she could answer, the deejay handed Dena the headphones and said, "Thank you, baby, I'll be right back."

Dena had learned all she needed to know about spinning from Hank, and Zebra reassured him, "She's good." He was relieved because he was able to take a break, and to see if he could dance with some of the gay women at the party.

Dena said, "Fuck it," and pulled out an album. She dee-jayed for about a half an hour. She kept telling Zebra, "It feels like old times when we used to go to the street jams in the Brooklyn parks." The deejays would open up the bottom of the street light box and plug in their equipment. So illegal, but who cared? It was always hours before the cops got the call and shut them down. They had heard great and unforgettable dee-jays of their time, like B-Rock Disco, Inner City Disco, and one time they had even seen Salt-N-Pepa with Spinderella. Dena and Zebra laughed together at the memory. What a treat those days had been. In the seventies, out of all the hundreds of street jams they ever attended, there had been only one shooting.

After the deejay came back, he complimented Dena on her deejaying and keeping the crowd alive.

"No problem, man." Dena winked at Zebra before leaving the room. She returned to the dance floor to look for Marcy. Oh shit. Marcy was gone. Marcy had left the party while she was spinning, probably to go to another house party. "Damn!" Dena thought wryly. " I sounded that bad on the turntables."

CHAPTER FOUR

Hilda and Dena became very close after the party. She went everywhere Hilda went. Hilda rarely kept a job. She really didn't have to. She had women paying her rent and her bills, and buying her expensive gifts. Dena remembered Hilda had been the first person she knew who had a Sony Trinitron television, courtesy of some dyke. "Shit, why should she work?" She thought, and wished her character would allow her to be feminine. She guessed she would one day have to treat her own girlfriend that way. Hilda's sister, Nikki, was bisexual. She would hang out with the girls from time to time.

One evening, while Dena was at Hilda's house watching television and talking about women, she asked Hilda if she could one day take her to the girls' clubs in Manhattan. Hilda told Dena, "There's this club called Better Days. It's a mixed club, mostly dominated by the boys, but a lot of women go there also. The girls love Better Days. It's roomy, easy parking, and the music is like the old Paradise Garage. Once you start dancing, you dance until you collapse. This is one club where you don't walk off the dance floor because they're not playing your song." Hilda said it was jumping with women on Wednesdays and Saturdays. "There's also a girls' house party in Brooklyn this Saturday on Eastern Parkway, by the Brooklyn Museum."

She looked at Hilda and said, "Today's Wednesday. You down?"

"Let me call Nikki. She asked me to let her know the next time we go out." Hilda told Nikki they would come by to pick her up around eleven. Even though it was a weekday, Better Days didn't start jumping until after midnight.

Dena had a driver's license, so Hilda had a steady driver. She never drove to the city or the clubs, not if she could help it, when Dena was around. It wasn't because Dena was the sober one. She wasn't. She'd have a drink at the club, a drag of weed here and there, but nothing stronger. But Hilda went all out drinking and having fun. Nikki, forget about it. Who knows what she had?

Back in the eighties, the Brooklyn Bridge road was plated with bumpy metal, so driving on it was slippery, wet or dry. Dena loved cars and liked to drive, but never liked driving home from the club, especially on the Brooklyn Bridge. She always wanted to have one more drink, or dance until she was exhausted, then fall out in the back seat. But she rarely did. So, she remained sober and responsible.

It never failed. Nikki was never ready when they got to her house, and Dena was impatient to get to the club. Not because of the actual party, but to see if she would run into Marcy. Nikki had to put her three kids to bed, talk on the phone a bit, then finish getting ready. So as soon as Hilda and Dena walked into Nikki's house, they would automatically make themselves at home.

Dena would channel surf while Hilda opened up Nikki's refrigerator. Nikki would follow Hilda and close the refrigerator door, and complain she was broke. She was always broke, or maybe it was just that she had her priorities wrong. Hilda snapped at Nikki, "I'm just scraping the top of your freezer for some ice. Go get ready already." That was something Hilda would constantly do with the old refrigerators. The top of the freezers would give you soft ice, like a snow cone machine—delicious.

Hilda drove to the city this time while Nikki and Dena talked about things, and about how they hoped there were some cute girls there that night, including Marcy. "Shut up already about this Marcy woman. You're never going to see her again, face it," Nikki told Dena. Nikki could be harsh.

"You're wrong," Dena retorted. "I am going to see her again, and I'm going to make her mine. Don't you understand? I have to have her."

Hilda understood completely, while Nikki, on the other hand, was so clouded by drugs, she would never understand.

Nikki laughed at Dena and said, "If you saw her again, you wouldn't even know what to do."

"Yes, I would, I think," Dena argued, although even to her it sounded lame.

It was cool because on Forty-Ninth Street after seven o'clock you could park your car on the street if you were lucky enough to find a parking space. Usually what the girls would do is double park and wait a few minutes to see if any birds were pulling out, either some early birds who had to go to work in the morning or some horny love birds who couldn't wait to get home. Ninety percent of the time it worked. Afterwards, they would wait in line to be searched and pay their cover, then go straight to the bar. They played the bar first because it gave their eyes a chance to adjust to the darkness, and to check out the view and buy a drink.

Dena only had enough money to enter the club and buy one drink. Still only working part-time on and off at the supermarket and going to school, she really didn't have enough money for herself after she got paid. She only made around ninety dollars a week. Every week when she got paid, she would spend half of her check on groceries for herself and Dolores. She knew Dolores' check was tight, without any child support or alimony, and wanted to help out and be responsible, even if it meant only one drink at the club.

Dena was all right with this because she knew it wouldn't be for long. One day soon she would get her GED, get a better job, and be able to drink all she wanted to, maybe even buy a cutie a drink or two. But right now she was content, and sometimes Hilda would buy her a drink or get free drinks from the bar and share them with Nikki and Dena. Nikki would always ask Dena for some money to buy a drink or some drugs and Dena never had enough to spare. She didn't mind Nikki getting high, because she thought it was just a party fad. In fact, if she'd had extra dough, she would have given it to her for a drink, but not for drugs.

They left the bar and walked toward the dance floor. "Wow," Nikki said to Hilda, "the club is jumping." Nikki would see three people on the dance floor and say the club was jumping. You could tell she didn't get out much. Nikki whispered something in Hilda's ear, then Hilda handed Nikki some money, and she went downstairs to the bathroom to make a purchase.

Dena asked Hilda if that was Nikki's normal routine. Hilda nodded her head and smiled at a beautiful woman walking by. Then she looked at Dena and said, "I'll be back" and went to dance. Hilda was used to the club, the music, the boys, the girls. Dena walked around the crowded dance floor, looking to see if she could spot Marcy. It was so dark. No luck. Before she danced with someone else, she had to inspect the whole club.

Maybe Marcy was downstairs in the bathroom. Dena went downstairs to check, and to use the bathroom. She was able to see faces again in the bathroom with the dim lighting. "Hi," a woman said to her. Dena disliked it when a dyke flirted with her. It was like taboo to her, like a man flirting with her. Yuk! She had cut her hair to a short, curly Afro. She wore a lumberjack shirt with a pair of jeans and some boots. What more could she do to look more boyish, grow a mustache? Dena kindly smiled back at the woman and said, "What's up?" and kept walking toward the stalls. Three stalls, all occupied, one with four legs. Dena smiled. The other one probably with Nikki's ass in it, and the last one for peeing only.

As one woman came out of the peeing only stall, Dena lifted her body off the wall and started to head for it when she saw this nice looking woman she hadn't noticed before and asked, "Are you waiting too?"

"Yes," the femme said.

Dena signaled for her to go first and she said "Thank you," and went in.

Dena was depressed. "Where the hell is Marcy?" she thought. "Doesn't she come out to party? I really want her to be my first." After she had gone to the bathroom, she noticed the nice looking woman still standing in the bathroom area. Dena said, "Fuck it" and asked her to dance. She said yes. "My name is Rita, and yours?" "My name is Dena. Nice to meet you."

As they made their way to the center of the dance floor, Rita wasted no time and brushed her body against Dena's. It made Dena a little nervous thinking Rita wanted to go all the way with her. If she did, she'd have to wait, because Dena had a hard-on for Marcy that would not go away. Boy, from couldn't wait to be with a woman to handing out numbers like a delicatessen. Dena felt the bass of the music and Rita's body on hers. She turned Rita around to make eye contact. Rita was beautiful. Damn.

At the end of the night, the lights always came on for the last two songs. It was a good idea because if the girl you were dancing with was not your type, you could just finish dancing with her, then say goodnight. If there was still time, you could look around to see if anyone else pleased you and try to catch them on the way out. When the lights came on, Dena looked for Hilda or Nikki. She spotted Hilda up ahead, then looked for Rita to say goodnight. As a line had formed to get into the club, a line formed to exit it, with everyone dragging their tired feet, looking for their rides, lovers, and train buddies and, of course, exchanging telephone numbers.

Dena saw Rita ahead of her and noticed this butch leaning over her. "Must be her lover," Dena thought as she saw Hilda standing outside. When she walked by Rita she politely said goodnight to the both of them. Rita said goodnight with a nervous grin on her face, and the butch waved her hand as if to say, "Step off." Hilda was not alone when she yelled at Dena to go find Nikki. Dena knew she could not re-enter the club, so she stood as close as possible to the exit door to put a rush on Nikki.

Rita came out by herself and asked Dena, "Are you waiting for me?"

Dena chuckled and said, "Hell, yeah." Then she said, "Nah, just playing."

Rita said, "That wasn't my girl. She was trying to hit on me all night. She's not my type."

"What is your type?" Dena asked.

Rita answered, "You're my type."

Dena asked Rita for her telephone number and if she could call her sometime. Rita wrote her number down, handed it to her, and said, "Call me," and went to catch up with her friends. Dena watched her as she ran off and thought to herself, "We could be friends."

As the crew was rounded up, Hilda handed Dena the car keys as usual and said, "You need the driving experience."

Dena mumbled, "Whatever." While driving home, Dena lit a cigarette. Everyone was talking over each other about what a great time they'd had. Nikki just wanted to know how many numbers they'd got. Nikki would never take anyone's number or give out her number.

"I got one friend number," Dena said proudly.

"What the hell is a friend number?" Hilda asked.

"I got this girl's number," Dena said, "but I only want to be friends with her, because I'm in love with Marcy." Nikki and Hilda laughed all the way home.

"Dena," Hilda said, "the gay world—the gay woman's world—is very small. So I don't doubt that you'll run into her again; but it may be next week, it may be next year. There're so many other women out there waiting to fall in love with you. Why does Marcy have to be your first—if you run into her again?"

"Yeah," Nikki added, "that bitch could be married with children and only come out every blue moon."

"You both are probably right," Dena said, "but I have to wait to see if I see her again. I can't give my heart a time limit. That one night changed my life, meeting her. My heart fell in love with her. Other women still excite me, so I'm not broken. I just want Marcy, and I'm going make her mine, mark my words."

Dena went back to her normal routine—school, her part-time job—but she still couldn't get Marcy out of her mind. She waited for and was excited about the house party that Saturday, hoping and praying she'd see Marcy there. Dena called Hilda every day to remind her not to go without her. Hilda told her that a friend of hers had invited her to a show that Saturday. The show started at eight o'clock and she would meet her there afterwards, and they would ride home together. Dena asked Hank if she could borrow his car that Saturday and Hank agreed. He really didn't have a choice, being that he'd bought the car from Dena's brother, Mike, and she had sweet-talked Mike into bringing the price down to fifty dollars.

Saturday night was finally here. Dena counted her little bit of cash: eleven dollars. Damn, not even enough to buy a bottle after she got gas. At eleven-thirty, she got five dollars worth of gas and had trouble restarting the car. "Come on, baby, not tonight. Start, please," she begged. It slowly started. Dena revved it a couple of minutes before she drove off. She assumed it was because of the weather. She hoped it wouldn't give her any more problems coming home after the party. But before she could even leave the neighborhood, the car stalled again. Dena kept trying to start it while at the same time trying not to flood the engine. It started for a moment, then stalled again. She just gave up on it and parked it.

She went to a pay phone to call Hank, but Hank's sister said he wasn't home. Dena explained the situation to her and told her, "If Hank comes home soon, tell him his car is on Atlantic Avenue." He'd have to see if he could start it or have it towed.

"All right," Hank's sister said.

"I'll call back in the morning," Dena told her. She had six dollars in her pocket now after putting in the five dollars' worth of gas that was worthless to her now. "Shit, I could have bought a bottle with that five dollars." Dena just walked to Utica Avenue and Eastern Parkway to catch the train. It was a long walk and it was getting late. She wasn't worried about walking by herself. "I'm a fast runner," she thought, and laughed. At least Hilda was meeting her there. Dena arrived at the train station at around twelve-twenty, looked around, and went under the turnstile. When the token booth clerk yelled, "Pay your fare!" Dena just kept running, hoping the token booth clerk wouldn't alert any cops. A quick look behind her and she was in the clear.

She finally arrived at the building and looked at the apartment number Hilda had given her: 3-L. She pushed for the elevator and rode up to the third floor and started looking for the apartment. Boy, one thing about Brooklyn apartment buildings, they could have as many as twenty apartments on one floor. So Dena listened for the music. She found it and just let herself in. No one would ever hear her knocking. It wasn't long at all before she spotted Hilda. Hilda was like, "Why so late? Trying to make an entrance?"

Dena explained to Hilda the car problems she'd had and quickly asked, "Is Marcy here?"

Hilda said, "I couldn't picture her anymore, but I think I would know her if I saw her, and I don't think I've seen her."

Hilda introduced Dena to Kitty, the woman who was giving the house party, and some of her friends. Afterwards, she headed right for the open bar, and Hilda joined her. Dena poured herself some vodka and cranberry juice. The shit felt good going down.

She felt bold and asked a couple of people if they knew a woman named Marcy. Hilda just shook her head and went off to mingle. One woman was ticked off and told Dena she had a lot of nerve asking her about another woman.

Toward the end of the night, while people were saying their goodnights, Dena asked one more person if she knew Marcy. It was the party giver, Kitty. Kitty said, "Yes, I know Marcy from Jersey," and described her down to a T, dimples and all. "She's my ex-lover," Kitty explained.

Dena asked Kitty if she could get Marcy's number or could she give Marcy her number? Kitty refused to do either and just got angry as if she was still in love with her, or as if maybe it had been a bitter break up and she did not want to do Marcy any favors. Dena kept harassing Kitty, until Kitty asked her to leave.

Hilda calmed Kitty down and said, "The girl's in love. What you going to do?" And they left.

Dena spent the night at Hilda's house. Sunday morning, Hilda asked Dena to take a ride with her to Nikki's house so she could take her food shopping at the supermarket. They got dressed and went to Nikki's, where they waited downstairs in the car for her. Nikki finally came downstairs. She was talking to someone on the street when Hilda yelled, "I'm leaving," and Nikki got in the car.

Dena couldn't wait to tell Nikki what had happened last night. "Nikki, we missed you last night. Couldn't find a baby-sitter?" she asked.

"Yeah, it's hard finding a babysitter for three kids."

Nikki always did a large grocery shopping, and Hilda didn't mind taking her once a month. The girls always had a lot of fun together. They always had a good time and made each other laugh. From the club to the supermarket, they were always being their crazy selves. "There're three good places to meet women besides the clubs." Hilda said, "One is the supermarket. Two, the laundromat, and three—"

"The library," Nikki interrupted.

"The Bronx Zoo," Dena added.

"No, simple," Hilda said, "the beauty parlor."

While they were shopping, two aggressive women approached and hugged Hilda. "Nice fucking party you gave, man," the cuter one of the two said. "When's the next one?"

Hilda was introducing all of them to each other when Dena blurted out, "Any one of you know Marcy?"

"Yeah, I know Marcy," Kerry said. "She's my friend. We were together the night of the party. I remember you."

"I like her," Dena said. "We met the night of the party and she left before I could give her my number. Do you think you can give it to her for me?"

"Sure," Kerry said, "I'll call her tonight and give it to her."

Dena grabbed anything she could find to write her number down on, and handed it to her.

"Will she remember you?"

"I hope so," Dena said. "I hope so. Thank you." When the two women walked away, Nikki and Hilda were shocked. Dena said, "You see, if you have enough faith, anything is possible."

Nikki said, "Shit, girl, you right. Now let's see if she calls."

CHAPTER FIVE

Dena must have counted every minute of the day since Sunday. "It's already Wednesday and still no call," she thought. "Oh well, maybe it was bad timing. I really did try." She came home from work around eight-thirty. It had been a long day, but she always had time for conversation with her mom. They always talked about each other's day, and Dena always asked Dolores if she needed or wanted anything, from money to a snack. She had great respect for her mother, and for women in general. She started walking toward her room and yelled out "Hey, Ma, did anyone call me?"

"No," Dolores said.

After Dena took her shower, she began preparing her clothes for the next day, when she heard the telephone ring. "I got it," she told Dolores. "Hello?"

"Hello, may I speak to Dena?"

"This is she. Who's calling, please?"

The voice on the other end said, "Marcy."

Dena became so excited, but forced herself to remain calm by taking a couple of deep breaths. They talked about everything. Marcy seemed interested, until Dena told her she had never been with a woman before. Marcy said she'd never had a virgin before and didn't know if she wanted to be Dena's first. She continued to explain that she was just having fun discovering this new world of women, and first timers were usually confused. "Eventually they run back to men, or they want a commitment; and I'm not looking to be tied down right now. What are your intentions, Dena? Are you looking for a relationship? Do you just want a fuck friend? Are you planning on being bisexual? What do you want?"

Dena said, "You know, I never thought about it. When I've fantasized about coming out and being with a woman, my thoughts have never left the bedroom. I just want to be with a woman. I always knew I would be gay, never bi. I just want to come out. And no matter what you say, Marcy, I still want you."

Marcy was moved by Dena's frankness, and also flattered. She loved an open and honest woman. "Let's just get together and see what happens," she said.

Neither Marcy nor Dena could decide where to meet, which house to visit. They lived so far away from each other, and in different states. Even with a car, it was at least an hour's drive, and that was with no traffic. They decided to meet at Dena's house, because Marcy's house in Teaneck was busy with her parents, brother, sisters, and her sister's kids. Not very appropriate.

"Is Thursday okay?" Marcy asked. "I can be over early, about eleven a.m."

Dena said, "That's fine."

Dena took her time to prepare for Thursday. She wanted to have something to drink on hand, just in case, something special; so she bought a bottle of Harvey's Bristol Cream and saved a joint from a bag of weed she'd bought earlier in the week. Now all she needed was some incense and she was all set. Shit, she had butterflies in her stomach, and it was only Tuesday. She had to keep her mind occupied. She decided to meet up with Zebra and kick it with her until bedtime. She went to bed thinking about Marcy. "Boy, what do I say to her?

What if she wants to do it on the first date? What if *I* want to do it on the first date?"

The alarm clock went off at eight a.m. Thursday morning. Dena wanted to get an early start to get things prepared. She was tidying up a bit when Marcy called and said she was running a little late. "I should be there around twelve," she said. They went over the directions again and hung up. Dena guessed she was nervous too. Around noon, the intercom rang and she just buzzed Marcy in. She wished she had a shot glass in her hand; 150 proof would be nice. The doorbell rang and Dena looked through the peephole and let her in. They embraced and tap kissed each other on the cheek.

"Come in," Dena said. "Let me take your coat." She showed Marcy the apartment. "And this is my room. Make yourself at home." Marcy sat in the only chair in Dena's room, her favorite beach chair. She noticed two turntables on Dena's dresser.

"Do you know how to mix?" she asked.

"Sort of," Dena replied. "This is mix equipment. Some belongs to me and some to a friend of mine named Hank. He's the real deejay. I just mix for fun. Would you like to spin a record?" Dena asked.

"No, I don't know how, but will you play something for me?"

"Sure," Dena said and turned on the stereo, put the headphones on, and thought for a minute about what she should play. She put "Love Is The Message" by M.F.S.B., which stands for Mother, Father, Sister, Brother, on the turntable, hoping Marcy would get the message. She started playing the instrumental version first, then mixed it with the newer vocal version by The Three Degrees. Marcy started dancing and told Dena she looked sexy at the turntables. Dena blushed and asked Marcy, "Would you like something to eat?"

"I already ate," Marcy said, "but don't let me stop you from eating if you're hungry."

But Dena couldn't have eaten even if she had wanted to. She was glad that she'd been wise enough to put something in her stomach earlier just in case Marcy didn't want to have lunch, because she had been told not to drink on an empty stomach. "Would you care for some?" Dena held up the bottle of sherry. Marcy continued dancing and nodded her head yes and smiled.

"I'll go get some glasses," Dena said. Would you light this for me?" She handed Marcy a joint along with a cigarette lighter. "But first, can you please light some incense?" She came back with the two glasses and opened up the small bottle. It was a two-drink bottle, but it was cool because having the sherry along with the joint, they were both feeling nice and mellow. They were higher from each other than from the substances. Dena was amazed at how beautiful Marcy was and felt special just to have her there with her.

Marcy and Dena sat on the bed and talked nervously, knowing soon they would be naked. It was inevitable. Marcy leaned closer and kissed her. No words were said when Marcy stood up and grabbed Dena's hand for her to stand, and started to remove Dena's clothes, while kissing her. Then she removed her own clothes. Dena let Marcy take control, only because it was her first time; but she couldn't wait for her turn. "It's magical how Marcy takes her time, knowing how nervous I am," she thought to herself. Dena felt a heartbeat between her legs, and with Marcy's help, it quickly flat-lined. It was a life decision; a fact that Dena was now and always would be gay. There was no comparison, no turning back.

Hilda and Dena spent the next couple of days together. Hilda was mouthing Dena's words along with her as she repeatedly told her coming out story about Marcy. Hilda told Dena she had to take a ride to the city that day, and Dena just shrugged her shoulders all right. "But first," Hilda said, "I have to stop at a gas station and put some air in my tires." Hilda only made repairs to her car when it was absolutely necessary. Usually she filled the car with gas, and that was it. Money was for more important things.

When they pulled into a gas station, Hilda looked for the air pump and pulled up to it as close as possible. There were three men just hanging around the car repair service area, and they asked Hilda if she needed any help putting air in her tires. Even though Hilda was gay, she was still fine and attracted men all the same. She was feminine, and liked femme women. She was aggressive on the inside. If she was alone with a femme, she knew how to take control.

Hilda and Dena waved them off as if to say, "Anything men can do, butches can do better." Hilda started to put the air in the tires, one by one, with no tire gauge as Dena walked around the car with her, running her mouth, until Hilda got to the last tire. Dena put both her hands on her knees and leaned forward to get a better looked at the tire and asked Hilda, "Are your tires supposed to have bubbles in them like that?"

"No," Hilda Said. "When I get a chance I'll have to find some lesbo to buy me some new tires." They both laughed, when suddenly a loud bang rang out. The tire had exploded. Dena quickly closed her eyes for safety. When she opened them, Hilda looked shocked as if to say, "What happened?" All of the guys were cracking up. One was even on the oil-stained floor from laughing so hard.

They yelled out, "You see, we asked if you gals needed any help," and continued laughing.

Hilda looked at Dena and said, "Are you all right?

Dena said, "I think so. Are you okay?"

"I'm okay," Hilda said, and they bust out laughing. After about a half an hour of laughing, Hilda said, "Because you were so close to the tire and facing the tire, you have a lot of black residue on your face. And because you have a curly Afro, you look like Buckwheat."

But by the time Dena and Hilda left Manhattan, they were both in a lot of pain. Hilda's arm was hurting and Dena had trouble blinking. She felt like something was constantly in her eyes. Hilda took Dena to the eye doctor. Dena did not have an appointment. She just walked in. When she approached the receptionist, she asked, "Could I please see the eye doctor today? It's an emergency."

"What's the emergency?" the receptionist asked.

She covered her mouth and mumbled, "A car tire exploded in my face."

The receptionist said, "Say what?"

Dena yelled out for everyone in the doctor's office to hear, "A Car Tire Exploded In My Face!"

Hilda looked up at Dena and laughed. So did the other patients in the waiting room. When a patient came out of the doctor's examination room, the receptionist called for Dena to be next, and no one complained. They were like, "Let that dumb ass go in next. We can wait." The doctor removed small particles from her eyes and told her, "You were lucky. It could have been a lot worse." Then he gave Dena some eyedrops. Until this day, Dena will not put air in a tires without turning the other cheek.

Marcy only wanted to bring Dena out into the life, and that's all. She didn't plan on falling in love with her, but she did.

Marcy knew Dena's love for her was genuine. And in her eyes, she planned on keeping Dena as her main woman, because she knew she herself could never be faithful. Marcy bought a used car, an Electra 225, and drove to Brooklyn to see Dena as often as she could. They sometimes double-dated with Hilda and her girl. Hilda fell in love around the same time Dena did, which no one had thought was possible. Hilda also kept her friends, who took care of her financially, close by. Her new girlfriend, Jasmine, never had a clue.

One day, Dena and Marcy pulled up to Hilda and Jasmine's house. Jasmine was there almost every day. Might as well say she was living there. Dena asked Marcy if she wanted to go upstairs and wait for them. Marcy said, "No, because I don't like Hilda's dog, Prince." Dena assured her the dog was only crazy outside.

Prince was a purebred German Shepherd, but something was wrong with him mentally. In the house he was the sweetest dog, but when anyone took him outside and walked him, he would flip if you came within ten feet of him. He would go into attack mode. Man, woman, or child, if Prince got a hold of you, it was all over. Hilda made sure whoever walked Prince was ordered never to take him off the leash. She loved Prince because he made her feel protected.

While Dena and Marcy waited in the car for them, Marcy explained to her, "You're not allowed in my home anymore. My father put two and two together about you and me, and now he doesn't want me to have any female company, except for my childhood friends. He wanted me to move out, but I talked him out of it." Then, Marcy started to laugh hysterically.

Dena kept asking her, "What? What is so funny?"

Marcy said her father asked her, "Why do you want to be with a woman?" And Marcy said she did not answer him.

Then he said, "What the hell do you do with a woman, smell each other's asses?" Dena and Marcy bust out laughing.

Hilda and Jasmine came downstairs, and off to the club they went. Dena thought Jasmine was somewhat weird; it was just something about her. Fine as hell, but weird. Besides, she was up Hilda's ass forty-eight hours a day. Dena thought, "Let the bitch breathe a little. Damn!"

Dena found herself being shy around Marcy in the club, and Marcy took advantage of it. Marcy walked around the club looking for women, dancing with other women, and then coming back to Dena to see if she was okay. Hilda pulled Dena to the side and mentioned the disrespect. Dena just said, "I will talk to her about it later." Dena and Marcy sat far from each other in the car on the way home from the club, while Hilda and Jasmine looked like one person in the back seat. Hilda insisted that Dena and Marcy spend the night. Marcy agreed, and thanked her because it cut down about an hour of the driving time for her.

When the girls entered the lobby, there were three teenage boys who actually looked like men just hanging out in the lobby. "It's three-thirty in the morning. Go home already," the girls thought. Marcy pressed for the elevator, and when it came down they all went in. All of a sudden, the three teenagers decided they were ready to go upstairs. "Too coincidental," the girls thought.

"So how you ladies doing tonight?" one of the boys asked.

Before the elevator door slid closed, Hilda kicked the elevator door back open and said, "Come on, ya'll, let's take the stairs." Hilda walked out first and the troops followed. So did the three assholes, popping shit now.

"Hey, you guys know what we have to do," Dena said out loud, when Jasmine shouted, "You motherfucker, you touched my ass!"

"Don't fight with them!" Hilda yelled out. "Wait right here, motherfuckers. I got something for you." No one knew which group of people she meant to be still, so Dena, Marcy, and Jasmine waited too.

A minute later they saw Hilda and Prince running down the stairs. Hilda let go of Prince's collar. "Get 'em, Prince!" You didn't have to tell Prince twice. Prince charged down the stairs growling and drooling, thirsting for blood.

Dena started laughing. "Where you sissies going?" she yelled out. Marcy put her hands together and prayed that Prince would just run by her and know who the bad guys were. Hilda told Jasmine and Marcy to go into the house. The door was unlocked. She asked Dena to go back downstairs with her to retrieve Prince. The bastards must have made it outside alive, because they found Prince in the lobby, scratching at the door to go outside and finish his task. Hilda grabbed Prince by his collar chain, looked at Dena, and said, "Touch my girl's ass again," and smiled.

"Thank God no one else was in the lobby," Dena said, "And second, I say we should let Prince outside and get those boys ready for the New York City Marathon."

Soon after that, while Marcy was spending the night at Dena's house one weekend, she began to feel unwell. She was throwing up. Dena took good care of her and jokingly said, "If I didn't know any better, I'd say you were pregnant."

Marcy looked at her, then put her head down and said, "I might be."

Dena said, "Excuse me?"

Marcy explained that about two months ago her brother Al had been home from the service and had invited his homeboy, who just happened to be Marcy's ex-boyfriend when she was a teenager, over for the weekend to hang out. They were drinking, and one thing led to another, and they slept together. Dena started to cry because she loved Marcy more than life and was willing to make and accept Marcy as her first and last lover.

Marcy made Dena happy, and she felt so special to have her in her life. She told everyone who was gay about Marcy. Even the women who tried to date Dena had to put up with Marcy this and Marcy that. That night Marcy and Dena sat down and talked about their problem, and Marcy told Dena that she wanted her to explore life, the gay life. It wouldn't be fair to her to be her one and only lover. "You have to experiment and go out and have fun, and be with other women—"

"I'm in love with you, Marcy. I don't want to be with anyone else," Dena protested. "I want to be with you and only you. Are you quitting me?"

Marcy thought about it for a second and quickly answered no. She wanted to be with other women, but couldn't see Dena with anyone else besides her. So Marcy asked Dena if they could have an open relationship, knowing Dena could never cheat on her. Dena knew she didn't want to lose Marcy. At least this way she could have her once in a while. So she agreed.

"I have one other thing to mention," Marcy continued.

"Okay," Dena said, "go ahead."

"Okay, you know when you go down on me? Umm, how can I say this? Okay, have you ever masturbated before?"

"Er, yes, Marcy," Dena said.

"Okay," Marcy said, "when I masturbate, I just focus on my clitoris and my clitoris only. That's what makes me come."

"Well, yes," Dena said, "among other things."

"But what I'm trying to tell you is, it's your clitoris that makes you come," Marcy said, stressing her words this time. "Okay, when you go down on me again, I need you to focus on that part of me only, and I'll talk you through the rest while you're doing it."

"Okay," Dena said.

"And try using your fingers too; that won't hurt either."

Dena got excited and couldn't wait to make Marcy come, and asked Marcy, "Are you feeling better? Would you like to try it now?"

"Yeah!" Marcy said, sounding breathless. "Just let me go to the bathroom and I'll meet you back here in the bedroom."

Dena really couldn't grasp the open relationship shit. It wasn't like Marcy disrespected her openly. She just started spending less and less time with her, while Dena wanted and needed more time with her. She wanted a full-time relationship. She wanted to be in love, and she wanted her Marcy. She could not take the pressure of Hilda and her friends telling her over and over again about how they saw Marcy in the club all hugged up with other chicks. Marcy knew Hilda was there and still didn't try to shield her being all over this woman. Dena put her head down and explained to them that they had an open relationship.

Hilda grabbed Dena's head with her hand and held it up high and said, "Yeah, the only thing open in your open relationship is Marcy's legs! All these women who approach you, you keep turning them down. Why? Dena, you have to start seeing other women. Marcy is, so why not you? Let me tell you something, girl, and I'm talking from experience. It's just a matter of time before you guys split up. I see it coming, Dena.

I'm sorry to be the one to tell you. I love you like a sister, girl, and I don't want to see you hurting anymore."

"I love Marcy so much," Dena replied, "and I can't sleep with anyone else right now because I don't want to. It's not like I can't. I don't want to, because I feel like I'm cheating on her, open relationship or not. I'm not a cheater. I just need some time."

Well, after about two years of on-again off-again, Dena was really unhappy and hurting. She tried to be Marcy's one and only, and it worked for a little while, but then opened up again.

On Valentine's Day all the girls went out together, and for the first time Dena seemed distant from Marcy. When the crew arrived at the club, Dena stayed by the bar most of the night and socialized. She was amazed at how many women in New York City were gay, and how she kept turning them down. "Boy, am I missing out," she thought. Dena saw Hilda at the other end of the bar and asked her if she had seen Marcy.

Hilda shook her head from side to side and said, "When are you going to wake up?" Then she put her arm around Dena's shoulders and asked her to have a drink with her. "I'll have a martini with two olives, thank you very much," Hilda said.

After her drink with Hilda, she missed Marcy and wanted to dance with her. She went to the bathroom first, because she had noticed the line was short. On Valentine's Day and only on Valentine's Day did you ever hear slow love songs in a club. This is where people came to dance, take off their shirts, swing them in the air and drop a purple haze every now and again. Dena thought a slow dance with Marcy would be nice and would get her in the mood for what was to come on their Valentine's Day.

When she finally found Marcy, she stopped right in her

tracks. Marcy was already slow dancing with this cutie-pie. Even Dena thought she was cute. "Damn, talking about bumping and grinding without a bed." And when Marcy started kissing her dance partner, Dena's heart seemed to stop. She'd never seen Marcy kiss another woman before, and open relationship or not, the shit still hurt. Dena went outside to cry, needing to keep her dyke image. She still loved Marcy.

She was wiping a tear from her eye when Marcy approached her. "Are you all right?" she asked.

"Would you be all right if the shoe was on the other foot?" Dena asked.

"Look, Dena, I'm sorry. I love you very much, but I don't want to be in a relationship with you anymore. I want to see other women, and I'm just hurting you by staying with you."

Dena told Marcy she did not want to break up. "I love you—"

But Marcy cut her off. "It's not meant for us to be, Dena. I see so many women peeping you. Go get them, girl. Explore, have fun, and be careful." Marcy gave Dena a hug and said, "See you around," and went back inside the club.

CHAPTER SIX

S aturday afternoon, Dena woke up to Dolores' muffled voice. "Dena, Dena, are you going with me to the hospital to see Nancy today?"

She wiped her eyes and yawned and answered her, "You know I wouldn't miss this for the world. Let me get dressed."

Dolores really appreciated Dena's devotion and dedication and how often she escorted her to the hospital, knowing she did not want to go alone. When Dolores was too busy to go, Dena would go with her dad or by herself. Timo had told her that it was good for the hospital staff to see that Nancy had family, and family who cared, so they would not take advantage of her and abuse her. After taking two buses, Dolores and Dena finally arrived at Kings County G Building, the crazy house.

Dena looked up at the building as they entered it and said, "What a fucking depressing place. I can't believe my sister's in here." They really couldn't bring her anything because she was still on the lowest level, and she would have to prove herself to the doctors by obeying the staff, making her bed, and getting along with other patients in order for her level to rise. Whenever they visited Nancy, she usually gave the staff a hard time. Dena never blamed her though.

Dolores and Dena would talk to Nancy about her behavior. They would tell her, "If you could just get to Level One, you could get transferred to another floor with less restrictions.

You could come home some weekends. And when we visited you, we could go outside and sit on the benches. Isn't that better than sitting up here in this locked ward with other patients disturbing us?"

After years of advising Nancy, she finally got to Level One and was transferred. But she kept going back down to Level Three because, from time to time, the staff would let her sit outdoors, which was allowed, and Dolores would find her knocking on her front door. No one knew if she hitched a ride, snuck on the train, or just walked home, but she found her way home every chance she got. Sometimes the hospital staff would call Dolores' house and tell her Nancy had escaped again and to expect her. Back down to Level Three she went. When she arrived home Dolores would notify the hospital, if they didn't call her first, and then call Timo, who would come by after work and drive her back to the hospital.

One afternoon Nancy was spending the weekend with Dolores and Dena, and it was a beautiful Sunday afternoon. They were waiting for Timo to come by and drive Nancy back. It was always better to take Nancy back by car. She had no patience with being taken back by bus. Most of the time, Dolores and Dena went along for the ride with Timo and Nancy, and they all went to the hospital together. It was a long walk from where Timo was able to get a parking space at the hospital to where Nancy's building was located, so one member of the family would take a turn escorting Nancy back to the building. Dena volunteered to walk Nancy back to the building this time and take her upstairs.

Kings County Hospital was a huge place, and the grounds were all long walks from building to building. They even had underground tunnels that went from one building to another. Dena guessed if they were escorting a notorious prisoner, or an escape artist, they would use the tunnels. When Nancy and Dena approached the building, Nancy sat down on the first bench she saw and lit a cigarette. Dena asked Nancy, "Can you make it quick, because Mom and Dad are waiting for me."

"You could go," Nancy said. "You know I have an outside pass, so it's okay if you leave."

"Nancy, you know I have to bring you back upstairs and sign you back in, and then they will give you a pass to go back outside. I'm responsible for you," she said.

"After I finish smoking a couple of cigarettes, Dena, I promise you I will go back upstairs."

Dena said okay, and kissed her. "Call you later, darling." She started walking back to the car.

Moments later, when she arrived back at the car, Timo asked her, "Did you take Nancy upstairs?"

Dena said, "Yes and no. I took her back to the building, but she wanted to sit outside and smoke a cigarette before she went upstairs."

"I thought I saw someone who looked like her running across the street up ahead," Timo said.

"She did not run past me, Daddy," Dena said, "and as far as I know, there's only one way out, and you have to pass a security guard in the booth. It couldn't have been her." Timo dropped Dolores and Dena off, not knowing that when he got home he would be receiving a call from Dena saying that Nancy needed to be taken back to the hospital again.

Dena received her GED. "No more school for a while," she thought. She applied for another part-time job at a Muslim owned and operated bakery. She thought the owners were cool. They were a young, handsome couple and they had it going on with their own business. They hired her part-time to work evenings from four to nine a couple of days a week. She managed to juggle her two part-time jobs. She felt that at twenty-two years old she was still not making enough money to be out on her own. One day her brother, Mike, mentioned to her that she might take on a city job. "The pay is good, and you get great benefits. I'll bring you some applications."

Dena said she would think about it. When she did think about it, she never thought of herself as a city worker. She had higher expectations, higher goals. But right now, she'd take what she could get. When she had been asked as a child, "What do you want to be when you get older?" Dena had always responded by saying, "I want to be a race car driver." She thought, "Maybe I could take a city job as a stepping stone for my dream job. I could go to school, or something. But if I do decide to take a city job, it will only be temporary."

Four-seventeen p.m. and Dena was reprimanded again by her boss, Mr. Jackson, for being late. Mr. Jackson really liked her, in a looking-out-for-her kind of way. She apologized, and said, "Mr. Jackson, I forgot my scarf. Can I borrow one from your stash again?" He told Dena to look in the closet. Instead of wearing hairnets in the bakery, Dena and the other female employees had to wear scarves on their heads. Dena didn't mind. She guessed it was a Muslim thing. The men wore baker's hats.

Dena and Joyce, her coworker, were total opposites. Joyce was around forty years old, married, and a little chubby after having had a few kids. She was very beautiful, with piercing eyes, and long eyelashes to match. She worked part-time just to get out of the house for a few days a week. Dena thought to herself, "Damn, if she wasn't married," and laughed to herself.

Dena had been born with a set of rules she could never

get out of her system. No one had taught her these rules. They were just lines she felt she could never in her life cross. One was cheating on her lover. The second was going out with a woman who was married or in a relationship. The third was to never date within your circle of friends, even if your friend gave you permission, even if you're drunk, or even if they'd been seperated for years. Never date within your circle of friends. Those were her rules.

The bakery was most famous for its carrot cake and brownies. Out of all the pastries and items sold there, Dena really only had to remember the price of those two special items. People bought them either by the pound or the whole cake. If someone wanted to order something else, there was a price list posted on the wall. On Thursdays the bank up the block was open until six p.m. One Thursday, Joyce asked Dena if she could run up the street and get four rolls of quarters, and handed her forty dollars even before she could say yes. Dena said, "Lazy," and headed for the bank.

Dena remembered she had a half a joint in her pants pocket and decided to take a couple of tokes after she left the bank. But instead of taking a drag or two, she finished the whole half a joint, went into the bodega store to get some gum, and asked the store clerk the price of the Visine eye drops. Two dollars and change. Dena asked him if he could give it to her for one dollar, "Because," she said, "you know the shit's expired, man." Bodegas always had expired shit. Expired or not, he said $2.29 and placed it back on the shelf. She knew her eyes were bloodshot, but she had better things to do with her change. "Besides," she thought, "Joyce won't say anything if she notices."

Back at the bakery, Dena handed Joyce the rolls of quarters, washed her hands and put her apron and scarf back on, and went back to work. "Joyce, what's the price of the carrot cake again?" she asked. "Joyce, what's the price of the brownies again?"

"Did you leave your memory at the bank?" Joyce asked.

"No. I just forgot," Dena answered.

After the customers left the store, Joyce pulled Dena to the side. "What's the matter with you, girl? Your eyes are red as hell. Did you—"

"All right, all right," Dena cut her off, "I smoked a half a joint. I know I shouldn't have, being at work and all, but I didn't think I would forget the prices."

"And you're giving the customers much more than what they paid for," Joyce added.

"Maybe I should get high more often," Dena said. "It would increase sales." They bust out laughing, and Dena was still laughing, being silly and all, when this woman walked in. Dena's antenna immediately went up, and she said to herself, "Damn, I got this order, Joyce."

"Dena," Joyce said, "the store is empty. I'm going to run to the bathroom. Be right back."

She nodded and turned to the customer and asked if she could help her. The woman was pretty. She looked Native American and had a curly Afro, much larger than Dena's. Dena stared into her eyes, waiting for her to look away so she could take a quick look at her breasts, because as she looked into her eyes, she could tell her breasts were filling up the rest of her view.

"What did she call you?" the customer asked.

"Dena. My name is Dena."

"My name is Sheryl. Nice to meet you. You live around here?"

Dena wondered what was going on, here. "Yeah, I live across the street, with my mom. And you?"

"I live in Queens, Jamaica Queens," Sheryl said. "Can I have two brownies? And may I borrow a pen, please?"

"Sure," Dena said, and handed her a pen, then grabbed a bag and put two extra brownies in the bag for her, just in case she had kids or something. "Will that be all?" she asked and turned around to ring her up.

"Yes," Sheryl answered, and handed her the money and her telephone number.

Dena placed her number in her pocket and gave her the change. Joyce returned from the bathroom and waited on the next customer, whom Dena hadn't even noticed. Sheryl exited the bakery without a "thank you" or "goodnight."

The next day, Dena was on her way to work at the bakery. She looked at her timepiece and said, "Fuck, late again. I just hope the boss isn't in." She walked past the bakery and looked through the glass window and saw her boss. She took a deep breath before going inside. Mr. Jackson asked to see her before she started work. Dena stood in the corridor waiting for Mr. Jackson to sign some delivery papers. She looked at her time-piece. "Oh boy, four-twenty."

Mr. Jackson said, "I don't know what your problem is with punctuality, Miss Vargas—"

"Mr. Jackson, you know I have another job," Dena said, thinking it would help her, mentioning her other job.

"Let me finish," Mr. Jackson said. "You're an attractive, smart young lady, but I have to fire you and get someone more reliable. I'm sorry." He handed her a white envelope and said, "Thank you."

Dena took the envelope and turned to leave when Mr. Jackson said one more thing, "Are you confused about anything? You have this look about you that says to me, you're confused."

Dena didn't answer him, but just walked away, gave Joyce a hug because she knew that Joyce had heard everything, and left. Dena thought that the only thing she was confused about was where she was going to get another job. Well, at least one good thing came of this job, and it was Sheryl. Now that she'd have time on her hands. "I think I'll give her a call tonight," she thought.

CHAPTER SEVEN

Dena waited until after nine o'clock to call Sheryl. They talked for an hour or so. They both seemed very interested in each other and decided to get together that weekend at Dena's house. Dena asked Sheryl if she could make it after seven because her father, Timo, was coming by with a couple of coworkers to drop off a sofa bed for the second time. He knew Dolores didn't need it, so he was secretly giving it to Dena, just in case she decided to move out one day. She had given her brother, Mike, the first sofa bed, because he was moving and needed a bed. At that time Dena didn't even have a real job to allow her to move out on her own, so she didn't mind giving it to him. But this one—this one she wanted to keep, just in case.

After Timo and his friends dropped off the sofa bed, Dena asked Timo if she could talk to him before he went home. He asked his coworkers to meet him downstairs, saying that he'd be right down. They waved goodbye to Dolores and Dena and left. She told Dolores, "You too, Mom. I want to talk to you both. Dad, I won't keep you long. I know your coworkers are waiting for you. I just wanted to tell you both, I'm gay."

"I kind of knew since your birth," Dolores said, "and I still love you very much." Dena could have told Dolores just about anything, and it wouldn't have fazed her love for her, not one bit.

Timo, on the other hand, well...Dena waited for his response. "Maybe it's a phase you're going through," Timo explained. "A lot of people go through these phases."

"Dad, it's not a phase," Dena said. "I know that for a fact."

Timo moved closer to Dena, gave her a hug, and told her he loved her too. "And you being gay, Dena, doesn't change a thing. Got to go. Call me later, Dena. Bye."

Dena told Dolores that she was having a friend over for a little while. "And it's not Marcy, okay? So please don't make a mistake and call her Marcy."

"Got it," Dolores said, and smiled.

Sheryl arrived around seven o'clock, and Dena introduced her to her mom. "We're going into my room to play backgammon," she added. Then she turned to Sheryl and asked her if she knew how to play.

"Sure do," Sheryl said. "Let's play."

"Do you mind setting it up on the bed? The game is right there on the dresser."

Sheryl grabbed the game off the dresser and placed it on the bed. Dena asked Sheryl if she wanted wine. She knew her mother had a couple bottles of Cani in the house.

"No, I don't really drink," Sheryl told her.

Dena thought that was unheard of. "Do you do anything else to compensate for your not drinking?"

"Yes, well, I smoke weed every now and again, but I really enjoy doing blow. I just can't afford it."

Dena asked Sheryl how anyone could possibly enjoy doing blow. "The first couple of times I tried it, it burned my nose so bad I couldn't even enjoy it."

"I just like the way it makes me feel," Sheryl said. "All I know is I get so excited sexually."

"Well, if you think you're going to do blow and have sex with me," Dena said, "you got another thing coming to you, sister," and they laughed.

Sheryl rolled the dice to see who would go first.

After two games, Dena said, "Let's make this game more interesting. If I win, you can give me a kiss, and if you win, you can give me a kiss."

Sheryl said, "You don't have to bet me to get a kiss. All you have to do is ask."

After about three more games, she asked Sheryl for a kiss.

Sheryl replied, "What took you so long?"

"I...er, guess I'm shy."

Sheryl asked, "How long have you been gay?"

"A little over two years," Dena said.

"Let me rephrase the question," Sheryl said. How many woman have you been with?"

Dena looked deep into Sheryl's eyes and held them there. "One, my first lover. We were in a relationship for about two years, and we just broke up."

Sheryl smiled. "That's why."

"That's why what?" Dena asked.

"Oh nothing. Come here and give me a kiss."

Dena placed her lips on Sheryl's and tap kissed her, then kissed her open mouth. She put her tongue in Sheryl's mouth and searched for hers. Sheryl's mouth felt so warm. When their tongues met, Dena got excited. She thought about Marcy for a second and said to herself, "Fuck her," and pulled Sheryl closer to her while they continued kissing. "Wow," Dena said to herself, "this is nice, kissing another woman besides Marcy. Didn't think it was possible, but I was wrong." She pushed the back-gammon game over and laid Sheryl across the bed. She did not want to lie on top of her, so she lay beside her and lowered her head to kiss her some more.

After a little while Sheryl sat up. "I like the way you kiss. Let me go before I get you in trouble."

"How are you getting home?" Dena asked.

"By train."

Dena grabbed her jacket. "Then I'll walk you to the station."

Sheryl kissed her. "You're such a gentleman."

Dena waited with Sheryl until the train arrived. She did not want the night to end. And the good thing was, neither did Sheryl. Sheryl told Dena that her mother was going away for the weekend. "Would you like to come over to my house Saturday?"

The platform started shaking, and Dena found herself yelling the word, "Yes," because of the rumble from the train. "Here comes your train." They hugged, and Dena waved goodbye.

Dena walked home high as a kite. She had not thought she could feel that way again. She wanted Saturday to be special. "Mom's gone. I know what her intentions are," she thought to herself. "I have to get a small package of blow. I want to meet this person she calls Buck Wild."

Dena really didn't know Queens very well. She had an aunt and uncle who lived in Jamaica, Queens, and she knew that Shea Stadium was in Queens, but that was all. But she knew the transit system very well. You just had to tell Dena your train stop and she'd open up a train map and know what train would get you there. Sheryl told her, "The train stop is Hillside Avenue." Dena had to transfer from one train to another to get there. Sheryl set the time for nine p.m.

Dena thought that was kind of late. "Oh well," she thought, "it's Saturday night. Maybe she'll ask me to spend the night, if I'm lucky." She estimated the time it would take to walk to the train station, wait for the train, train ride, switch trains, train ride, and find her house. "Hmm, I'll leave around seven-thirty." Dena asked a friend of a friend about buying a small package. She had put twenty dollars away for this purpose. She found a twenty-dollar package and it looked like more than enough to her. She made sure she had it hidden deep in her jacket pocket, grabbed her keys, and headed out the door.

Dena liked being single, but she yearned to be in a relationship. She always liked having someone special and steady in her life. "Maybe Sheryl is the one for me," she thought. She was nervous and it showed. She had seventy-five cents ready for her train fare. This was not a good time to sneak on the train. If she got caught, she would probably be searched, and that was not a good idea with a package of cocaine in her pocket. Dena could never understand how a perp with contraband would take a chance and sneak on the train, when you just exchanged your misdemeanor for a felony if you got caught. She got off the train and went to the store to get a pack of gum and ask the clerk for directions. She found the house and rang the doorbell.

"Coming," she heard through the door. They embraced, and Sheryl asked her to come upstairs. To her surprise, Dena felt like she was entering a daycare center. There must have been at least six kids and two teenagers sitting in the kitchen. Sheryl introduced all of the family to Dena and signaled with her finger for Dena to follow her to one of the bedrooms. It was a small room with a large bed, pink walls, a pink bedspread, and clothes all around the room.

"So this is your room, huh? Do you share it with any other family members?"

"No," Sheryl answered, "this is a five-bedroom house, and since I'm the oldest, I have my own room."

"Wow, your mother must be raking in the dough, boy."

"She does pretty well," Sheryl said. "Give me your jacket and make yourself at home. Are you hungry?"

Dena said, "I don't want to take any food from you guys," and laughed.

Sheryl said, "We have plenty of food. Are you hungry or not?" and grabbed Dena by her waist and pulled her closer.

"No, darling, I'm okay. Do you have something to drink? Oh, that's right, you don't drink."

"It's okay, Dena. I'll send my brother to the store so you don't have to go back out. What do you want?"

Dena wanted something strong but good. "Hmm, Old E...too strong. I don't want to get sick. Okay, a quart of Colt 45," Dena said, digging into her pants pocket. "Here's two dollars. Tell your brother I said thank you."

Dena and Sheryl sat down to talk, and she told Sheryl she had some blow, and asked if it was all right to pull it out. She didn't want Sheryl's siblings walking in and seeing the substance. Sheryl was surprised when Dena told her what she had. It was a happy surprise. She went into her drawer and pulled out a round mirror with no edges and a razor blade. She asked her to pass her the package and said, "How much did you pay for this?"

"Twenty dollars."

"It's a nice-sized package for twenty dollars." Sheryl took a two-on-two, and then passed it to Dena. Dena took a one-on-one and quickly handed it back so she could grab her nose to ease the burn.

"Shit," Dena said.

About a half an hour later, Sheryl's brother knocked on the door and Sheryl invited him in, forgetting about the blow. He gave Dena her beer and her change. When he saw the mirror, he asked for some. Sheryl quickly stated it wasn't hers, and left it up to Dena, who bluntly said, "No." She figured if she said no, he would soon leave and she could be alone with Sheryl. If she gave him a hit, she figured he wouldn't want to leave until it was all gone. Not happening.

He started to beg, "Please, please, please."

Sheryl got up off the bed and escorted him out and locked the door. She apologized for his behavior and lifted the straw to Dena's nose and gave her another hit. She told Sheryl, "That's enough for me. You can have the rest. I know you'll probably say no, but do you want any beer?"

"No, baby, enjoy."

Dena knew she was hot-blooded, but this feeling between her legs was overwhelming. She could not control her desire once she was aroused. Sheryl stood up and took off her sweater. She had a wife beater on under it with no bra. When Sheryl went to sit down a little ways from her, Dena grabbed her arm and pulled her closer to her.

Sheryl said, "I'm glad you're here." She closed the rest of the gap between them and kissed Dena. "If I'm going to be your second lover, I want you to remember me. Women always remember their first lover and their last lover, but they never remember the ones in between. You will remember me. Let me take charge of you tonight."

Dena was shaking with excitement, and her voice cracked when she whispered, "Okay."

"Lie down on the bed, but leave your clothes on. I want to remove them." Sheryl stood up at the edge of the bed, never taking her eyes off Dena. She looked so sexy. Sheryl licked her lovely lips while taking off her top. She winked and removed her pants and underwear, then climbed aboard Dena. They kissed. Neither one of them needed much foreplay. Sheryl removed Dena's shirt and started to kiss her neck. Dena blushed, then moaned when she realized how sensitive she was around her neck area. Sheryl gently placed her lips on Dena's breast. Then she sprinkled some blow on her other breast, and within a split second she was licking the powder off it.

Dena thought, "Damn, that shit feels good," and ran her fingers through Sheryl's hair. Sheryl removed the rest of Dena's clothes now, and Dena felt a chill from being both excited and cold. Sheryl separated Dena's legs and gently kissed her, then she used her tongue to find Dena's clitoris. Once she found it, Sheryl moaned with excitement. Dena gasped for air, then shook with pleasure. She relaxed her body and focused her attention on the movements of Sheryl's tongue. Sheryl knew exactly how to please a woman. Her tongue was like a brushless car wash on Dena's clitoris, and she sucked her until Dena exploded. Dena glanced at Sheryl's clock. She had come in a matter of minutes. "Damn, she's good," Dena thought.

Dena never had a chance to catch her breath. Sheryl got on top of her and used her hand to spread Dena's juices around her pussy, making it more slippery for her to ride. She licked Dena's juices off her fingers and started to ride her. Dena moaned while opening up her legs wider to enjoy Sheryl's body rubbing against hers. Dena started to grind Sheryl back and get into her rhythm. But Sheryl was like a wild woman, a buck wild woman, and Dena loved the way she let herself go when making love. Sheryl started humming and breathing heavier. Dena knew she was coming, so she squeezed and massaged her ass. Sheryl screamed and her body jerked, then she slowed down for a moment to catch her breath. Then she slowly started grinding Dena again, while whispering in her ear, "I'm just warming up, baby."

Dena felt excited again from the weight of Sheryl's body bouncing on top of her. She felt a spark of electricity shoot up from her pussy to the tip of her breasts. It made her tighten up into what she thought wasn't possible, another orgasm. She had only read about women having multiples. This was the first time she had experienced it. "Damn, Sheryl is right. I will never forget her. Two o'clock in the morning and still going strong. Guess I'm spending the night."

Dena had decided to get up around six a.m. and try to leave before the kids got up. She opened one eye and glanced at the clock. "Six-fifty. Let me get up." Sheryl was knocked out. She went to the bathroom and washed up and brushed her teeth with her fingers, a reminder to carry a toothbrush. She left a note, which read, "Had a fabulous time. You were awesome. Call you later." And she went on her happy way. While Dena was riding home on the train, she imagined herself being in charge and in control like that one day. She really liked Sheryl. "We'll just have to wait and see what happens," she thought.

Dena arrived home that afternoon and Mike was there. He seemed to be a little tipsy. Mike told Dena he was moving again. Things weren't working out with him and his lady. "I'm sorry to hear that, Mike," she said.

"The reason I'm telling you this is because I need to borrow your sofa bed."

"What happened to the last one I gave you?" Dena asked. "It should still be in good condition."

"Well," Mike explained, "I left it at Lisa's house."

"Mike, this is the second sofa bed Daddy has given me, and he was kind of upset that I gave you the first one. Plus, I'm planning on moving one day soon, and I plan on taking it with me."

"So you're not going to lend it to me?" Mike asked.

"Lend it to you? No, Mike, I'm taking this one with *me*."

"But you don't even know when you're moving out—"

"But I do know I'm moving out one day, and this sofa bed is coming with me." Dena saw a strange look came over Mike's face.

"You fucking lesbo. I'm ashamed to say you're my sister," he said, and left the house.

"That went well," she thought to herself. "Damn, my parents took it better. He didn't really think he was going to get the second sofa bed, so he could leave it with some chick when he decided to break up with her and move out. But what does being a lesbo have to do with anything? Lesbo, sofa, sofa, lesbo, hmm."

CHAPTER EIGHT

Dena hadn't heard from Hilda in a while and decided to give her a call. "What's up, baby?" she greeted Hilda when she answered her own phone for a change.

"I'm in the middle of something, Dena."

"What's wrong? She asked.

"Well, you remember Joan?"

"Of course I remember your dyke pimp," Dena said and cracked up. So did Hilda.

"Stop fucking around and listen. Joan knows that I'm seeing Jasmine, and she's not too happy about it. But she's still around. Now she's found out I slept with Vera, and she's going to tell Jasmine, hoping she will leave me so she can have me all to herself again. Can you come over? Jasmine's not here yet, and I don't know how she's going to react."

"Be right over." Dena hung up the telephone and left her place.

She arrived at Hilda's house and let herself in. Then she walked through the house to the bedroom, said hello to Joan and Hilda, and went back and sat in the living room. She overheard Hilda pleading with Joan not to say anything to Jasmine. "Why would you do that, knowing how much I love Jasmine? It's not going to make any difference between us." At that moment Jasmine let herself into the apartment. Hilda and Joan came out of the room and met Jasmine in the living room. Hilda just stood there and waited to see if Joan had the audacity to reveal her secret.

"I have something to tell to you," Joan said to Jasmine. "Would you like to sit down?"

Neither Jasmine nor Joan liked each other, so Jasmine said, "Just say what you have to say." Dena had a snickers bar in her pocket and decided this was a good time to eat it. "This is going to get good," she thought.

"Jasmine, aren't you the least bit curious where Hilda was all last night?"

Jasmine looked at Hilda and said, "I called you twice last night. Where were you, baby?"

Hilda just looked at Jasmine as if to say, "You'll find out in a minute from this bitch."

Dena loved how her candy bar was packed with peanuts.

"Jasmine," Joan said, "she was at Vera's house all night long fucking her brains out."

"Is this true, Hilda?"

Hilda hesitated as if searching for the words, then said nothing.

Jasmine put her hands on her face and screamed, "Noooooooooooooo!" and dropped to her knees crying.

Dena looked up at Hilda to see what she was going to do. She was actually trying to hide a smile. Dena discreetly laughed at Jasmine's performance, then looked at Hilda again. Hilda told Joan to get the hell out and then tried to work things out with Jasmine. Jasmine headed straight to the bedroom, grabbed some of her belongings, and left.

Hilda mimicked Jasmine by grabbing her face and falling to the floor. "What was that about?" she said, and sat down next to Dena on the sofa.

"Looks like true love to me," Dena responded. Then she asked Hilda, "Why are you in a relationship if you can't be faithful?"

Hilda said, "I don't know. Don't worry about it, baby, she'll be back."

Then Dena changed the subject. "Are there any other clubs besides Better Days? I'm getting tired of partying with men. They seem to dominate the club now. Last time I went there, there were only a handful of women. It sucks."

"Girl, you just missed this really nice club called Bonnie and Clyde," Hilda said. "They closed about a month ago." Then she explained, "Women's clubs always seem to fly by night. They never stay open long. Gay women don't want to spend money in New York. Whereas, the men—the men's clubs have and will always have longevity, because they know how to spend money and leave big tips. I'll check around to see if the owners of Bonnie and Clyde have opened another club somewhere else."

Dena hung out with Sheryl a couple more times, but she noticed that Sheryl had lost interest in her and had gained more interest in getting high. She could not continue to see her. She could not afford her anymore. It seemed to her the only time Sheryl wanted to make love was when she was high. Not good. So Dena moved on. One night, when Dena was at the club, she ran into Sheryl. When Sheryl approached her, Dena almost didn't recognize her. Sheryl looked more aggressive than Dena did. She had cut off all of her hair, and had on a jersey with jeans.

Out of all the city exams Dena had taken, wouldn't you know it was the New York City Department of Traffic that called her first. "Damn, a meter maid," she thought. "The pay is good, the benefits are nice...it's like five times more money than what I'm making at the supermarket. But those brown uniforms! Oh well, I'll go for my physical examination next week and that's that."

Dena went to work at the supermarket to discover her register was short ten dollars again. She was suspicious because every time this certain female manager was on duty, her fucking register was short. "Too coincidental, I'll say. But what can I do about it?" she thought. One thing Dena knew how to do was count. "I'm the fastest one on these registers, and I know I'm never short. I'm going to talk to the manager about this shit." Dena was slow moving at work that day. "I only make ninety dollars a week," she thought, "and she keeps taking ten dollars out of my pay. I'm glad I'll be starting a new job soon."

Dena saw the manager's sister, Lily, and asked her if her sister was working that day. "No, Dena, she's off today."

"Thanks," Dena said as she noticed this fine young woman in her line, three shopping carts back. She became nervous. She glanced at the woman every chance she had. When the young woman was finally next in line, Dena looked up at her and smiled and said, "How you doing?"

The woman smiled back and shyly said, "Okay." She was slimly built, with a beautiful face and corn rows braided front to back, hanging past her shoulders.

She thought to herself while ringing her up, "Damn, she is fine fine. What do I have to do to have a woman like this? Dream on, girl. She's probably straight. Oh well." Dena said thank you and handed her the change and receipt, and slyly watched her walk out of the store. "Sometimes I wish I was a man so I wouldn't have to conceal my attraction for women," she thought.

Dena's little packer, Brian, made a quarter tip and yelled out, "I'm going on a break!"

Dena yelled back at Brian, "Every time you receive a tip, you run to the candy store to spend your earnings. Save some money, boy." A lot of customers would ask Dena if Brian was her son, because they looked so much alike. She never had a chance to answer, because Brian would cut everybody off and say, "Yes, that's my mother, so give me a good tip." And they would say, "Smart kid."

As she turned away from the register to pack the next order, she looked out the store to watch Brian go into the candy store and she saw that fine woman come out. Dena thought she was long gone when she saw her reenter the supermarket. "Forgot something, I guess." But the woman was headed directly toward her. Dena looked around her counter area to see if Brian had forgotten to put an item in her bag. Nothing. She had stopped looking at her and had gone back to working when the cutie-pie tapped her on the arm, handed her a piece of paper, smiled, and walked out of the store.

Dena put the paper in her jeans pocket for fear of losing it if she put it in her smock. She kept telling herself, "Nah, it can't be her telephone number. Things like this don't happen to me. I know she realized I was flirting with her. She's beautiful." The suspense was killing her, so she stopped right in the middle of an order to see what was on the piece of paper. It read, Tammie, 555-3256. She looked up, squeezed the piece of paper in her hand, and said, "Yes!"

Back at Hilda's house, things weren't going so well with Hilda and Jasmine. Dena asked Hilda if she could use her telephone to call Tammie, but she couldn't concentrate with Jasmine yelling in the background. She came out to the living room to see what all the commotion was about. Hilda's mother was staying with her for a couple of days, and Dena could not understand why Jasmine was yelling with Hilda's mother in the house. Jasmine was packing her belongings again, and while she was packing her stuff, she was bitching pretty loud about how Hilda was treating her.

She didn't like the fact that she was cursing in front of Hilda's mother. She approached Hilda and tugged at her sleeve and pointed to Jasmine with her eyes as if to say, "Aren't you going to do something?" Hilda just rolled her eyes at Dena. Dena bit her tongue, because she loved Hilda's mother like her own. Jasmine blurted out again, "How could you have treated me this way, when all I did was fucking love you?"

Dena had had enough, and told Jasmine, "You have to go, and you have to go right now. Hilda's mother is here, and you're disrespecting her. Either you leave right now willingly with whatever's in your bag, or I will throw your ass out and your bag will follow you out the door." Jasmine looked at Dena and noticed her toes were tapping, and grabbed her bag and left.

Relieved, Hilda said, "Thank you, Dena."

Hilda's mother just shook her head and said in Spanish, "I never liked that woman."

She told Hilda she was sorry about Jasmine's behavior, then quickly changed the subject. She told her about meeting Tammie and that her father was buying a new car and, "He wants me to have his old Chevy."

"Are you going to take it?" Hilda asked.

"I might as well," she replied. "Timo and Mike don't get along, and Nancy can't drive it. I priced the car insurance and it's only eighty-six dollars a month for liability. I figured I could afford it with my part-time job at the supermarket. And soon I hope to be starting a city job. So I told him I would take it. I expect to be driving by Monday."

"Cool," Hilda said, "maybe you can chauffer me around now."

"Now," Dena said and smiled, "I'm going to use your telephone." She dialed Tammie's number. "Hi, Tammie, this is Dena, the butch from the supermarket."

Tammie laughed, and said, "Dena, huh? I like your name." The voice on the other end sounded so sweet.

"Do you live around the supermarket, Tammie?"

"Yes, across the street. I live with my dad, but he's always at work. Would you like to come over tonight?"

Dena answered, "Not tonight, sweetie. I'm not home. How about tomorrow? I'm off tomorrow. Anytime after three o'clock is fine with me."

"Can you make it around seven?"

Dena said, "I'm there. See you tomorrow, okay? Bye."

Dena entered Tammie's home, and could not believe how beautiful her apartment was. Every piece of furniture looked brand new. She sat down, and Tammie handed her a cold drink. They talked for hours. She asked Tammie, "Where's your mom? Do you have any brothers or sisters, or are you an only child?"

Tammie's eyes became watery when she said, "I don't have any brothers and my mother and sister died in a house fire two years ago."

Dena said that she'd never known anyone who had died in a fire. "I'm so sorry," she said, and held Tammie until she thought she felt better. Tammie went to the bathroom to clean herself up. Dena now realized how serious a fire really was. Tammie asked Dena if she had a lover and vice-versa. Neither did. For a moment, she thought Tammie was straight or bisexual—just something about her. Dena asked, "Are you bisexual?"

Tammie said, "No, I'm gay. I recently turned gay, I mean—"

"How long have you been gay?"

"Around a year," Tammie said.

Dena thought Tammie looked stunning and leaned forward to kiss her. Tammie responded by kissing her back. Then Tammie said, "It's getting late. My father should be home soon."

Dena said, "Okay, let me go. I have to get up early."

Tammie walked her to the front door and they kissed again. This time Dena held Tammie and squeezed her tight. She felt Tammie's breasts on hers and wanted to go back into the living room. "Goodnight, Tammie."

"Goodnight, Dena."

"Can I call you tomorrow?"

"I'll be waiting for your call."

Dena and Dolores sat down one morning at the kitchen table for coffee and rolls. "You know, Dena, ever since you came out to the family, three other family members have also announced they're gay," Dolores chuckled.

Dena said, "First of all, Barbara Walters, I told you and Daddy I was gay, not the entire family. Second, it must be in our genes, because every family member that you named— Mimi, Irene, and Ariel—is on your side of the family. Are you gay, Mom?" Dena asked and laughed. Then she looked at her mom and said, "Mommy, you know I love you very much, and all we have is each other. Dad left, Mike is on his own, and, unfortunately, Nancy is in a hospital. I just want you to know, no matter what, I will never leave you, even if I move out one day. I will always be here for you. And, God willing, when I buy a house, you will move in with me. Okay?"

Dolores cried, and said, "I love you very much, Dena. And do you think when Nancy gets better, she can live with us too?"

"Yes, Mommy, Nancy can live with us too. Now give me

a hug and stop crying." She gave her mom a hug, and just then the telephone rang. "I'll get it, Mom."

"Hey, girl, what you doing?" Hilda asked.

"Having coffee with Mom."

"Guess what? I found this new club for women in the Village on Christopher Street. Heard it's jumping on Friday nights. In addition, the bartender who worked at Bonnie and Clyde is bartending at this new club."

"All right," Dena said, "now you're talking. What's the name of it?"

"I think it's called The Duchess. I have everything written down. I'm going this Friday. You want to come?"

"What time should I pick you up?"

"Usual time," Hilda said, "around eleven."

"If I don't talk with you before then, I'll call you Friday to confirm. Thanks for the info. Have a good day, baby." Dena hung up the telephone and walked back to the table to finish her coffee, just to do an about-face when the telephone rang again.

"Hello?"

"Hi, Dena," Tammie said, "what you doing?"

"Just cooling out."

"Can I see you today?"

"Okay, what time?"

"Is six okay?"

"Six o'clock is fine."

Dena got all dolled up, then patted her neck with some cologne, thinking about Tammie, and walked to her house. "This is cool," she thought, "no trains and no buses—just a hop, skip, and a jump to Tammie's house." Dena thought about commitment and wondered how many more women she would have to date until her next relationship. She really didn't believe that Tammie would be the one. She had all the qualities. "But, I don't know," she thought. She stopped at the supermarket where she worked and picked up some flowers, and called Tammie to see if she needed anything from the store. Dena got a chill anticipating what was to come.

Tammie put the flowers in water and invited her into the living room. Dena thought, "It's a small lesbian world," when she found out that Tammie knew a woman in Hilda's building. Dena described Hilda to Tammie, but Tammie said she didn't know her. "What time are you expecting your father home?" Dena asked.

"It's six-thirty now," Tammie replied. "Around midnight, so you have me for hours."

Dena thought, "Still not enough time."

After making love to Tammie for hours, Dena left her house around midnight, hoping she wouldn't run into Tammie's father. She arrived home and sat in her room, drinking some cheap wine and thinking about her night with Tammie. "Damn," she said to herself, "I forgot to check the mail. Oh well, I'll check it tomorrow. Boy, I'm sore from all that grinding."

Dena called Hilda the next day and confirmed that eleven o'clock was a good time to meet. "See you later."

That night, Dena knocked on Hilda's door. Hilda waved for her to follow her into the bedroom and wait for her.

"I'm almost ready. Plus, my friend, Sharon, is here. She wants to go to the club with us."

"Cool," Dena said, "the more, the merrier." Sharon was one of Hilda's brother's ex-lovers. After they broke up, Sharon started hanging out with Hilda and Dena big-time. Dena guessed she'd tossed the boys to the side and was experimenting with women.

Hilda asked Sharon to answer her telephone while she finished getting dressed, adding, "Or else we'll never get out of here. When the telephone rings," Hilda told her, "say the person's name out loud, and I'll decide if the call is important or not."

The telephone rang. Sharon answered, "Hello, who's calling, please?" and yelled out Hilda's name. Hilda and Dena both looked at each other. Hilda was handed the telephone still clueless about who was on the other end of the telephone.

"Hello?" Hilda said. "Abdul, I can't talk to you right now. I'm walking out the door as we speak. Talk to you tomorrow." She hung up and turned to Sharon. "Sharon, are you losing your mind? I said, say *their* name out loud, not *my* name. I'm ready, you guys. Let's go. Dena, get off the bed and let's go." But she couldn't stop laughing. Once Hilda had thought about it again, she joined her on the bed, laughing at Sharon.

"I'm never going to live this down, am I?" Sharon asked Hilda and Dena.

"Hell no, you won't," Dena answered her.

When the girls exited the building elevator, Dena, Hilda, and even Sharon were amazed to see two women entering the building all hugged up. At first, Dena thought to herself, "That's cool." But then when she zoomed in to have a closer look, she looked into familiar eyes and noticed one of the young ladies was Tammie. Tammie noticed Dena and was surprised, and whispered something in the other woman's ear. Dena stopped right in front of Tammie and said, "What's up, Tammie? What's going on?"

The other woman stepped in and said, "Who are you?"

Dena said, "I'm a friend of Tammie's, and I'd like to talk to her for a minute." Hilda and Sharon stood to the side.

"What's going on, Tammie? You have me on Wednesday and her on Friday?"

"Look, hater," the woman said, never taking her arm off Tammie's shoulder.

But Dena interrupted her and said, "I'm finished."

"Tammie, do you want to talk to her?" the woman asked.

Tammie said, "No," and they walked away.

Dena turned around and yelled, "Ho!" then said, "Let's go, I need a fucking drink."

Once in the car, she informed Sharon and Hilda that she had to warm it up. She reached into the glove compartment and pulled out a tape, put it in the tape deck, and pressed "play." "Pillow Talk" by Sylvia started playing and Sharon asked her, "What the hell are you listening to?"

Dena explained that every time she got depressed or needed some inspiration, she could always rely on this record to cheer her up. Hilda just shook her head because she was used to it. Sharon said, "Put on some Fonda Rae, 'Over Like a Fat Rat,' or something fast." The girls didn't realize Dena was hurting after that incident with Tammie.

"How could she break my heart and act so nonchalant about it?" Dena wondered. "Damn, women are just as crude as men."

Dena liked this new club—wall-to-wall women, just what she'd wished for. A guy here and there, but women dominated this club. They even had two women bartenders. Dena danced, mingled, and had a great time, although her mind was elsewhere—on Tammie, of course. Dena did not give out her telephone number, nor did she take anyone's number. Instead she socialized and met a lot of new friends. She knew she would see the same women there the next week. There were a couple of cuties Dena had her eyes on, but she was too upset to talk to them tonight.

After leaving the club, the girls were walking to the car when they noticed some women arguing down the block. Sharon said, "Slow down, let's see what's going on."

"Obviously nothing," Dena said, "if the two women are yelling at each other from across the street.'

Hilda said, "Let's wait to see what happens anyway."

It was a clear night, not cold.

"Okay, let's wait," said Dena.

There were about five women on one side of the street with a femme woman, most likely the girlfriend, and about five women on the other side of the street with the aggressor. Only the femme and the aggressor were arguing, though. One woman was holding the aggressor back, but she broke out of her grip and started running across the street in her cowboy boots. She made it only halfway across the street when she fell. Everyone started to laugh and the fight that never began was over, because once the cowboy boot girl got up, she started walking back in the same direction she came from, still yelling and cursing out the femme. "You didn't knock me down, bitch!" She must have been drunk or just could not walk in her boots, because there was nothing in the street to make her fall.

The girls had a good laugh on their way to the car. Dena dropped off Hilda and Sharon and decided to go home and spend the night at her own house, where she could be alone. She did not want to hear anyone's advice about women. She found a parking space and, before she went home, she played "Pillow Talk" again, this time without any flack, and then headed upstairs.

CHAPTER NINE

Coffee!" Dolores yelled as she knocked on Dena's door.
"Be right there, Mom." She went into the bathroom, then went to join Dolores for coffee.

"Dena, next month we're having a family reunion in California. Everybody's going and everybody's purchasing their tickets now. Do you want to go?"

"How much is the airfare?" Dena asked.

Dolores said, "If you want to go, I will charge our tickets, and you pay me back when you can."

"Okay, Mom. I want to go. I will pay you fifty dollars every payday until I pay it off."

Dolores said, "You don't have to pay me back."

"I know I don't have to, Mom," Dena said, "but I want to. Who are you staying with, Mom?" Dena had two cousins in California, and she knew she would stay with her gay cousin, Mimi. Dolores, of course, would stay with Dena's older cousin. Most of the older family members would stay there, or in hotels nearby. "I am going to call Mimi now, Mom, to see if it's okay for me to stay with her." Mimi could not wait. She told Mimi she would call her back with the details. "Okay, Mom, it's all set. I'm going to be staying with Mimi. After I take a shower and get dressed, we'll go the travel agency and make our reservations."

Even though it was her first time on a plane, Dena was not afraid. She said a prayer and asked the flight attendant for a drink. The flight attendant informed her that drinks would be served shortly. Dena could not wait that long, so she pulled out a small bottle of gin, opened it, and drank it straight.

Dolores looked at her and said, "Oh my!"

Dena laughed. "First time flying, Mom, and besides, it's after nine a.m."

Mimi picked Dolores and Dena up at the airport. Dena was so happy to see her younger cousin. Mimi was happy too. She informed Mimi that Hilda could not make it this trip. Mimi told her Aunt Dolores that she would drop her off first at their Cousin Mona's house. "We'll stay there for a bit. Then we'll head back to my house in Crenshaw."

"Crenshaw, Mimi?" Dena said. "I've never been to Crenshaw. Can't wait. Now I can tell people I've been to Crenshaw, California." The big family dinner and gathering wasn't going to be held for two more days, so Dena kissed Dolores and told her she would see her then. Mimi and Dena walked back to the car hugging each other.

"Damn, cuz," Dena said, "we live so far from each other now, we don't see each other anymore."

Mimi's family used to live in the Bronx. But Mimi had recently moved to California with her lover. After they broke up, Mimi decided to stay. Then her mother and stepfather moved to Florida. So she only came to New York for special occasions. Mimi's father and Dolores were brother and sister. He had died very young, at age thirty-seven, on Dena's birthday. He had been handsome. Dolores used to say, "The girls were always after him." Dolores told Dena she had eyes just like her brother. Mimi resembled her mother, with a nice complexion, brown eyes, and real tight curls—not a curly Afro like Dena's.

Mimi gave Dena the itinerary for the next couple of days. She said, "I have to work tonight at this club called Catch Two. You know I don't get high, so I work at the juice bar on the main floor. Would you like to make a few dollars? My boss is always looking for workers."

"Off the books?" Dena asked. Dena was always worrying about the books.

"Yeah," Mimi said, "off the books."

"Hell yeah, then." Dena replied.

"Why don't we stop by the club first, before we go home? Do you mind, I mean with jetlag and all?"

"I'm okay. Let's go to the club."

Mimi stopped and greeted most of the workers inside the club, and introduced them to Dena. "Has anyone seen John?" she asked.

"He's in the office," one worker replied.

Mimi knocked on his door and introduced Dena to her boss. She told John that she was staying with her for a couple of days. Before Mimi could ask, John interrupted her and asked Dena if she wanted to work that night. "I need all the help I can get. I'll pay you seventy-five dollars, plus any tips you might get."

"Well, I really wasn't planning on working when I got here," Dena said, "all the way from New York. I still have a little jetlag—"

"One hundred dollars for the night. All you have to do is walk around the club selling shots."

"Okay," she said, "I'll do it."

Mimi had a cute apartment on the first floor in a court-yard type of place. Dena couldn't even call it a building, because it only had two stories. Not even close to an apartment building, compared to New York City. Mimi knew every tenant. "Hey, throw me my videotape you borrowed from me last week," some woman yelled from the balcony. Mimi complied, reaching into her bag and throwing the videotape up to the second-floor balcony. The woman caught it on the first try.

That night, Mimi and Dena were getting dressed for work when one of Mimi's ex-lovers kept calling her on the telephone, insisting she ditch work and come over to her house. Mimi told her, "Work is work and I must attend, and the boss is already short staffed." Mimi told Dena, "Let's get out of here before this crazy woman calls again."

Dena got her instructions: "Only work the top floor. As soon as you run out of shots, go back to the bar and restock. Your work is complete when all the shots are gone. Could be an hour, could be all night, depending how fast you sell them, got it? If you want to socialize, no problem—just sell the shots while you socialize."

"Okay, John," she said.

Mimi showed her the juice bar where she'd be working, "Just in case you need a break and want to chitchat."

"Okay, I got it, Dena said. "Just tell me where the bathrooms are located."

"There's one right there," Mimi said, "and one right above it on the second floor."

"Okay, I'm going to work," Dena said, kissed Mimi, and went upstairs.

Dena was selling her shots quickly. She figured she would be done in under two hours. She mostly approached women. Every now and again, a guy would wave to her to purchase a shot. She would just ignore him and make him run after her. She laughed, "Have to make the job interesting."

She looked up at what you would call a music video screen. She had never seen a screen that big in the clubs before; the movie theater, yeah, but never the clubs. When the deejay played a music video of Janet Jackson, Dena did not move. "I guess these shots will have to wait, because I have to watch this life-size video of Janet," she told herself. After the video was over, she asked herself, "Why don't they have stuff like this in New York?" She sold all of her shots and turned in her serving tray, collected her money, and went to the bathroom. Then she went downstairs to see how Mimi was doing.

Dena saw Mimi when she reached the stairwell. Mimi looked like she was enjoying her job. She waved for her to come down. "What's up, culito, working hard?"

"Just finished. Now I want to relax and socialize."

"Want something to drink?"

"Nah, I'm going to go upstairs and have a stiff one, thanks anyway. While I'm here, would you like to take a bathroom break?"

"I just went, baby, thank you. Go mingle, have fun."

Dena took in a breath and headed upstairs. "Budweiser and a Jack Daniels, please." She grabbed the shot of Jack and held it up to the light. She was amazed at the amount of liquor in the shot glass. "Hey," she said to the bartender, "do you normally pour this much liquor into a shot glass, or is it on account of me working here temporarily?"

"That's how I pour all my drinks," the bartender said.

"Damn, that's cool." She downed the shot and chased it with the beer, and asked for another shot. Dena said to herself, "This is like three shots in one compared to New York, for less fucking money. After this next shot, I should be feeling nice. Then, I'll be ready to mingle."

She scoped the top level and noticed this gorgeous, very tall woman. She was at least five-foot-seven. "Wow, I would move to Cali for her," Dena thought. She was standing very close to two guys, maybe her bodyguards, because she was that fine. Dena knew that some women, especially feminine women, would travel with male friends, mainly gay guys, because when the femmes left the club at two, three o'clock in the morning, they felt protected going to their cars and going home with men. So dykes didn't find it unusual to see femmes with men, nor were they intimidated to approach a woman with a group of guys in the club. Well, she kept looking at Dena, so she decided to approach her.

"Hi, my name is Dena," she said, and nothing else came out of her mouth. She really didn't think of what she was going to say after that, or maybe she did. But when she realized how beautiful the tall woman was up close, she forgot what she was going to say. So instead of saying something corny, she just stopped her flow of words.

The tall woman smiled at Dena and said, "Hi, my name is Faye. Nice to meet you. This is my friend, Gerald, and this is Rodney."

"Nice to meet you," Dena said, being polite. One of the two guys waved hello in a feminine way. The other guy nodded a hello, then rolled his eyes. Dena nodded a hello back, while saying to herself, "Fuck you too."

"Can you buy me a drink?" Dena said jokingly.

Faye laughed and said, "A white wine, please?"

"Sure," Dena said, "be right back." "Wow, she is beautiful," Dena thought. "I hope I don't screw this up while walking back to her with her drink." When she got back, she said to Faye, "Here's your drink."

"Thank you, Dena. Why didn't you get one for yourself?"

"I already had two drinks. I'm good."

"So where you from?" Faye asked.

"Where am I from? Like where are my parents from?" Dena asked.

"No," Faye said, "where do you live? Because I know you don't live out here in Los Angeles."

"You're right, I live in New York. I'm here for a family reunion. My cousin works here in the club. She's working the juice bar downstairs. Do you know her? Her name is Mimi."

"No, I don't know her. I really don't go out much." Faye grabbed Dena's face with her hand and brought her face closer to hers, and said, "I think you're really cute—kind of my type. But there's no future between us, you living in New York and all. I'm sorry." Then she waved to the two young men and walked away.

"Give me your telephone number just in case I relocate." Dena shouted.

Faye turned around. "Sorry."

"But I really like you," Dena said.

Faye did not turn around this time. Dena whispered, "I'll be here for three more days," as Faye vanished into the crowd. "Damn it," she said, and just shook her head in disappointment.

Friday morning, Mimi woke Dena up early so they could go help out at the homeless shelter. Mimi had a special place in her heart for the unfortunate. She would go to a shoe store and buy shoes and sneakers in all different sizes and put them in the trunk of her car. When she saw a person needing shoes, she would go to her car trunk and have them pick out a pair of shoes in their size. After working all morning and afternoon, the girls headed to Mona's house in Harbor City.

It was nice seeing Dolores and the other family members. All the family members requested that they do this every year. Easier said than done. Dena hit the open bar and chatted with her family. "Boy," she said, "what a fine family we have." Everyone was so positive and happy, and no one snubbed Dena or Mimi off for being gay. Even though Dena and Mimi didn't know when to stop talking, the family listened with interest to every story they had to tell.

Saturday morning came and Mimi woke Dena up early again. "For someone who doesn't have a fucking job, you sure wake up early," she said while scratching her head and walking toward the bathroom.

"I do have a job, you bum."

"Oh, that's right, three part-time jobs equal one full-time job. I forgot." They laughed.

"I'm giving a house party tonight," Mimi explained, "so we have a lot of things to do today."

"A house party? Why didn't you say so? I would have been up hours ago!" Dena made a funny face. "Not!"

Mimi and Dena cleaned the house from top to bottom, then went outdoors to pick up last minute things. On the way back, Mimi didn't realize how fast she was going on the highway and got pulled over for speeding. The officer told Mimi to step out of the car and told Dena to remain in the car. While Mimi tried to talk her way out of the summons, Dena was fumbling with the stereo and accidentally hit the horn. She was still changing the car radio stations when the police officer and Mimi approached the vehicle. Dena became nervous when the officer asked, "Is everything all right?"

Dena looked at him dumbfounded when Mimi cut in. "Sir, she's from New York. She doesn't know that blowing your car horn on the highway is illegal."

Dena jumped in. "Sorry, officer, I didn't do it on purpose. It was an accident."

He handed Mimi back her license and registration and said, "Drive safely."

Mimi got back in the car and thanked God, then slapped Dena on the back of the head and said, "What the hell is wrong with you, beeping the car horn like that? I already had the ticket squashed when you beeped the horn. Then I said, 'Oh shit, now he's going to change his mind.'"

"First of all," Dena explained, "I told your ass it was an accident. What do you think? I'm that crazy I'm going to rush the cop when he's making up his mind about giving you a summons? Second, how can blowing your horn on the highway be illegal?"

"I know, I know," Mimi said.

Dena added, "Damn, in New York, drivers ride their brakes and their car horns."

On their way home, Dena asked Mimi if she would have any liquor at her party. Mimi said she wouldn't, so Dena asked if she could swing by a liquor store on the way home.

"No problem," Mimi answered.

"What time does the party start?"

"Around nine o clock."

"That's one of the things I miss about New York," Mimi complained, "that you could arrive at the club as late as you want and still have hours to party before the club closed. Here in Cali, all the clubs close at two in the morning, no exceptions."

Mimi's posse started rolling in around eight-thirty. She had a small dance area, a movie area, and a card game going on, and if you just wanted to socialize, you could go into the kitchen where it was quiet and well lit. Dena scoped out the party. "Hmm, more aggressors here than femmes. Come to think of it, there were more aggressors than femmes in the club where Mimi worked too. Therefore, if you're a femme in California, you got it going on. I bet the butches fight over the femmes." She laughed to herself.

Mimi introduced Dena to everyone at the party. Dena asked who had next at the card game. They were playing spades, which she knew how to play well. Who didn't? They informed her she had next after next, and pointed to the team who had next before her. "Okay," Dena said, and went to the kitchen to pour herself a drink. She opened the cabinet and pulled out her stash. Most of the women there frowned at her, because they were on a no-drinking program. Dena wanted to say aloud, "Don't be mad at me if you guys can't hold your smoke." But she noticed these L.A. women were fucking buffed, and she didn't want a beat down that night.

A woman touched Dena's shoulder and asked if she could pour her a drink.

"On the rocks, please," the woman said nonchalantly.

Dena thought to herself, "Oh, my goodness, a femme, a cute femme at that." "I thought I was the only drinker in here tonight," Dena said.

"You and I probably are," the woman stated. "Friend of Mimi's?"

"Mimi is my cousin. I'm visiting her for a family reunion. I live in New York, and I'll be here until Monday." Dena thought she'd get it all out in one breath.

"That's cool," the woman said. "You told me your whole life story, but you didn't tell me your name," she added, and smiled.

"Oh, damn," Dena thought, "I thought I did mention my name. I must be nervous." She said aloud, "Dena's my name, and yours?"

"Tonya, nice to meet you. Would you like to dance?"

Dena peeped around the kitchen wall and told Tonya she was waiting to play cards, that she was next.

"Do you have a partner?"

"No, Tonya, I don't. Would you like to be my partner?"

"Sure."

"Well, we had better wait over by the card table before somebody jumps us."

Dena looked at Tonya and said to herself, "She's pretty," while they were playing cards and sitting across from each other. She noticed Tonya flirting with her. She would wink at her from time to time, and Dena found it arousing. Dena found anything a woman did arousing. Some of the other women knew Tonya, and approached her a couple times during the card game, probably trying to rap to her. Mimi came out of the kitchen with a birthday cake, wishing a femme woman happy birthday. One of the women playing cards with Dena and Tonya asked if they could pause the game for a moment, while she gave the birthday girl her present.

"Not a problem, go get your gift on, girl," Tonya said. Tonya got up from her chair and said she'd be right back, came around to Dena's side of the table, and asked if she wanted a refill of her drink.

Dena said "Sure," took the bottle out of her pocket, and handed it to her.

Dena could not believe how many presents the birthday girl received. She had at least seven aggressors lined up to hand her their gifts. She received a diamond tennis bracelet, cash, gift certificates, and a fur coat. "What the...?" She wondered if all these women were in competition for her heart, or had they already slept with her? "I'm confused. I must ask Mimi about her later," she thought. Tonya came back with Dena's drink, sat on her lap, and asked her if her drink was all right.

She tasted it and said, "It's fine, thank you."

Tonya yelled out, "Can we finish this game already?"

"Not yet," Dena said, "Casanova's still in line."

"Well, let me look over my cards again," she said, and gave Dena a kiss on her lips. "We better win."

Dena said, "Well then, you better have both jokers in your hand, because we're losing by over two hundreds points."

The party was over at two o'clock sharp. Tonya asked Dena if she could walk her to her car, and she agreed but went to ask Mimi for a sweatshirt first. Dena couldn't get over how cold it got in Los Angeles at night. How could it be eighty degrees in the afternoon and forty degrees at night? Dena and Tonya walked fast to her car. Tonya welcomed her in while she warmed it up. Dena admired her car, and saw a job identification card hanging up on her rearview mirror. She looked at the picture and asked, "Who's this?"

Tonya started to laugh. "You know, that's me. I just got my hair cut a couple of weeks ago and haven't had a chance to change my ID. I look better with longer hair, right?"

You would look fine to me bald-headed, because you have a very attractive face. So you look good with your hair short or long."

"Thank you, Dena. You're so sweet. Would you like to come home with me and spend the night? I'll have you back at Mimi's house in the morning."

"Wow, what an offer," she thought. The heat was kicking in now, from Tonya's car *and* from Dena's body, and it felt good. Dena did not want to leave. "I like you, Tonya. I think you are a very special lady, and good-looking. And if I lived here in California and knew you a little better, I would want to be with you every day. But, baby, I don't live here and I don't know you, so I can't. I'm sorry."

Tonya said, "I have my own place. It's not far from here. You'll never forget Los Angeles."

Dena had to rethink the situation. She always wanted some pussy, and Tonya was beautiful. "We'll have our privacy," she thought. "But I've never done anything like this before. I don't have any feelings for her. How can I make love to a woman without feelings?" she thought. "I'm sorry, Tonya, I must have feelings for someone in order to sleep with them, nothing personal."

"It's okay, Dena, I understand. But can I have a kiss good-night?"

Dena leaned over to the driver's side to kiss her. It was a long, wet kiss, and she was reconsidering again, or maybe the liquor was. Dena tap kissed her while reaching for the door handle. Then she placed her lips by Tonya's ear and whispered goodnight. She stood outside and waited for Tonya's car to pull off. She noticed about four or five aggressive women just standing across the street. "They must be waiting for the birthday girl to come outside to see who has the winning lottery ticket," she thought. Tonya finally drove off and Dena wanted to chase her car, but thought it was for the best. "Sex with no feeling—I don't think I could ever do that in my life," she thought. "Besides, she could have been a dominatrix or something."

Dena folded her arms for warmth and started to walk back to the house when she overheard one of the women across the street say, "Didn't she just get out of your ex-lover's car?"

Before another woman could answer, she was too far away to hear them.

Once back in the apartment, Dena asked Mimi if she wanted to straighten up a little bit, so there wouldn't be so much to do the next day, being that it was only two-thirty. Mimi's lips were locked with this other woman's. "So, I guess that means no," Dena said. She wondered if maybe she should have spent the night out to give Mimi some privacy.

Mimi came up for air. "Could you give the birthday girl a hand with all of her presents?"

She looked at all her presents and said out loud, "Damn, I'd rather clean the house." Then she looked at the birthday girl and said, "You have a lot of admirers. No wonder you don't have a lover around birthday time. You'd only get one gift." She laughed, but the birthday girl really didn't find it to be too funny, so she just said to her, "Between you and me, we're going to have to make at least two trips to your car. Are you ready? Grab what you can."

They grabbed as many bags as they could on the first trip and just set them by the car trunk. After the second trip, Dena just wanted to walk away after she'd set the last bag down on the ground. But the birthday girl asked her, "Could you start the car and pop the trunk?"

Dena thought, the birthday girl should know where the trunk lever was better than she did. But it was a Porsche, so she wanted to start the car to hear what the engine sounded like. Dena looked across the street to see if any of the dykes had any balls to come over and give them a hand and talk to this woman.

Across the street it looked like a football huddle. All her bags were loaded in the car, and the birthday girl was thanking Dena with a hug when one of the jealous aggressors from across the street yelled out, "Who the fuck do she think she is coming around our way and getting all the girls?"

"Yeah," another joined in, "I say we all should go over there and kick her fucking ass."

Dena was like, "Whoa!" She turned around to face them. "Look, lesbos, I'm just helping the birthday girl carry her gifts to her car, which is what you guys should be doing if you like her like that, instead of standing across the street all scared." The birthday girl rushed back toward the house. Dena thought, "Maybe she forgot something or she didn't want any trouble." Looking back at the crowd of aggressive women, she said, "Shit, I'm going to get my ass kicked. But one of them is getting fucked up too, because I'm going to grab one of them and I'm not going to let go."

Then Mimi came running out of the house with the birthday girl. "What's the problem, guys?" Mimi asked. "This is my cousin." And that's all she had to say, nothing more. Some of the women even apologized. Mimi and Dena laughed about it later.

Monday morning, Mimi drove Dolores and Dena to the airport. "Group hug," Mimi said. They kissed and cried and said their goodbyes. Dolores always corrected Dena when she said that.

"Never say 'goodbye,' Dena, always say 'so long.'"

CHAPTER TEN

Saturday afternoon, Dena had nothing to do. It was a beautiful May day, so she called Hilda to see what she was doing, but Hilda was busy. Dena asked about her sister. "How's Nikki doing? Do you think she might want to take a ride to the park?"

"Nikki's falling behind," Hilda said. "She hasn't hung out with me or the crew in a long time. She's busy with her kids."

So Dena decided to go to Greenwich Village by herself, to walk around, windowshop, and sit in Washington Square Park and read a book, just to get out of the house. On her way out, she checked the mail and found a letter from the City of New York in the mailbox and put it in her back pocket. "I'll read it in the park," she thought. She put the rest of the mail back in the mailbox and went to her car. She started her car, lifted her ass up off the car seat, and reached into her back pocket to get the letter.

It said that she had passed her physical examination with the City of New York, Department of Traffic—damn, out of the entire set of city tests she took—had hired her. "This is the first job to call me and the worst job," she thought. "I'll take it. Better money than what I'm making now, and with benefits. I start the academy in six weeks. Cool. The academy is located in downtown Brooklyn. Good, I don't have to go to Manhattan. I could even drive to work sometimes if I want to."

Then Dena read the fine print: Must have the list of uniform equipment or a receipt for the equipment on order before the starting date at the academy. Listed below are three licensed uniform stores, one in Brooklyn, one in Manhattan, and one in the Bronx. The price for the complete list is approximately three hundred and fifty dollars.

"Shit, where the fuck am I going to come up with four hundred dollars?" She figured it would come to that with tax and all. "Timo, have to ask Timo. Let me worry about this on Monday."

Dena sat in the park and read a book, and watched the women go by. Most of the cuties who walked by flirted with her, even with their lovers close by. "The cuties are always with their lovers," she thought. "It's hard to catch a woman who has it going on, in between lovers." Dena got up and decided to take a walk. She went windowshopping and spoke to a couple of women who appeared to be straight. "What do they expect if they come to Greenwich Village to shop?" she thought. Dena winked and said hello. One woman rolled her eyes at her in disgust.

The other woman smiled at Dena and said, "I'm not gay, baby."

Dena said, "Aside from your flaw, you are still very attractive."

"Thank you," the woman responded, and for a moment it looked like she was going to give Dena her telephone number, but she kept on moving.

"Wow, I've never had a straight woman before. Now I know what Marcy went through—exciting."

Dena saw four women standing around the basketball court on Sixth Avenue. She knew the women were gay and slowed down to take a look at each one of them as she passed by, when she recognized one of them as Kelso. She could not believe her eyes. She stood there waiting for Kelso to notice her. Kelso must have felt someone looking at her and turned around, and the look on her face was a good one. She screamed Dena's name and they hugged each other. "Oh, my goodness!" Kelso said.

"What the fuck! I always knew you were going to follow in my footsteps!" Dena said, and laughed.

Kelso's friends looked a little surprised. Kelso turned around and introduced Dena. "This is my childhood friend, Dena. We were best friends until our parents separated us. Dena, this is Simone, Lisa, and Kris."

"Hi everybody," she said. "You cut all your hair off, Kelso. It looks good on you. You can get away with it with your handsome face."

"I see you haven't cut your hair since I last saw you," Kelso said.

"You know my hair is my trademark, girl."

"Listen," Kelso said, "we're getting ready to go. Lisa has a blind date and we're tagging along for support, just in case, and we're running late."

Dena pulled out a piece of paper and a pen, and wrote her number down. "Here's my number," Dena said. "Give me yours and I'll call you tomorrow, okay?" Dena squeezed Kelso's bald head and made the sound of sucking out Kelso's brain. "Call you tomorrow." Dena walked to her car and contemplated returning to the Village that evening to party. "What the heck, seems like I have more fun by myself anyway," she thought, and went home to get ready to come right back.

Dena dressed lightly in a pair of khaki pants, a brown, short-sleeved linen shirt, and brown high-top boots. She put a jacket in her car just in case it got cold at two or three o'clock in the morning. She arrived in the Village and found a parking space. "Boy, it seems like all of New York City is here in the Village tonight," she remarked. She entered the club, paid her five dollars, and went straight to the bathroom. She scoped the club, but it was so dark and crowded that she really couldn't get a good look.

She waited in the bathroom line, knowing she did not have to go, thinking she'd just look in the mirror and pat her hair. While in line, she noticed some women already dressed for summer. Dena laughed and said to herself, "Couldn't wait to break out their summer clothes. Halters, belly blouses, skirts—lovely. I love seeing skin." She patted her hair, lit a cigarette, and went upstairs to the bar. This time she had to fight her way across the dance floor to get back to the front of the club. Seemed like everyone was dancing now. "Good," thought Dena, "the bar is empty."

Dena spoke to the bartender, who was very patient and polite. She said she used to bartend at this club that just closed down called Bonnie and Clyde. "Well, I'm glad you're here." she told her. "I like to see women bartenders at the clubs." Dena gave her a tip and took a step away from the bar so the next person could order drinks as easily as she had. Dena had never seen a woman in a club with a fur coat on before, let alone one who brushed it against her face when she raised her arm to get the bartender's attention.

"I'm sorry," the woman said and grabbed Dena's arm, "did I hit you in the face?"

"Damn, she's cute," Dena thought. Aloud she said, "It's okay, my face was wondering if your coat was real or not. Now it knows."

The woman laughed at Dena's response, and said, "Would you like a drink?"

"That's a change," Dena thought. "A Budweiser, please. My name's Dena. What's yours?"

"Karen. Nice to meet you. Here's your beer, dear."

"Thank you, Karen. You live around here?"

"No, I live in Queens, you?"

"I live in Brooklyn." Dena did not mention her mother, but thought if she got to know Karen better, she would.

"I own a house in Queens, and my lazy brother stays with me most of the time."

"You own your own house already? But you're so young. How did you manage that?

"It was my parents' house," Karen explained. "When they died, they left it to me. I'm blessed because the house is paid for and I'm able to maintain it by working for the city."

"What kind of city job do you have, if you don't mind my asking."

"I work for the Department of Social Services."

"That's cool."

"A lot of stress though," Karen said.

"I just got called by the Department of Traffic. It's just a stepping-stone for me though."

"Finish your beer so we can dance, Dena."

Dena did what she was told, and led Karen to the dance floor. "Are you going to take off your coat?"

"I'm looking to see where my friends are sitting so I can leave it with them."

"Do you want me to hold it for you?" Dena asked.

"No, baby, I see my friends over there. Be right back." When Karen returned, Dena could now see her tight jeans and sleeveless top.

"Sexy," she thought. Dena noticed a couple of dykes who were dancing with their girls following Karen's ass with their eyes. One chick took it upon herself to forcefully turn her woman's head with her hand. Dena and Karen danced most of the night together. Then she stood close by while Karen danced with some of her friends. Dena remained dance faithful and did not ask anyone else to dance. But one woman asked her to dance and she did. Couldn't be that faithful to someone she didn't even really know. Karen kept looking over at Dena dancing as if to say, "Keep it simple, girl."

Dena read her vibes and winked to let her know, "I silently hear you." After Dena danced, she went to the bar and refreshed Karen's drink and got herself another beer, and went to sit this one out. Karen was still dancing, and Dena thought, "Maybe she's not into me if she's dancing with so many other women. Then again, it's just a dance." Around three-thirty in the morning, the music got corny. Dena guessed they did that before closing. An announcement sounded off for last call for alcohol. Dena knew she had had enough to drink and passed on the thought.

Karen was walking around the club with a fresh drink in her hand. After saying her goodnights to some of her friends, she started walking toward Dena. Dena put a piece of candy in her mouth. "Watermelon smells better then hops and barley, that's for sure," she thought. Karen kissed Dena on her lips, and asked her if she'd had a nice time.

"Yes, great time, baby."

Karen asked, "How are you getting home?"

"I have a car." Dena said. "Do you need a ride home to Queens?" She didn't mind the drive because Queens and Brooklyn were so close to each other, like Siamese twins.

"My friends are driving me home."

Karen and Dena continued talking until the lights came on and they were asked to leave. They were told, "You don't have to go home, but you have to get the fuck out of here."

Dena chuckled and thought, "That was funny," then got up to leave. She asked Karen to walk outside with her. Karen agreed and told her friends to meet her outside. They were all drunk. Some of them had to go to the bathroom, another was gathering her things, and one of them was arguing with one of the bouncers, saying, "All right, all right, man, we're going. I just dropped fifty dollars on drinks in here, man. Can I at least use the fucking bathroom? Did you see my sweater, bouncer man?"

Dena and Karen walked outside and found out their cars were parked in opposite directions, so they had to say their goodnights there outside the club. Karen acted first and told Dena, "I like you, and I had a really nice time with you. I would like to get to know you better. Is that possible?"

"Sure is," Dena said. "Can I have your telephone number?"

"Okay, and give me yours."

Karen searched her bag for pen and paper. Dena used Karen's back to write her number down, and vice-versa. They exchanged numbers, and Dena leaned closer and kissed Karen on her cheek and said goodnight. As Dena started walking to her car, she realized how cold it was for early May. "Glad I brought my jacket. Glad I did a lot of things."

Dena liked Karen a lot, not because she owned a house, but because she had a lot of the qualities she was looking for in a woman. Plus, she had her own house. They got along really well. They were both silly and laughed a lot, and she spent a lot of time, and nights, over at Karen's house. But there was one problem: every time Dena went to Karen's house, her brother, Darrel, was always there, never giving them any privacy. He would ask her, "You want to see my paintings?" or "Do you want to see my handmade jewelry?" or "Do you want to play some cards?"

Dena thought Darrel was gifted, because his paintings and jewelry were nice. The man had talent. But because he did most of his work in the basement of Karen's house, he was always at home. Any time he heard company upstairs, he would stop painting or making jewelry, go upstairs, and intrude, whether it was Dena or some other of Karen's friends. Karen didn't mind, or maybe she'd just gotten so used to him hanging around, or got tired of asking him to leave. If she wanted to be alone, she would just go into her bedroom and close the door, which is what she did a lot with Dena.

One evening, Dena and Karen were in the kitchen being intimate when Darrel entered and asked, "Do you guys want to chip in and get some weed and a couple of six packs?"

Dena was dazed by Karen's kiss, and asked Darrel, "What?"

Darrel repeated his question.

"Okay," they responded, "how much?"

"Give me five dollars each, because Lance is coming over and he'll give me five dollars too. I'll buy two nickel bags and two six packs. That should be enough."

Dena dug into her pocket and handed him the money, and Karen told him, "Go into my room and get five dollars out of my bag, and only take five dollars, motherfucker," and went back to kissing Dena.

"I'm going to meet Lance at the train station and then go to the store," Darrel said. "See you guys in about a half an hour, hint, hint."

After Darrel left the house, Dena made a bedroom gesture with her eyes. She still felt a little uncomfortable with Darrel in the house. She always had to walk around dressed. Karen grabbed Dena by her hair. "I'll take care of you tonight, baby. Can you set up the card table while I take a shower?"

"Okay, okay," Dena answered.

Soon Dena was at the card game bitching at Darrel. "Why the hell would you buy this cheap ass beer? You know it tastes like gasoline!"

Darrel didn't answer. He assumed she was just PMSing, so he left her alone. It was the girls against the boys, and every time a team lost a hand, they had to drink a can of beer, nonstop. Karen would kiss Dena every time they won a hand, and Dena happily kissed Karen back. She was so happy when they won a hand, because she did not have to drink that nasty ass beer. After playing cards for a couple of hours, Karen whispered to Dena, "Let's go to my room." The girls got up and said their goodnight to the fellows.

Lance was saying, "One more game," and Darrel was inquiring about a couple of joints that were left over. Karen took one of the joints, grabbed Dena by the hand, and led her to the bedroom.

Dena became excited immediately. Karen was a few years older than Dena and it showed, because Karen was nasty in bed, never shy. While Dena, on the other hand, was still a little restricted and shy. Dena sat on the bed, and Karen placed the joint in Dena's mouth and lit it. She took a couple of drags and felt she could not get any higher, so she just held the joint in her hand. Karen grabbed a blanket from her closet and dropped it on the floor in front of Dena, then got down on her knees between Dena's legs, unzipped her pants, and motioned for Dena to stand up so she could take off her pants. Dena complied.

Karen pulled down Dena's pants and underwear at the same time and pushed Dena by her stomach back down on the bed. Dena sat as close to the edge of the bed as possible.

Karen started to kiss Dena from top to bottom, then she licked her. Dena moaned and dropped the now well-extinguished joint to the floor. Karen put her hands on Dena's thighs and opened her legs wider. She separated her lips with her tongue, and found Dena's clitoris to be hard and swollen. Dena grabbed the back of Karen's head with both hands and gently pushed her face closer to her body, and she came. Dena came hard and twitched, and held in her scream because of Karen's company. "That was enchanting, baby. Wow!" Dena exclaimed.

"Take off the rest of your clothes," Karen said. "I'll be right back."

Dena had to pee. She'd put her pants back on when Karen entered the room in a sexy nightie. Dena was aroused all over again.

"Not so fast, Dena," Karen said.

"Baby, I have to use the bathroom. I wouldn't miss this for the world. I'll be right back," Dena said as she got off the bed.

When she came back into the room, she took off her clothes. Karen was lying in bed on her back with her legs spread apart. Dena climbed on the bed when Karen directed her to get on top of her. Dena complied and kissed her, a nice long tongue kiss. Dena loved kissing. Then she went down to her neck and gently sucked it until she bruised. Karen's body moved under her, and Dena smiled, knowing she was working her. She reached down to feel her breasts and kissed them until they were erect. Dena had been told that you can never give a woman too much foreplay. It's better to give too much foreplay than to give too little or none at all. Plus, a woman would always tell you or show you when she'd had enough foreplay and she was ready for love.

Dena felt Karen's pussy and she was ready. Dena got on top of her, missionary style, but with one leg in between her legs and one on the outside of her leg. This was a better position for women, because it allowed their clitorises to touch and kiss and come. Dena was surprised to feel herself coming again so quickly but knew she couldn't stop, because she hadn't heard Karen coming yet. So she continued to ride Karen. Karen started breathing heavy, then threw her head back and pulled Dena closer to her. She started to move faster, grinding Dena harder while gasping for air. She tightened up and let out a scream. Karen and Dena kissed and hugged and laughed, trying to catch their breath.

Karen reached into her night table drawer and pulled out a cigarette. She told Dena, "I wish you had a strap-on."

Dena asked, "What's a strap-on?"

Karen giggled and said, "You joshing, right?"

Dena just looked at Karen.

"Oh my gosh," Karen said. "You really don't know what a strap-on is! It's a dildo, a rubber penis with a strap. A woman straps it on around her waist and legs and then penetrates another woman."

"You kidding me, right?" Dena asked.

"Nah, girl, I used to have one, but when my ex-lover and I broke up, that bitch took it with her, and it wasn't even hers."

"Damn," Dena said, "I always wanted to penetrate a woman. I thought I had to get a sex change to do it, though. Now I don't have to."

Karen laughed. "You're kidding, right?

"Imagine, I can give you the best of both worlds: the best oral sex you ever had, and now penetration. Even if I come first, I can still continue to penetrate you, so you can come repeatedly. Where can I get one?"

"If you could be quiet for a second, I'll tell you. I think you could work a strap-on, girl. I like the way you move. Do you mind, Dena?"

"Hell no, I don't mind."

"I think it's about time, because I like penetration."

"Again, baby, where can I buy one?"

"The last one I purchased, I bought it on Forty-Second Street, in one of those novelty shops. I was with a group of friends and they dared me to buy it. Little did they know I was going to buy it regardless." Dena and Karen laughed.

Dena told Karen how bad she wanted to make love to her with a strap-on, and that the first chance she got, she would go to a Forty-Second Street shop and purchase one.

Dena finally completed the Traffic Academy, and had to repay Timo for the money she had borrowed for her uniform. So she could not buy the dildo until her next payday. She called Timo and asked if he would meet her for lunch to thank him again and pay him back. When she handed Timo an envelope with the money, Timo asked, "What's this?"

Dena said, "Daddy, it's the money I borrowed from you for my uniform, every penny. Thank you again."

Timo smiled and said, "I'm glad you're a woman of your word like your dad, but I don't want the money back. Take it and use it for something you need."

Her eyes lit up and she thought, "Like the dildo." Aloud, she said, "Thank you, Daddy. I love you."

Dena could not wait to go to the city to buy the dildo. She knew she could not drive there because you could never find a free parking space in the morning or afternoon. If you parked your car illegally, either you received a parking summons or your car was towed. So she decided to take mass transit. When she arrived on Forty-Second Street, strangers approached her. "Hey, Mommy," they yelled.

Dena just ignored them. They assumed a woman walking alone on this avenue must be looking for some action. She thought to herself, "Let me make this quick." She weaved in and out of the novelty stores until she finally came across a store that sold strap-ons. "Shit," she thought when she looked at the price and it read $75.99. "Motherfucker." Dena knew she shouldn't have dropped the envelope off at the house. She did not want to travel with so much money, so she had left the money at home and only taken out fifty dollars, thinking that would be enough. Well, she had thought wrong. She already knew she couldn't talk the man down twenty-five dollars plus tax. So she headed home and told herself she would come back and get it on Friday.

On Thursday, Dena had an appointment to get her first tattoo. She had made this appointment after Timo had told her she didn't have to pay him back the money. She'd found a picture in Dolores' dresser drawer of Rosie the Riveter and had decided that's what she wanted on her right arm, so she grabbed the picture and headed to a friend of a friend's house. Joe was his name and Dena introduced herself as a friend of Zebra's. "Where's the picture?" Joe asked.

She showed him. "But, damn, you have so many other drawings on your wall I'm starting to think twice about my picture."

"Well," Joe said, "it's going to take me a couple of minutes to trace this picture. So if you want something else, let me know before I start, because once you make a choice, it's a lifelong decision."

She decided on Rosie the Riveter, after all, so Joe got started. Dena thought it stung a little bit, but it wasn't that painful. "Can't wait to show Karen and wear a short-sleeved shirt," she thought. "Next one I'm going to get will say 'Lesbo Forever.'" Dena laughed out loud.

Dena called Karen and asked if she was doing anything on Saturday, if she could come over and spend the night. She told Karen she had a special treat to give her. Karen knew exactly what she was talking about and said, "I can't wait. Come over early, baby." First, Dena went to the liquor store and bought a small bottle of wine, because she knew she would be a nervous wreck and thought the wine would calm her down so she could make this night special. Saturday came and Dena packed everything in a bag and left for Karen's house.

When she arrived, they headed directly to the bedroom and locked the door. Dena and Karen talked for hours, Dena in a chair and Karen on the bed.

"Do you want to see my tattoo?" Dena asked.

"Sure, baby," Karen answered.

Dena unbuttoned her shirt and lifted her sleeve.

"Who is she?" Karen asked, "your mom?"

"No, silly, she is the famous icon, Rosie the Riveter. She, along with several other women, worked in the manufacturing plants when the men went to war in 1941. You never heard of her? Then I guess you never heard of Wendy the Welder either?"

Karen just shooked her head.

They were both feeling the wine, but Dena felt good, not too drunk where she could not perform. Karen finally came over to her and sat on her lap and started moving slowly in a circle. It didn't take long for Dena to respond. She squeezed Karen's breast from behind and kissed the back of her neck while grinding her in the same circular motion. Karen could not wait any longer and she stood up and asked Dena to put on the dildo. Karen sat on the bed and observed Dena strapping it on. It made her wet. "Okay, baby," Dena said, "I'm ready."

Karen asked if she had any KY.

Dena thought she had everything, but she didn't have any lubricant. When she told Karen she hadn't brought any, Karen instructed her to look in the top dresser drawer. "There should be some on the left side." Dena opened the drawer and reached in to retrieve it when she noticed a large picture in a frame tucked underneath some underwear. She pulled it out to take a look, because Karen didn't have many pictures of herself around the house; so Dena thought she would have a good laugh. It was a wedding picture, a wedding picture of Karen and Darrel. Dena dropped the picture in shock.

Karen turned around and asked, "Are you drunk, woman?" She looked over and saw the expression on Dena's face, then down on the floor where she saw the picture.

Karen must have forgotten the picture was in there, and her lips moved the words, "Oh, shit," but no sound came out of her mouth. She hesitated for a moment, then said, "Dena, I can explain."

"Go ahead," she said.

"Well, umm, okay, you see, alright, it's like this. Darrel and I were high school sweethearts, and we got married very young, at nineteen. As we grew older, we grew apart. I fell out of love with him, and became gay."

"So, are you still married?" Dena asked.

"Yes, we never got a divorce. We're like separated, but living together. He claims he's still in love with me, and he thinks this is a phase I'm going through. So he's on standby."

Dena had to laugh it off in amazement, and said, "You selfish bitch, do you know what the hell you just said makes no fucking sense? Why couldn't you just be open and honest with me from the beginning, and let me make my own choice if I wanted to be in your house fucking you when your damned husband is in the next room listening to me making his wife come."

"Dena," Karen pleaded, "we've been separated now for about four years. I haven't been sexual with him since then, baby. You have to understand, I love you and want to be with you. He just has to realize that this is who I am. I want to be gay."

"You're not making sense to me," Dena said.

"How can I prove it to you, Dena? Do you want me to ask him to move out?"

"Yeah," she said, "ask him to move out."

"I can't," Karen said, "he owns half of the house."

"Again, I thought you said your parents left you the house, not you and your husband." Dena started to get dressed when Karen grabbed her to stop her.

"We can work this out, baby. I was going to ask you to be my woman tonight. Please, Dena, let's work this out."

Dena finished getting dressed and picked up her things. Before she opened the door to leave, she turned around. "You wanted to make a commitment with me tonight? Do yourself a favor. Make a commitment with yourself to be truthful with people, especially people you are intimate with. Have a splendid life," she said and left.

CHAPTER ELEVEN

When Dena got home she needed someone to talk to, so she called Kelso. She told Kelso what had just happened. "The nerve of these bitches," Kelso said. "Damn, how did her husband feel? You were drinking beer, playing cards with him, all up in his house, and all up in his wife."

"I really didn't have a clue. That's not even my style. Kelso, I don't like women anymore. I'm tired of them using me and abusing me and getting over on me. I'm at my wits' end. All I want to do is love someone and settle down with that special woman and become her hersband. Is that asking too much? I'm never going to let that happen again in my life. I want to be a step ahead of them from now on. You know, Kelso, my new motto is, 'If you can't beat them, join them.' Well, I'm going to join them. I'm going to join the 'I don't give a fuck about women' club."

"Don't you think you're jumping to conclusions?" Kelso asked.

"No," she said. "That's it. My heart is tired."

"Well," Kelso said, "your timing couldn't have been better, because the Gay Pride Parade is coming up, baby. Let's go together."

"You bet," Dena said, "it's the last Sunday in June, right?"

Kelso said. "Mark your calendar, player."

The last Sunday of the month of June finally arrived. Dena

spoke to Kelso and planned to drop by her house to pick her for the Gay Parade around three o'clock. Dena was so excited she was sweating like a pig, so she decided to wear shorts. She picked out a pair that fell down to her knees, with pockets on the side. She put on her boots and a white button-down shirt. Then she accessorized her outfit with a white gold chain. She'd had it on layaway for months. She didn't mind spending a little more for white gold, because she'd never liked yellow gold and she could not afford platinum yet. So white gold had to do. She put on her timepiece and some cologne, then called Kelso and told her she was on her way.

Kelso met Dena outside and, as she was walking toward the car door, Dena checked out her little brother. No matter how hard Kelso tried to be a boy or follow in her footsteps, Dena thought Kelso still had many feminine ways about her. Dena didn't mind. "She's trying or maybe that's just her style," she thought.

"You ready to meet the honeys?" Kelso asked.

"Sure am," she replied.

"I see you got the rainbow flag on your antenna. Hey, Dena, we got the three H's out here today."

"What do you mean?" Dena asked, "Hazy, hot, and humid?"

"No," Kelso said, "hazy, hot, and horny lesbo."

She told Kelso she had two six packs of beer in the cooler and she had to get some ice at the bodega. "You don't mind buying the ice, Kelso, since I brought the beer, baby?" Kelso reached in her pocket and pulled out what Dena thought was cash, but it was actually a half pint of whisky.

"We'll both chip in for the ice," Kelso said.

She collected a couple of dollars from Kelso and double-parked her car outside the store and ran inside. Kelso had her window rolled down and was smoking a cigarette. Dena turned around. "Whisky! You must want us to pass out in this heat, man!"

Kelso yelled back, "That's why I only brought a half a pint, motherfucker!"

Dena came out of the bodega with the bags of ice dripping. "Damn," she said, "it's hot. It's at least ninety-six degrees. We're going to hide somewhere in the shade." They arrived at the outskirts of the Village, where it was easier to park the car.

"Wow, look at all the beautiful women here at the parade," Kelso said.

"Yeah, but it's like twenty men to one woman. We should have our own parade for women," Dena commented.

Dena and Kelso were excited about the parade. But before they began their journey, they walked to a small park on Christopher Street where statues representing fallen heroes had been placed as a monument to the Stonewall riots. They stood in front of the statues and lowered their heads and said a prayer, and thanked them for their courage. They proceeded to pour some of their whiskey on the ground. "We are still fighting," Kelso said, and took the rainbow flag out of Dena's hand and placed it on one of the statues. They toasted each other and knocked out the half pint of whiskey with their first beer. Then they walked back to the car.

Dena suggested they carry two beers each, so they wouldn't have to keep walking back to the car. Kelso grabbed a must-have pen from Dena's car, and they started on their way. They enjoyed the parade, the floats, and all the people. They were proud to be lesbians. They ran into some people they knew, a couple of ex-lovers, and some admirers. Kelso asked Dena if it would be all right if there was an admirer that she did not care for, could she hold on to Dena and act like they were lovers just until they got the message.

"I don't see why not," she replied, "if they believe us. Two aggressors together, Kelso, that's kind of unheard of. But no problem."

"I'll act very femme and be the girly girl if we cross that bridge," Kelso said.

"Isn't it funny," Dena added. "You see an aggressive woman with a femme woman or you see two femme women together, and don't even blink. But when you see two butches together, you do a doubletake. Why? Why is that so unusual to see?"

"Don't know," Kelso said with glossy eyes. "Maybe it's like seeing two guys together. Anyway, who gives a fuck, Dena? Look at all these beautiful women we got here." Now Dena knew she was drunk. "Say, let's find a bathroom."

"You know once we go to the bathroom, we'll never stop peeing," Dena speculated. "It's like turning the handle and opening up the beer barrel." They laughed and headed off in search of a bathroom.

After they were turned away from two restaurants, they decided to walk into the next restaurant and just head straight for the back to where the bathrooms were located. No one said anything to them this time. They guessed they'd gotten tired of saying no. When Kelso and Dena headed back to the parade, they decided to walk toward the pier.

"Let's walk down Christopher Street," Dena suggested as Kelso was approached and stopped by some of her friends. As Kelso was introducing the women to Dena, Dena could not take her eyes off one of them. She stopped their conversation in mid-sentence and asked, "What's your name again?"

"So-So," she replied.

"Are you two lovers?" Dena asked, referring to the butch standing close to her.

"Yes, we are," So-So said.

"So-So...I like your name," Dena said. "No disrespect, but I think you are gorgeous." There was something special about So-So that Dena picked up on immediately. She had a lovely golden-brown complexion, sexy black eyes, and a beautiful smile that worked its way right into Dena's heart. She was classy and very feminine. Dena thought to herself, "There are a lot of women out there that call themselves a femme, but a real femme wears heels." She could not close her dropped mouth.

The aggressor did not get mad, but she grabbed So-So by the waist, pulled her closer, and said, "Thank you."

When they walked away, Dena told Kelso, "I'm in love with So-So. She's beautiful. Where do you know her from?"

"She's a friend of a friend of my ex-lover."

Dena hadn't even heard what Kelso was saying when she said, "You have to hook me up with her, Kelso."

"How the hell can I do that? Hey, didn't you just see her with her lover?"

"I know, Kelso. I have much respect for relationships and all, but I just want to be friends with her until that day comes around when she breaks up and needs a shoulder to cry on. Whether it's next week or next year, I'll wait. Remember, relationships are history for me, so I won't be spoken for. I have to have her."

That day, Dena was handed a lot of telephone numbers, but could not get So-So out of her mind—typical. She went into the diner to buy some coffee to try to sober up before driving home. She'd stopped drinking liquor hours earlier but thought a cup of coffee would do her some good anyway. Kelso was drunkenly flirting with every cutie-pie who passed by. Dena asked her if she wanted to go to the after party.

Kelso said, "And do what there, throw up?"

"Feeling kind of woozy?"

"Yeah."

"All right, Kelso, night is falling anyway. We had better call it a night. Let's head back to the car." Dena walked Kelso to her door, gave her a hug, and waited for her to lock her door. Then she said, "I'll call you tomorrow, bro."

Dena was reprimanded at her new city job on her three-month evaluation for two tardies and four absences. Her supervisor liked her and was always complimenting her on the way the brown uniform brought out her eyes. Dena knew she was gay. But she was a dyke, and she must have underestimated Dena in her uniform. Dena brushed her off gently, because she was still her supervisor. She warned Dena that if she continued, she would lose her good city job. She had Dena sign the evaluation papers and told her as she walked away, "Stop hanging out so much." Not that Dena didn't care about her job; she just cared about women more.

Dena dropped by Hilda's house to see what she had been up to. When she arrived, Hilda said, "Jasmine is moving out as we speak. She's here with her brothers, and they're taking her furniture. She's moving to the Virgin Islands on Monday."

"But today's Thursday," Dena said.

"I know," Hilda said. "*Which* Monday the bitch is moving, I don't know," and she cracked up.

"Don't let her take that expensive painting you bought her," Dena said.

Jasmine's brothers stood in the hallway and waited until Jasmine came back upstairs. Jasmine asked Dena nicely, "Would you please get up off the sofa?" She complied and when she stood up, her brothers each grabbed one end of the sofa and carried it downstairs to the moving truck.

"Damn," Dena said to Hilda.

"Well," Jasmine said, "that's everything." Then she looked at Hilda and left.

Hilda started to yell, "You could at least say goodbye! You and your son have fun in the Virgin Islands. What kind of education is your son going to get out there, huh? What is he going to do for books, read coconuts?"

"Want to go have a drink, Hilda?" Dena asked.

"Nah, I'd rather just sit here on the hardwood floor and mope. Hell yeah, I want to go have a drink."

Dena went to the club on Wednesday and called in sick again Thursday. She just could not wake up. Her supervisor approached her Friday morning and said, "There's a position opening up for the control room radio dispatcher. Are you interested? You don't have to work outside if you don't want to."

"What about the summers?" Dena asked. "It's nice working the streets of New York in the summer."

"If you want, I can arrange for you to switch positions in the summer. Plus, you'll be inside with me where I can keep an eye on you."

Dena knew she had ulterior motives, but at that moment she didn't care. Maybe a change in positions would help her bring her ass to work. "All right," she said, "I'm game. See what you can do."

Her supervisor smiled, patted Dena on the back, and said, "Great choice."

After a long, hard workweek, Dena went home, took a nap, took a shower, got dressed, and went right back to the city. She went to the movies first. She figured by the time the movie finished it would be around midnight—perfect timing for the club. Hilda had told Dena she would meet her at the club. Kelso was hanging out with some woman she'd just met. When she arrived at the club, there was a line to get in. "Cool," Dena said, "a line is good."

She entered the club and slowly walked to the bathroom, checking everyone out, head moving from side to side. It was crowded, smoky, with the music blasting. "Now this is what Friday night and the end of the workweek is all about." Dena saw this goddess sitting at the bar, looking annoyed. She smiled at Dena and mouthed the word "hi." Dena nodded back, but she was still tempted to scan the rest of the club to see who was there. She went to the bathroom and did an about-face, and actually hurried back upstairs to meet the woman at the bar. Dena thought she would just go slide in next to her, order a drink, and try to make conversation.

The woman was fine. She had a dark complexion and very alluring eyes and full lips—a little too skinny for Dena's taste, though. She squeezed in next to her, and smiled and said hello, then said, "You don't look like you're enjoying yourself. Well, I'm here now." They laughed. Dena asked the bartender for a Budweiser, then turned to the woman. "Can I put a head on your drink?" The bartender turned her eyes to the woman to read her lips, because she could barely hear.

"A Hennessy on the rocks, please."

Dena wanted to touch her, so she held out her hand and said, "My name is Dena."

She placed her warm hand in Dena's, but kept turning around before she could say her name. "I'm so sorry. My name is Terry. This woman is hawking me. I'm really feeling uncomfortable here."

"It's okay," Dena explained, "a woman as attractive as you

must have that occur quite often. Would you like to pretend we're lovers, you and I, just until you get rid of her?"

Terry looked Dena up and down, then put her arm around her. Dena put her hand on her thigh. Every time the crazy woman walked by, they would move closer to each other—face-to-face closer—and Dena enjoyed that. "I could get used to this," Terry said. Dena smiled. After the woman walked by several times, she stopped and tapped Terry on her shoulder. Terry took her time turning around and asked her, "What do you want? Let me introduce you. This is my lover, Dena. Dena, this is...What's your name again?"

The woman didn't even answer and said, "That's not your fucking lover. Why you playing games with me?"

Dena thought to herself, "Damn, this woman is fine, but is she worth fighting this woman for? Hell, yeah!" She yelled in her mind. Dena stood up and said, "Did you hear what my girl said? Don't you see we're together?" As loud as the music and talking were, you could still hear the woman suck her teeth. Then she sized Dena up before she walked away.

"Thank you," Terry said. "I owe you one."

"How about dinner?" Dena asked. "Would it be okay if you and I had dinner one day?"

"Well, okay," Terry said. "Would you mind walking me to my car? I've been in here since ten o'clock. I don't want to obligate you."

"Oh," Dena said, "that would be a pleasure. Being your lover for a night, I would have been all over you, pretending." Dena laughed and added, "You sure you want to call it a night?" Terry held Dena's hand and escorted her out of the club. "Which way to your car?" She asked. Terry pointed toward Seventh Avenue. She stopped at a red sports car. "The car's awesome," Dena thought to herself.

"Come on in," Terry said.

Dena sat down in the passenger seat, looked around, and said, "Smells good in here."

"Let me drive you back to the club."

Dena had never seen a woman in a skirt drive a stick-shift before, legs spread apart and moving on the pedals, shifting gears. "Oh, my goodness, what a fucking turn on." She felt a shiver in her body. When Terry pulled up to the club, Dena wanted to ask her to spin around the block a couple more times. "I noticed you have New Jersey license plates. Do you live in Jersey?"

"Yes," Terry said, "in Fort Lee. Is that a problem?"

"No," Dena said, "I would walk to Atlantic City to see you again."

Terry jotted her number down and handed it to Dena before dropping her off in front of the club. Dena went directly to the bar to have a stiff drink. While drinking, she observed the crazy stalker woman walking by her several times, rolling her eyes every chance she got. Dena laughed and went to dance, and then she realized there was nothing happening in the club that night. Or maybe there was something happening there, but now she was gone. Dena had already started to have feelings for Terry, and she was glad they had exchanged telephone numbers. She decided to go home, thinking she could not do better than Terry that night.

Dena and Terry talked constantly on the telephone. In fact, all they did was talk on the telephone. Dena could not get a date with Terry to save her life. She worked for the U.S. Post Office, and she worked all the time, even weekends. On her days off, she would sleep all day, do domestic chores, and watch repeats of "Columbo." Then she would go right back to work the next day. Terry said she wanted a change in her career. She had a college degree, and soon, she said, she would quit her job at the post office to start something new. However, it seemed that until then, Dena just had to be patient and wait.

So Dena called Terry often. She wondered if Terry had a girlfriend and was using her job as an excuse. One night she asked Terry, "Be truthful with me. Do you have a lover?"

" I'm single," Terry explained. "I don't have to lie. Dena, one day we'll take a ride to New Jersey so you can meet and visit with my family. I'll prove to you I'm single."

"So when can I meet your family?" Dena asked.

"I'll let you know," Terry said.

"Figures...she'll let me know," she thought to herself.

CHAPTER TWELVE

While Dena waited impatiently for Terry's love, she decided to call Rita, a woman she had met at Better Days years earlier, before she had even had her first experience with Marcy. As she dialed Rita's telephone number, she crossed her fingers and hoped that her number had not changed. It hadn't, and Rita was happy to hear from her and asked her if she wanted to go to dinner with her that Friday, then out to a club. Dena agreed, and they decided to meet in Greenwich Village around nine o'clock.

Dena always called up Hilda and Kelso when she was going out to a club. That way, if she got stood up, her friends would be there to hang out with, or just in case they wanted to bring their dates out. Undecided about what to wear on her date, she put on a pair of jeans with a white t-shirt and a navy blue blazer, and, of course, boots. She drove to the Village, parked her car, and stood waiting on the corner of West Fourth Street for Rita to arrive. Dena looked at her timepiece. Nine twenty-two. "Just like a woman, always late," she smiled to herself while she thought about all the preparations that femmes had to go through: hair, makeup, shaving, polishing—all the things a dyke never had to do, except the shaving. "No wonder they're always late," she concluded.

Someone grabbed Dena from behind, covered her eyes with their hands, and said, "Guess who?"

Dena said, "I hope it is a rich homosexual woman who will take me out to dinner."

Rita laughed and said, "Well, part of your answer is right."

"I hope it's the rich homosexual woman part."

While Dena and Rita walked to the restaurant, Dena placed her arm around Rita's shoulder. Rita looked at her and smiled, then asked, "What took you so long to call me?"

Dena answered, "Circumstances." That was her new answer for everything.

Rita ordered a bottle of merlot while they waited for their dinner to arrive. She was impressed. She had never been wined and dined by a femme before. "Wow," Dena said, "you have a healthy appetite. I think I'd rather clothe you than feed you."

Rita smiled.

Whenever the bill arrived, for some reason the waiter would always place the bill closest to Dena. It never failed. There could be ten people at a table having dinner, and she would always receive the bill. Dena pulled out her wallet and insisted on paying when Rita waved her hand at her and gave the waiter her credit card. Dena placed the tip on the table and waved her hand back at Rita. Rita then informed Dena that she was going to the ladies' room to freshen up before they went to the club, and winked at her.

Dena's sexuality always worked and thought much faster than her brain. Sexually, her body knew exactly what Rita was talking about. But she just sat at the dinner table and watched Rita walk away, until it registered in her mind what Rita had really meant. About ten seconds later, she stood up and followed her into the ladies' room. One thing Dena liked about being gay was that you and your girlfriend could always enter the same bathroom together.

Dena and Rita flirted with each other while they washed their hands. Then Rita grabbed Dena by the waist of her jeans, pulled her into the bathroom stall, and locked the door. Dena always got nervous when she was about to kiss a woman. She leaned back against the wall in the stall as Rita pressed her body against hers, and they kissed. Their kissing became so overwhelming that they decided to stop and continue later. When they exited the stall, they saw that there was a line forming now, and what a look they got from the ladies waiting in line. She held Rita's hand and led her out of the bathroom.

They took a slow walk to the club and decided to take a short cut and were walking down a quiet street when they passed a group of men sitting on a stoop. Dena's first thought was to remove her arm from around Rita's shoulder, but she decided not to. They started yelling at Rita, asking her for her telephone number and calling her a "fine bitch." Dena felt uncomfortable. The men seemed drunk. She instructed Rita to walk a little faster. She noticed that the men had left the stoop and were walking behind them. Dena got scared, because the men were disrespecting her mostly. But she didn't care about the disrespect, as long as they didn't touch her.

She thought, "If we were on a busy street, this would not be happening; there would be so many other people around."

The men caught up and surrounded them.

"What do you guys want?" Dena asked.

One of the men responded, "We don't want anything from you, dyke. We have the real thing right here," and grabbed his crotch.

"What do you see in her?" one of the men asked Rita.

Rita stood silent, shaking. When one of the men grabbed Dena around the neck and pulled her closer to him, she held his hand with hers to prevent him from choking her. Rita screamed, "Let her go!"

"I like you," the man told Rita, then turned to the other men and said, "Let her go." He looked at Rita and said, "Bitch, do you have to be told twice? Get the fuck out of here!" Rita's frightened face looked at Dena, then she turned around and ran like hell. Dena continued to remove the man's hand from her neck. It was irritating her now as she watched Rita run down the block, praying she would go get help...

The next day Dena awoke as a nurse asked her for her name. She tried to remember what had happened. "Please," the nurse asked, "do you remember your name?"

Dena lay silent in the bed and looked nervously around the room. Then she said, "My name is Dena Vargas. Where am I?"

"You're at Saint Vincent's Hospital. An ambulance brought you here last night. You didn't have any identification on you."

Dena said, "Last night—" then felt her ribs and asked the nurse, "Are my ribs broken?"

She looked at Dena's chart. "Yes, you sustained four broken ribs." And then she looked at Dena's chart, again. "I guess I don't have to mention your eyes."

She realized she was only looking out of one of them. The other was swollen shut. "What happened to me?" she asked.

"I don't know." When you arrived at the hospital, you were mumbling something about some men."

"Did anyone ride to the hospital with me in the ambulance or escort me here?"

"No," the nurse said. "The police want to ask you a couple of questions. They think you may be the victim of a hate crime."

"Look at me, nurse. Somebody was definitely hating." Dena smiled, then grabbed her jaw and said, "Ouch. Nurse, can I have some pain medication, please?"

"My name is Jean, and yes, you may. I will be your day tour nurse. Ring me if you need anything."

"There is one thing I need," she said. "Is this telephone operable? And if it is, may I use it? I would like to call my family and let them know I'm okay."

"Sure," Nurse Jean replied.

Dena first called Dolores and told her she was all right, and that she was staying at a friend's house. Then she tried to remember Rita's telephone number, and when she did, she dialed it. The recorded message stated that the number was disconnected. "Typical fucking dyke," Dena thought and slammed the telephone down. "I guess Rita is still looking for help. How could she leave me there and not get help? I knew she was not going to defend me, but she could have at least gone for help. I will run into her ass one day."

Dena looked around the room and spotted a bed pan, and chuckled. Nurse Jean entered the room and told Dena, "The police are here to see you."

"I have to use the bathroom first. Can you please lower the bed rail so I can get out of bed?" Dena climbed out of bed holding her ribs, and walked slowly to the bathroom. Nurse Jean grabbed her arm to help her. When Dena entered the bathroom she turned around and said thank you, then said, "The back of my nightgown is open, right?" and laughed.

Dena told the police she was alone when she was attacked, and that she didn't remember anything, which she didn't. She did not want to get Rita involved. They informed her that this was the third incident in that neighborhood in the past four months.

Once Dena felt strong enough to get out of the house, she went to her city job to fill out her resignation papers. She had been told she was not going to successfully complete her one-year probation, so she resigned and decided to take some time to recuperate. Her supervisor helped her out by giving her the opportunity to resign instead of being fired. This way Dena could still apply for another city job and get hired. If she had been fired, she would have had a very slim chance of being hired by the City of New York again. Dena thought, "I am still on the list for a couple of other city jobs, so hopefully they will call me soon." In the meantime, she applied for a security guard job while she waited to hear from the City.

One day, while she was walking in her neighborhood, she was thinking, "It's been months and still no call from them. Damn, I didn't realize what I had with the meter maid job. The pay was good and I had my own medical benefits. Now I have no coverage whatsoever. I have to make sure I don't put any air in my tires until I have a job again." Dena smiled. "I hope I get a call about this security guard job soon, because I'm broke."

She was so heavy into her thoughts, she did not notice her ex-coworker, Lily, from the supermarket. Lily walked right up to Dena and pretended to bump into her. When she looked up, she smiled and gave Lily a hug.

"How have you been, girl?" Lily asked.

"Fine as wine," Dena replied. "How you been? You look good, Lily. Still working at the supermarket?"

"Yes, I'm still there, girl."

"How's your sister doing?" Dena asked. "Is she still at the supermarket too?"

"No," Lily said, "she was fired. Speaking of my sister, Dena, there is something I want to tell you."

"Yes?" Dena asked.

Lily looked down, and then she looked directly into Dena's eyes and said, "Do you remember when your register used to come up short?" Dena did not respond. She just felt a flame of fire go though her body. "Well, my sister took the money. She took the money from a couple of cashiers' registers. That's why she was fired, because she was caught."

"I knew that bitch was stealing money from my register. I knew I wasn't crazy, Lily, because every time your sister was working, my register would come up short. So where is your sister now? Because you know I am going to kick her ass."

Lily just laughed and said, "That's why I am not telling you."

Dena hugged Lily and thanked her for being honest, and said, "I know you were not going to snitch on your own sister, no matter how fucked up she was. Take good care of yourself, Lily."

"You do the same, Dena."

The security company finally called Dena and hired her. "You will start orientation this Monday. Please be here at eight o'clock, and not a minute after." She did not have any choice but to take the job. She was once again strapped for money, and seven dollars an hour sounded pretty good to her. She decided it was time to start looking for a studio apartment. She needed her privacy. She figured she would be called for a city job soon. Dena thought, "I will get an apartment close to Dolores so I can keep an eye on her and have dinner with her every other night. I will start out with the sofa bed Timo gave me, and then purchase some more furniture as soon as possible."

Dena started the security job and she enjoyed it. She liked her boss and her coworkers, one gay female in particular. Her name was Donna. Dena and Donna worked side by side every chance they had. They talked about women, the clubs, women, fast cars, and, oh yeah, women. She went apartment hunting in the neighborhood on her days off. She finally found one on Highland Boulevard in Brooklyn, one she thought was comfortable, in a safe building, and not far from Dolores. The rent was $375 a month, plus one month's rent as security deposit.

Dena had $800 saved up, so she got a money order for the $750 and took the balance of the money and opened up a checking and savings account. Dolores had always told her about establishing good credit. She told Dena, "The first chance you get, open up a checking account and a savings account. If you just put twenty dollars in your saving account and forget about it, it will grow up. Because you're young right now, only apply for one credit card, and only charge what you really need. And pay all, you hear me, all your bills on time. That is so important for the future if one day you want to buy a car, go on vacation, or purchase a home." Dena absorbed all of her mother's good advice and kept her credit line clean and intact.

Meantime Dena became frustrated waiting to be called for a city job, and for Terry to take a damn day off. One day, Kelso called her. "I have a surprise for you. Be at my house tonight around eight." Dena disliked surprises, but decided to go anyway.

She arrived at Kelso's house with a bottle of wine, not knowing what to expect. When she entered Kelso's house, she first hugged her "little brother" and asked Kelso, "What's up?" Kelso grabbed Dena's arm and led her into the living room. To Dena's surprise, So-So was there without her girlfriend. Dena's eyes lit up when she approached So-So. She stopped right in front of her and held out her hand and said, "Hello." So-So's hand was warm and Dena felt like she was shaking the hand of a queen on a throne. So-So pulled Dena closer and kissed her on the cheek.

Kelso said, "I invited a couple of friends over, so take off your jacket and stay a while." There must have been at least five other women there, and Dena could not even remember their names. So-So was there and that was all that mattered to her. She sat next to So-So and chatted with her, refilling her drink when it was empty. Dena would have gone to the bathroom to pee for her if she could have. She was mesmerized.

So-So explained, "I'm flattered by your infatuation for me. I think you are so sweet, but I am still with my girlfriend you saw me with the day of the Gay Parade. Anyway, here is my telephone number. I would love to be friends with you, if you can handle being friends."

Dena quickly snatched So-So's number out of her hand before she changed her mind, and said, "So-So, I don't know what I'm capable of, but I do know I would like to get to know you better."

Dena and So-So became good friends. Dena respected So-So and her relationship, and So-So kept their friendship on the down low. Her lover would never understand that they were just friends. Dena frowned whenever So-So would cancel their plans so she could be with her woman, and So-So would get a tad jealous when she knew Dena had a date. They loved each other as friends. When So-So finally broke up with her lover, Dena and So-So still remained just friends. Dena kept her feelings moving and she never thought twice about a true love again. She was becoming a jaded lover. But she began having feelings for So-So that she could not control.

One night Dena and So-So went out to dinner and a movie. Then she drove So-So home and pulled up in front of her house and shut off the car's engine. They sat in the car and talked for a while, and then she asked So-So, "Can I come upstairs to your house? So-So, you're not in a relationship now, and you know I've been wanting you since day one. I have never even kissed you."

So-So replied, "I love you, Dena, and one day we will make love, I promise you. But right now, sweetie, I'm not ready. You just have to wait."

Dena became a little emotional, and said, "All right, baby, if that's what you want. I really didn't think I would ever want a relationship again until I met you. But if you're not ready… there's nothing I can do to change your mind?" She asked.

So-So just shook her head and leaned over to kiss Dena, at the same time saying, "Goodnight." She noticed So-So's lips were headed straight for hers. So-So kissed Dena open-mouthed. A nice, long tongue kiss. Dena held the back of So-So's neck to keep her lips there as long as she could, thinking maybe it would change her mind. After they stopped kissing, So-So opened the car door and blew her a kiss.

Dena yelled out, "You know I'm going to hold you to your promise, girl!"

So-So smiled and said, "I never break a promise."

CHAPTER THIRTEEN

Dolores' sister, Elsa, and her husband, Lewis, announced they were selling their brownstone in Brooklyn. They had purchased a house in Puerto Rico and would be moving at the end of the month of September, in about six weeks. "Lewis is handing in his retirement papers as we speak," Dolores told Dena. Elsa had also told Dolores she would be taking their mother and father, and their Aunt Josie, to live with them. "Elsa has invited all the New York family members to get together and come over and say our goodbyes." Dolores asked Dena if she could drop her off if she was too busy to go.

Dena told her mother that she would go and stay to the end. "We'll drive back together, Mom, and I'll spend the night with you. Just let me know the date when you find out."

Saturday, September 29th, was the day of Elsa's farewell gathering. Dena went to pick up Dolores and they were on their way. The gathering went well. "There are so many family members and friends here, it's a nice but sad event," she thought. There was plenty of food. Everyone had made their secret specialty recipe, and Dena ate until she felt her top pants button pop open by itself. She didn't know when she would have a tasty home-cooked meal again.

After dinner, the gang began to tidy up a bit. Dena asked if they needed any help, then asked Dolores, "Can you ask Grandma Rosa in Spanish if she needs any help?"

Grandma Rosa barely spoke English, and Dolores and Timo had never taught their children how to speak Spanish. In addition to Spanish and English, Timo knew how to read, write, and speak Papiamentu, a Creole dialect based on Portuguese, which his mother had taught him. Dena could have been trilingual instead of just trisexual. Grandma Rosa responded that she could gather up the dishes and take them to the kitchen.

Everyone would always go into the living room to chit-chat and tell old tales and stories after dinner. Coffee and dessert were always served. "I am going to miss you guys," one of Dena's cousins said.

"Where will we all go now for the holidays?" someone asked.

Elsa said, "I am going to miss all of you something terrible, and all of you will always have an open invitation to come to Puerto Rico to visit. Just give us a call first." Everyone laughed, because they had some family members who would ring your doorbell in the middle of the night.

Cousin Ted said, "Elsa, if you don't mind me asking, how much did you guys pay for this three-story brownstone back in the sixties?"

Uncle Lewis chuckled when he answered, "You would never believe what we paid, about sixty thousand dollars. With the money we sold it for, we're buying a house in Dorato, Puerto Rico, and we're buying our son, Lewis, Jr., a house in Arizona, and we still have thousands to spare."

"Damn," Ted sighed.

"Elsa," Dena said. "I have two things to say to you tonight. One is, is there any way I can have a copy of the picture of Grandpa Gregory?" She pointed to a picture of her grandfather. He was in his boxing trunks. The picture was signed by her grandfather, "Battling Rosa." Rosa had been his last name. Dena had heard the story about her grandfather introducing boxing to Puerto Rico.

"No problem," Elsa said. After I settle in, I'll make you a copy and send it to you."

"Second, I want to talk to you about this brownstone basement. I remember when I was a child, you took Mommy, Nancy, and me downstairs to the basement to show us something. All the rooms' doors were closed. Then you took us to this one room and unlocked the door. Every piece of furniture had a sheet over it, except for one baby carriage, and the baby carriage looked like one of those models from the eighteen hundreds. The whole scene was spooky. I never forgot that day. I've been afraid of the basement ever since.

"I remember on rainy days after we got on you and Mommy's nerves, you would tell Nancy, Lewis, Jr., and me to go play in the hallway. We would play ball in the hallway, and when the ball would accidentally fall down the stairs, we would take turns going downstairs to the basement to retrieve it. When it was my turn, I would be so scared, I would run as fast as I could down the stairs to look for the ball. Nancy and Lewis, Jr. would yell out, 'Run, run, he's right behind you!' I would grab the ball and run so fast back up the stairs. Sometimes we would end the game early because Nancy or Lewis, Jr. would refuse to go downstairs and retrieve the ball when it was their turn. Or sometimes, you would tell us kids to go play in the backyard until dinner was ready.

"We would ask, 'Can one of the adults escort us downstairs and through the basement?' Most of the time, one of you adults in the house would escort us. But then there were times when you guys were busy cooking, and you ordered us, 'Go by yourselves, and take the dog with you.' So, Lewis, Jr.,

Nancy, and I would all count to three and charge down the stairs, screaming at the top of our lungs. Whoever was at the end of the line would grab the person in front of them and pull them back, behind them. I remember being tripped and falling many times. Whoever was the first person to reach the doorknob, the other two would yell, 'Open the door, open the door! Here he comes! Open the door!'

"Once we arrived outside in the backyard, we would all be out of breath and one of us would yell up to the window, 'Ma, Ma, we made it safely! We was not dragged away by the monster!' You or Dolores would stick your head out of the window and say, 'What?' We would say, 'Mom, we made it to the backyard safely!' 'Oh, okay,' you would reply, then go back to cook. When you called us to come back upstairs for dinner, we would not budge until one of the adults came to get us. We were never hungry enough to come back upstairs by ourselves."

Dena and the rest of the family laughed. "Elsa, we were silly, crazy kids to be so afraid of the basement, right? And Lewis, Jr., who lived here."

Elsa looked at her, then said, "You know what, Dena? I lived here for many years, and I was afraid of the basement too."

Terry at last called Dena and made a date with her. She invited Dena to her house for dinner, and to meet her family. "Finally," she thought to herself. She put on a pair of jeans and a black mock-neck sweater. She looked for a pair of dress shoes, but decided to put on her black-on-black Adidas sneakers that matched her sweater. "Parents or no parents, I still have to be myself and put on my gay apparel," Dena thought. She took about a half an hour to polish her sneakers. She always shined her shoes and her sneakers. Dena thought if your shoes are shined and your hair is done, your outfit is complete. Her grandmother had always told her, "Your hair is like your crown, so why don't you comb your hair sometime?"

Dena was nervous. She never enjoyed meeting her lover's family, and she knew the feeling was mutual. "Should I bring her mother some flowers? That is the question," she mused. "I will bring some flowers and a bottle of white wine and give them to Terry. Let her decide what to do with the flowers." She found Terry's house and parked her car on the street closest to it. "Damn, what were my parents doing with their money?" She wondered while looking at Terry's house. "Their house is nice. Looks like a two-family." She took a deep breath and rang the doorbell.

Terry greeted her with a smile and a hug. "Please come in. Let me introduce you to my family. This is my father, who refuses to get up off his chair except for dinner."

"Hello, Mr. Nicks, nice to meet you."

"My father is a college professor. These are my brothers, Bruce and Steve. I have another brother who lives on his own, not like these two bums. This is my sister, Ruth, and my grandmother." Terry led her into the kitchen, and there she was, Terry's mother. Terry was a carbon copy of her mother. "Wow, Terry is going to be a fine ass woman in her later years," she thought.

"Thank you for the flowers," Mrs. Nicks said.

"You're welcome," Dena replied. "It's nice to meet you. Do you need any help with dinner?"

"No, thank you," Mrs. Nicks told her. "I will let you know when it's time for dinner."

"Come on, Dena, let me show you the house." Terry showed her the rest of the house, including her bedroom.

"You have a nice room and a nice house."

"Thank you," Terry said. "How do you feel about meeting my family?"

"Nervous, nervous as hell. You and your sister don't look anything alike. You look so much like your mother, beautiful."

"Thank you, you're so sweet. Listen, I'll be starting a new job soon. I'm going to become a loan officer. I start in two weeks."

"That's great, Terry. Are you sure you want to leave your job at the post office?"

"Positive," Terry answered. "I told you that job would be history soon."

"Okay, I am happy for you. Where's your girlfriend?" Dena asked.

Terry said, "Right here."

Dena turned and looked around the room. "Where? You have a blow-up doll under your bed?"

Terry laughed, and said, "It's nice outside. Let's go to the backyard and wait for dinner there. Do you want something to drink?"

"No, thank you, Terry. I don't want to spoil my appetite." Dena sat in the biggest lounge chair in the yard and kicked up her feet. She talked about her life, how long she had been gay, and how she was continually trampled on. "That's why I'm not looking for a relationship anymore. Women have become so fucking cutthroat. I have my friends and my job, and that's enough to keep me occupied."

"Then why are you here?" Terry asked.

"I don't know. I like you, and—"

"Well, I've been gay since I was twenty-two—" Terry interrupted.

146

"And how old are you now?" She asked.

"Twenty-six. And my first lover was forty-three. We were in love. She taught me everything I know. She was offered a job in Virginia, and she took it and ran. I haven't seen or heard from her since, and that was two years ago. I've been single ever since."

"Have you ever been with a man?" Dena asked. "I'm just curious, because I have."

Terry laughed, and said, "That's a good question."

"Why is it so good?" Dena asked, and made an ugly face.

"First of all, I haven't been with a man since my first girl-friend. I am gay. I am not bisexual. I do not have a desire for men. Do you?"

"Hell no," Dena replied.

"So," Terry said, and paused for a moment while looking around the backyard like she was thinking and gathering her thoughts. "When I was with my boyfriend, we were engaged to be married. He was so in love with me, and I was very un-sure about marriage. I thought I was way too young. I wanted a career. I wanted to do some traveling and date other men outside my neighborhood before I tied the knot. He knew I was uncertain about marriage, so he got me pregnant." Tears came to her eyes when she announced she had terminated the pregnancy. She took a minute and said, "I think he was in love with me because I was boning him."

"What do you mean by 'boning him?' You mean you were having sex with him?" Dena asked.

"No," Terry said, "I was boning him. I mean, I would strap on a dildo and fuck him in the ass. He said he had found the best of both worlds in one woman. You see, he didn't have to be on the down low with other men. He had his woman bone him. And from what he said, most men love getting hit from behind, even straight men. And if they tell you they don't, it's a lie. He said he would have become bisexual if his girl wouldn't bone him. When he asked his old girlfriends to do it, they looked at him as if he was crazy, called him a homo, and left his ass. I understood him. That's why he loved me so much and wanted to marry me, I think."

"Wow," Dena said, "you learn something new every day."

Dinner was announced, and Dena and Terry went to the bathroom to wash up. She enjoyed dinner and Terry's family. They seemed to like her as an individual, but not as their daughter's lover, as expected. Terry walked Dena to her car and asked, "Can I see you again?"

"Call me if you would like to come to my house for dinner to celebrate your new job," Dena offered.

"Will do," Terry replied.

Dena shook her hand and said goodnight. Terry held on to Dena's hand and put her head through the car window to kiss her goodnight. "Call me and let me know when you're available," Dena said, then drove off. Terry watched her car pull away, and noticed her brake lights come on. She put her car in reverse and pulled up alongside Terry.

Terry asked, "Did you forget something?"

"Yes," Dena smiled, "which way to the George Washington Bridge?"

CHAPTER FOURTEEN

Dena arrived home and checked her mailbox. In it was a letter from the City of New York. Dena could not wait until she entered her apartment. She opened up the letter and it read: "You have been hired by the City of New York, Department of Correction." She laughed to herself and said, "Jail guard. I could have been hired by the Police Department or the Transit Department. I wouldn't have minded being a police officer or a train conductor. Shit, a jail guard. I don't know if I can work with criminals. Hmm...the starting salary is twenty-five thousand a year, plus paid overtime and benefits. Right now, I'm only making seven dollars an hour. I need some damn furniture. When do I start, baby?"

She read on. In six weeks she was to report to Riker's Island Training Academy, at seven o'clock a.m. "I will be there on time. I am not messing up this job," she told herself.

The day before starting the academy, Dena made sure she had everything ready for her big day. She had her receipt for her uniform. Her clothes were ironed and laid out. She set two alarm clocks, just in case. She decided to take the train to work for the first couple of days, until she scoped out the parking situation. Dena sat in the kitchen and opened up a New York City Transit map to see what route she would take to get to Riker's Island. Dena had to call the Transit System help line. They informed her that once she got off the train at the Queens Plaza Station, there was a special bus, the Q-101, that would take her directly to Riker's Island. "Damn, that means I'll have to leave my house at four-thirty in the morning, just to arrive at work on time." Dena reset her clocks for three-thirty and went to bed.

July 15, 1985. "Well, at least it's warm outside," Dena thought to herself while walking to the train station at four-thirty in the morning. She put on a hooded sweatshirt and walked with a bop. "Maybe they'll mistake me for a dude." But just in case, she carried her jackknife. "I won't fight anyone for my jewelry or my little bit of cash. But I will fight for my life if some crazy Son of Sam type motherfucker approaches me and tries to harm me."

Dena got on the Q-101 and paid her bus fare, and sat at the back of the bus to get a window seat. For some reason she got this uncomfortable feeling in her stomach thinking about Riker's Island. She wondered if the other recruits had the same feeling. She thought about Timo instructing her not to take this job. He said that this city job was at the bottom of the barrel. "You're putting yourself in danger," he had warned her. "There are riots, stabbings, and hostage situations. Are you sure you want to take this job? Why don't you wait for another city job to come your way, like the Transit or the Parks Department? It is a shame how you let the meter maid job slip away."

"Look Dad," Dena responded each time, "I am twenty-four years old and I am taking this job. And if I cannot handle the job, I will stick with it until another city department calls me. Dad, the meter maid job is history now. Why do you keep dwelling on it?" She had already quit her security job, so there was no turning back.

There was a large sign on the street corner that read New York City Department of Correction, Riker's Island, New York's Boldest. Dena had never heard the term before. She had heard of "New York's Finest," which referred to the Police Department, and "New York's Bravest," which referred to the Fire Department. Then the bus made a right turn and stopped at a small booth with one correction officer in it. The bus driver opened up his window and yelled out to the correction officer in the booth, "Twenty-seven." Dena guessed it must have been the number of passengers on the bus.

The bridge was a little under a mile long, and the smell of the water pierced her nose. She looked at the water. At the beginning of the bridge, the water was filthy and murky. Then it seemed to clear itself of the murk but not the filth as they drove closer to Riker's. She smiled when she imagined a convict escaping by swimming through the water and stopping when he reached the murky section of water, and begging the officers in their speedboats, "Help, help, I give up! I give up! Just get me the hell out of this water!"

When Dena exited the bus, she asked a couple of other lost and scared faces, "Are you here for the academy?"

"Yes," a handful of people said. "Do you know which way to go?"

"Well, let's go inside this building and ask for directions," she suggested.

The building was called the Main Control Building. All of the workers, from correction officers to cooks and medical staff, entered and exited this way; occasionally an inmate attempted to escape through this building and failed. The recruits showed the correction officer their driver's licenses and academy letters and were allowed to pass through the turnstile. They were told the academy was right behind Riker's Island Hospital. "Take the Route 2 bus," the correction officer told them.

Once they exited the main building, there were five buses outside with numbered cardboard signs on them. Some signs were on sideways. Each bus went a different route to a different jail on the island. Dena said good morning to the bus driver and to her fellow officers riding the bus. No one but the bus driver returned the good morning. The officers seemed to be dazed and in another world. Two stops later, the bus driver yelled out, "Academy! This is your stop, recruits!" Dena squeezed the metal bar on the seat in front of her to let the other recruits get off ahead of her, thinking about changing her mind. Then she stood up and walked off the bus.

The first couple of days were orientation: filling out paperwork, being fingerprinted again, and getting a weekly schedule. They were told their class number was 413 and that they would be the last training academy class taught on Riker's Island. The instructor stated further that they would be completing a brand new training academy in Queens, so they should feel special when someone yelled out, "Can I renege on my appointment date until the next class? At least the new training academy will have air conditioning!" Everyone laughed, because it was hot as hell in the training classrooms. They tried to cool the rooms off by using two propeller-looking fans that just blew the hot air around.

The first thing they were taught at the training academy was how to search for weapons and contraband. The recruits also trained outside, singing and marching from jail to jail. The inmates would yell out from their cell windows, "Hey, new jacks,"— that's what they called brand new officers—"we're waiting for you!" and throw bread and garbage at the recruits. One female recruit almost passed out because of the heat. The recruits were told to wear their sweatsuits on Fridays, because every Friday was physical training day. The first Friday, they were told to form a large circle around the mats and sit and wait for the meanest black belt instructor in the department's history. His name was Instructor Wright.

Dena and her classmate, Fran, sat together. As Fran was saying, "Thank goodness he's on our side," Instructor Wright entered the room. He called the recruits one by one and told them to put on boxing gloves and step into the circle. Within sixty seconds, each recruit had been knocked down to the floor. One recruit stood in a fighting position with his hands by his sides. Instructor Wright and the other recruits started to laugh. Instructor Wright asked the recruit, "Are you sure you're ready to defend yourself?"

The recruit said, "Yes, this is my fighting position."

"Son, you have to put your arms and hands up and cover your head and face to protect yourself," Instructor Wright insisted.

"I said, 'this is the way I fight.'"

"Well, all right," Instructor Wright said, and landed at least five punches in a row to his head and face, and down he went. The whole class could not stop laughing.

"Enough of the men. I want a female volunteer." Every female was afraid, even Dena, so the instructor picked the puniest female recruit of the bunch.

"I have to give it to her," Fran told Dena, "because she didn't back down."

The instructor was hitting her like she was a man, and everyone was complaining, "You're hitting too hard, man."

The instructor said, "Do you think the fucking inmates are going to care that she is a female officer? Hell no. The inmates just see a blue uniform."

When Dena stood up, and yelled, "Why don't you pick on someone your own size?" Instructor Wright turned to her while beating the shit out of the female recruit and said, "You're next." When the fight ended, Instructor Wright threw the boxing gloves at Dena's feet, punched his two gloves together, and said, "Put them on, loud mouth."

She asked Fran to tie the stings on the boxing gloves, and while Fran was tying the gloves, Dena whispered to Fran, "Tell my mother and family I love them, and they will be compensated dearly after he kills me."

Fran laughed and said, "Go get him, girl."

Well, Dena took a couple of punches to her head and face. She just wanted to get one good shot in. No recruit had been able to hit him in the face. She swung her right hand with all of her might, and the instructed threw his head back. When he brought his head forward, Dena backhanded him with the same right hand, all in one motion, and landed the punch on the right side of his face. Dena was so excited she threw her hands in the air, and the instructor took advantage of it and knocked her down with combination punches in retaliation for her one good shot to his head. Everyone clapped and cheered while the recruits pushed Dena off of them. After the sparring was over, Instructor Wright shook Dena's hand and said, "I never expected you to come back with that backhand punch. Good work, because if you're defending yourself against an inmate, you have to do whatever it takes to stop him or her." Then he yelled, "Got it, class?"

Dena's car broke down one day on her way to work. She quickly replaced it with a used car for six hundred dollars. She didn't care how it looked. It took her to and from work. That made the difference between a twenty-minute car ride and a two-and-a-half-hour train and bus ride, and that's what mattered.

The recruits had to study and pass each course in order to graduate. Dena wanted training to go on forever. One day, the instructor announced, "Company A and only Company A will report to the Brooklyn House of Detention for Men for on-the-job training Monday morning, so do not come here. Go directly to the Brooklyn House Jail on Atlantic Avenue and Jay Street."

On-the-job training was not so bad, Dena and Fran thought, until they were locked in an actual jail cell so they could see the world from the inmates' point of view. One recruit yelled out, "Okay, okay, we get it! Unlock the cell door and let us out!" while another recruit hollered, "Who gives a fuck about the inmates' perspective?"

The academy training went smoothly. They were told, "Enjoy every weekend you have, because once you finish the academy and transfer to your assigned jail, you will only have one weekend off every six weeks; that is, if they don't cancel your weekend off, which is what they do from time to time if they are short of staff."

Fran told Dena, "I'm going out to party Friday night, and I am not returning home until Sunday evening."

Dena smiled and said, "I'm with you."

"Fran, my cousin is giving a house party on Saturday. If you're not doing anything, here's the address. Dena tore a page from Fran's memo book and scribbled the address down. You and your girlfriend are welcome."

"Friday afternoon is the last day of the training academy," the instructor said. "Saturday morning is the graduation ceremony. Then Monday morning, you report to your assigned jail. Here is the list. Everyone have a pen ready and write it down when I call your name and jail."

Dena was hoping to be assigned to the Brooklyn House because it was close to home. "But fat chance," she thought. "They consider the borough jails and the city hospital jails a privilege."

"Dena Vargas," the instructor stated, "C.I.F.W., Correctional Institution for Women."

"Damn," she said, "Riker's Island. Bastards!"

The ceremony was nice. Dena invited Timo and Dolores to attend. She was surprised when her father showed up. She introduced her parents to everyone, and they informed her parents, "You have a tough daughter here."

Dolores responded, "Yes, we are very proud of her."

Everyone took pictures, then said, "See you guys on the Island," because every last recruit had been assigned to a jail on Riker's Island except for one female officer who had an uncle who was a warden. Since she had juice, she had been sent to a borough jail, the Queens House of Detention. Dena and Fran hugged each other and exchanged telephone numbers.

Dena kissed Timo and thanked him for coming. She told Dolores she was going home with her. "My car is around the corner, Ma." She was exhausted. She needed a nap before she could even think about going to Hilda's house party that night.

CHAPTER FIFTEEN

Dena arrived at Hilda's house around five o'clock. She was happy because she found a parking space right in front of her building. She went with Hilda to pick up Nikki at her house, but Nikki changed her mind and decided not to attend the party. "I have better things to do," she said. Then Hilda and Nikki started quarreling.

Hilda told Nikki, "You could have called me to let me know you weren't coming to the party, saved me the trip of driving over here."

"Oh, whatever, bitch," Nikki responded. "You had to come outside anyway for some supplies."

Hilda just shook her head. "Come on, Dena, let's go."

They shopped for some last minute things and went back to Hilda's. Hilda was telling Dena about a woman she had met and invited to the party that night. "Her name is Gwenda. I've been seeing her for about two weeks now. Maybe I shouldn't have invited her to the party."

"Why?" Dena asked.

"I don't know. She's very attractive. I—"

"Okay, what's wrong with her?" Dena cut her off.

Hilda cracked up at how good she was getting at reading her. "Well," she said, "okay, we've had sex twice. The first time, I went to her house in Brooklyn, and it was great. The next time we decided to get together, I invited her to my house and, because she doesn't drive, I figured I'd swing by her house and pick her up, and we'd come back to my house. I had dinner ready and a bottle of Moet on ice."

"You must really like her," Dena commented.

"Well, I did until—let me finish telling you the story. Gwenda asked me if I could pick her up at her sister's house in the Bronx, and I agreed. After I picked her up, she asked if we could drop off some food her sister made at her mother's house in Queens. What the hell was I going to say? No? I wanted some pussy, so I drove her to her mother's house in Queens. When we finally got to Brooklyn, she told me she had a surprise for me, but we had to go to her house and get it. She must have seen the look on my face, Dena, because she told me she'd brought a sexy nightie and it was for my eyes only. Of course, we drove to her house to pick up the nightie."

Hilda laughed and said, "I felt so bad because I was so frustrated from driving in bumper-to-bumper traffic. There was this man crossing the street with his dog, and the light had just turned green, and I yelled out the window for him to get the fuck out of the way. By the time we arrived at my house, four hours later, I wanted to go to sleep, the dinner was cold, and the champagne was hot."

"Damn, Hilda, you could have just about drove to Washington, D.C., in four hours. But I still don't think that's reason enough not to like her. When she wants to get together again, just tell her you are not driving to Washington today, and let her meet you at your house."

"That's not the reason. We get back to my house and she goes to take a shower, and I go to take some Geritol intravenously along with a nap." Dena could not stop laughing. "She came out of the shower in this black, nasty-ass nightie. She looked beautiful. You should have seen how fast I jumped out of the bed. We start kissing and messing around, and she asks me to hit her. So I slapped her on the ass, no big deal. But then she asked me to punch her. I punched her lightly on her back. Then she ordered me to punch her harder. I told her, 'I'm not punching you any harder.' She turned around. I thought she was possessed when she said, 'Punch me, Hilda. You won't hurt me. Punch me in my face. Please.' Dena, every time I punched her, she said, 'Harder, harder.' I got scared. Then she came. I couldn't come because I was freaking out."

"Damn," Dena said, "I never met anyone like that before. Now I hope I never will. You know, Hilda, a light slap on a woman's ass while you're making love to her, or a slight tug on her hair, a light bite on her nipple, no problem. But I feel that should be the extent of it. She's coming here tonight. I can't wait to meet her. When I'm introduced to her, instead of shaking her hand, I'll say, 'Hello, nice to meet you,' and punch her in the face."

Dena started laughing, when Hilda sternly said, "Please don't say anything about this to her."

"I won't," Dena said, "I won't."

The party was going smoothly. A lot of women, as usual. Dena noticed this certain woman could not take her eyes off of her. She seemed too shy to approach her, or maybe she felt femmes should not make the first move. She stepped over to her and introduced herself. "Hi, my name is Dena. What's your name?"

"I'm Belle," the other woman said.

"Nice to meet you, Belle. Do you know Hilda, the hostess who is giving the party?"

"No," Belle replied, "I'm here with a friend of a friend."

"She's my cousin," Dena said.

"I don't go out much," Belle said. "I work long hours. I'm opening my own beauty salon soon. "Wow-wee," Dena said, "a business woman. That's cool."

She asked Belle to dance. She thought she was attractive, sweet, and very shy. After their dance, they went into the kitchen to have a drink when Belle said, "I love your hair. Can I touch it?"

"Okay," Dena said, "go ahead, get it, Belle, go ahead." Dena always laughed hard at her own jokes.

Belle touched and massaged Dena's hair and head. Dena was in ecstasy. Belle's hands were like magic on her head and scalp. "Your hair is so soft. What do you use?"

"What?" She asked. "I use gel and coconut oil, that's all.

Just then, Hilda approached Dena. "I have a problem."

Dena introduced Belle to Hilda, and said, "Can it wait?" and pointed to her hair with her eyes.

But Hilda grabbed Dena. "Excuse me, dear, she'll be right back," she said as she escorted her away. "Dena," Hilda said, "Gwenda arrived about a half-hour ago."

"Cool," she said, "I want to meet her."

"She's here with her ex-lover. She said she doesn't want to be bothered with her. She's afraid of her and thinks she followed her here."

"Did you invite her to your party, Hilda?"

"I don't even know the bitch."

"Well then, she is going to have to leave. This is your house. Where is she?" Dena asked. "Let's escort her out."

Hilda led the way and stopped right in front of Gwenda and her ex-lover. Gwenda looked nervous. Dena told the woman, "My cousin and I are giving this party, and neither one of us invited you, so I am going to have to ask you to leave."

The woman said, "No problem, man," and left the apartment.

Gwenda stood at the top of the stairwell and gave a sign of relief. Dena watched Hilda escort her ex-lover down the stairs, then went to the kitchen to pour herself a drink, then another, when Belle ran up to her. "Your cousin is fighting downstairs."

Dena ran down the stairs and found her cousin hugging Gwenda and asking her, "Are you okay?"

"What happened?" Dena asked Hilda.

Hilda was discreetly laughing when she said, "After I escorted her ex-lover out of the building, Gwenda came outside to get some fresh air. All of a sudden, her ex-lover came out of nowhere and slapped the shit out of her. I went to break it up, and she ran."

"There she goes," Gwenda said, crying. "She keeps driving by in her car."

"Which car is hers?" Hilda asked.

"The burgundy one. I don't know the model."

She drove the car by the building and slowed down to shout out, "You bitch, I am going to get you!" Then she sped up the block, put her car in reverse, and said the same shit again while driving in reverse.

Dena went to the curb and told her, "Get the hell out of here!" When the woman noticed Dena, she sped off in reverse and hit the passenger side of a parked car, which happened to be Dena's car. Dena threw her hands up in the air and said, "Out of all the fucking parked cars in New York City's fifteen million streets, this butch had to hit my car! I knew that parking space was too good to be true!"

The woman drove by a couple more times and Dena and Hilda chased her, but to no avail. "Oh well," Dena said, "we'll never catch her on foot. Let's go back upstairs."

They went back to the party. Then Hilda went to drive Gwenda home, and Dena looked for Belle. When she found her, she said, "My cousin was not the one fighting, but thank you anyway."

Belle asked Dena, "Would you like to come by the salon one day so I can wash and condition your hair?"

"Yes, of course. I would love to, but you cannot cut my hair."

Belle laughed and said, "I won't."

"Why is someone as special as you not spoken for?" Dena asked.

"I do have a lover," Belle answered. "We've been together for nine years. But lately, we've been having problems."

"Wow, I never knew any gaybody in my life that has been in a relationship for so long. My congratulations. I have much respect for you and your relationship. You and your lover fuck around on each other, right?"

"Sometimes," Belle answered.

"I see," Dena replied, "that explains it. Look, I do not and I will not mess around with a woman who is married or in a relationship. If you want to be friends and condition the shit out of my hair, that will be all right. But that is the extent of us. If you don't want to, I understand."

"I would like that very much," Belle said, and they exchanged telephone numbers.

Dena reported for work, her first midnight to eight a.m. tour. She had no clue as to what her job description was. It seemed things were run very differently from how she had been taught at the academy. She was working with two other officers in a dormitory of female prisoners, and the other two officers kept to themselves.

One of the officers explained to Dena, "This office here is called the A station. I am the A officer and this is my post. When the supervisors make their tours, it's best if you're not in the A station, but at your post in the dormitory area. You are the C officer. That side of the dormitory is your post, the C post. I will hit the button and pop you inside your post. Go inside, make a tour, then have a seat inside. If you need to use the bathroom, knock on the window and let me know. I will pop you back inside the A station. Sign the log book that you are in the station to use the restroom." Dena took a deep breath and swallowed and told the officer to pop the door and let her inside the dorm. "Oh, one more thing," the A officer said. "I will let you know when the captain is making a tour." Then she popped the door and let her inside the dorm area.

It was dark inside the dorm. Dena stood near the door for a moment to let her eyes adjust to the darkness while patting the side of her utility belt to make sure she was carrying her flashlight. Then she made a tour through the dorm area. She started in the bathroom area, then walked up and down the aisles of the dormitory beds. Some of the prisoners were whispering that she was a cutie-pie, while other prisoners shouted, "Bitch, go back inside the bubble!" That is what they called the A station. "And go to sleep like all the rest of your coworkers. There's nothing for you to see in here."

Dena grabbed a chair and placed it with its back against the wall, so she had a clear view of everybody and everything. She announced, "I will be sitting here for the duration of my tour, so go to bed."

An inmate approached Dena and asked, "Can I speak to you for a minute?" She nodded. "When your captain makes a tour, he's going to reprimand you for this card table being out here in the dorm area. It should be inside the dayroom, and the dayroom door should be locked." Dena had the female inmates move the table back into the dayroom and locked the door. When the captain and the warden made their tour, there were no complaints. Dena thanked the inmate and the inmate replied, "Your coworkers should have given you that information. I like you, Officer Vargas. I think you're nice. I am going to be discharged in two days. So take care and look out for yourself, because some of your coworkers will not."

Dena's used car broke down shortly after she got her site assignment. It was back to mass transit and the Q-101 bus. She would have to get another car as soon as possible. She kept a low profile at work during her one-year probation. On her six-month evaluation, the captain said, "You are doing well. Keep up the good work."

After announcing roll call, Dena made a second announcement to her fellow officers. "If anyone sees inmate Janet Rivera, please do not tell her which post I am working at."

Janet Rivera was an adolescent inmate, a seventeen-year-old detainee who had been arrested for selling drugs for her boyfriend. She was a very attractive female, but it was against department rules and regulations to fraternize with the prisoners, even after they had been discharged. Janet was in love with Dena. She would ask her housing officer for a movement pass, then she would forge the movement pass so she could wander through the entire women's prison looking for Dena. Once she found her, she would hang out at her post or at the gate to talk to her and bat her eyes at her. Even after being told repeatedly by officers and captains to leave the area, she would only leave for a moment and then come right back to Dena's post.

Dena would talk to her and advise her, "You're still young and you have a good chance at turning your life around. When you get discharged, don't go through that revolving door and come back to this ugly place like I see a lot of other inmates do."

All Janet Rivera wanted to know was, "When I get discharged from jail, will you marry me?" Dena would just laugh.

The first time Dena reprimanded a female prisoner by writing her an infraction, which is written charges, she handed it to the house captain and the captain ripped it up right in Dena's face. She was fuming. She asked the female captain, "She cursed me out and threatened to cut my face. Don't you think she should be disciplined for that?"

The captain responded, "This is a good working inmate dormitory. I don't believe she said those things," and walked out of the area. All the inmates started laughing at Dena.

Realizing that the house captain for their dormitory area would not allow her workers to be reprimanded, Dena called over to her coworker, the A officer, to open up the gate to let her inside the dormitory area where the inmates were located. The A officer popped the gate with the control button and told her, "Don't do anything stupid."

Dena went inside and walked right up to the female inmate who had threatened her, put her hand in her face, and looked her right in her eyes. "I first tried the power of the pen, and that didn't work. Threaten me again, bitch, and I will kill you." Dena turned around and walked back to the station, using a wired glass window to watch her back through the reflection. While the inmate continued to talk shit, Dena yelled to the A officer, "Pop the gate."

Dena never dated any of her coworkers. She knew better than to mix business with pleasure. She had witnessed the fights in the locker rooms and parking lots, and had seen brand new cars keyed, and did not want any part of it. There were too many women in New York City for her to date an officer.

On Dena's next day off, she decided to go to Manhattan to a gun shop to purchase her first firearm. All she had to do was show her job ID, fill out some paperwork, and wait two weeks for her background check to clear in Albany, and she would be strapped in more ways than one. At the time, correction officers were only allowed to purchase and carry .38 caliber handguns. She did not want a sissy gun, like the Lady Smith and Wesson. She wanted a real gun, so she purchased a Colt Detective Special, a six shot with a three-inch barrel.

Then she went to the Chevrolet dealer and purchased a brand new Chevy Blazer, black on black. She needed a good working car to get her to and from work, and another used car was not going to cut it. When she worked overtime, and she had to take the train and bus, after traveling, she would only have about five hours in between her work tours. This meant she would only get about two hours' sleep before returning to work. And she liked working overtime. For just having an equivalency diploma, she was bringing home pretty good money.

Meanwhile, Dena called Terry all the time to see how her day was going and to complain about her day. She liked to hear her sweet voice at the end of the day, and she always wanted to know when they were going to get together. One evening, Terry told her, "I'm going out with some of my friends this Saturday. Do you want to meet me at the club?"

"No, not really. I want to see you alone, without your friends."

"You will, Dena. Are you going to meet me at the club or not?"

"All right, all right, the same club I met you at fifty years ago?"

Terry laughed and said, "That's the one."

A brand new prison for women was completed on Riker's Island. All the female prisoners would be transferred to the new jail. The current jail would only house male prisoners and would be given a new name, The George Motchem Detention Center. It was named after an officer who had been killed in the line of duty. The officers were given the option of transferring to the new jail. To fill any empty posts, they would start drafting officers from the bottom of the seniority list. Dena had three years on the job, so she did not have to worry about being drafted. She decided to stay put and work with the male prisoners for a change.

Every chance Dena had she would go on a hospital run, taking prisoners to nearby hospitals. One thing different about working with male prisoners, you had to stay alert because of riots, assaults, stabbings, and escapes. The first time she took a prisoner to Bellevue Hospital for treatment, she found out there was a mini prison ward there that was kept very quiet. Dena automatically knew she wanted to work in that ward. As soon as she returned to her assigned post, she put in for her transfer to Bellevue Hospital and crossed her fingers.

CHAPTER SIXTEEN

Saturday morning, Dena called Kelso and woke her up at six a.m. "Kelso, I found a new apartment. I'm moving today. I need help with a couple of boxes. Can you come by and help me? Hello?"

The moving men moved the heavy furniture, so the girls only had to move a couple of small boxes.

"What part of Brooklyn is this?" Kelso asked.

"Caroll Gardens," Dena replied. "It's close to the highway, the Brooklyn and Manhattan bridges, five minutes from Timo, and twenty minutes from Dolores." It was a large one-bedroom in a quiet building in a great neighborhood with a fire escape and a beautiful view overlooking Lower Manhattan and the twin towers. "Kelso, do you have a date tonight? Why don't you come out to the club with me? We can relax here for a bit, then we'll go out. I'm supposed to be meeting a woman named Terry there tonight. She said she'll be coming with some of her friends. So, want to go?"

"Bet," Kelso said.

"Kelso, before we go to your house, I just have to drop by Timo's house. I'm going to give him a spare set of my house-keys just in case I get locked out the house. He lives close by, I can walk to his house and pick them up. You want to come upstairs with me and say hello?" Kelso answered Dena's question with a look.

After dropping the keys off at Timo's house, the girls went to Kelso's house. While Kelso was getting dressed, she asked Dena to get her a beer out of the refrigerator. Dena opened the fridge door and saw five open, half-full bottles of beer and one that was unopened, so she grabbed the unopened one. She handed the beer to Kelso, and Kelso looked at her as if she were crazy. "What is wrong with you, girl? Didn't you see a six-pack of opened beers?"

"Yes, flat, opened beers," she said.

"Well, put this one back and hand me an opened beer."

"What is wrong with you?" Dena asked. "You're the only one I know who drinks day-old beer."

"Just go get me a beer, man."

Driving to the city, Kelso asked Dena, "Suppose your friend wants to come home with you?"

"I really don't expect that to happen," she replied, "because we didn't make plans for it to happen. It's only our second date. Plus, she's coming to the club with some friends, so I really doubt it, Kelso."

Kelso squeezed Dena's chin and said, "Nothing is impossible. And if she's smart, she will give you some tonight. Just in case, Dena, will you still drive me home?"

"Kelso, you know I will."

Dena introduced Kelso to Terry and her friends. Kelso pinched Dena on her leg and whispered in her ear, "She's fine." Dena and Terry laughed about the last time they had been there at the club and looked around to see if the stalker was there too. Terry bought rounds of drinks for everyone, including Kelso. While standing by the bar, Dena saw this woman leave the bartender a twenty-five cent tip. "No wonder women's clubs don't stay open for long," she thought.

"She is cute and rich. You better marry her," Kelso instructed Dena.

Dena snapped back, "I am not marrying anyone. No matter how good a woman appears in the beginning, she will hurt me in the end."

Terry asked Dena to dance. She threw her arms around Dena and hugged her tight. She was breathing heavy in Dena's ear when she asked, "Can I come home with you tonight?"

Dena pulled her back to look into her eyes. "Do you want to spend the night with me?" she asked.

"Yes, Dena, I want to spend the night with you."

"What about your friends?"

"They all have their own cars, and the ones who don't can ride with someone who does."

"My friend, Kelso, doesn't have that option. She left her car at home. I have to drive her home."

"It's cool, Dena. I'll follow behind you in my car. Just don't drive too fast."

"Okay," she answered with excitement.

When Dena mentioned her plans to Kelso, Kelso smiled and said, "You dyke, I told you."

"I am not cutting your night short, Kelso. Whenever we're all ready to go, we'll blow this popcorn stand."

"Cool," Kelso said, "because I'm trying to get this cutie-pie's telephone number."

Dena smiled when she saw Hilda enter the club. They hugged, and Hilda said, "I have a surprise for you. Come outside with me for a moment."

"I have to let Terry and Kelso know where I'm going first," she said. Dena introduced Hilda to Terry and then told Terry and Kelso that she would be right back. Dena and Hilda had their hands stamped and left the club.

"Okay, remember the bitch, Gwenda?"

"Yes, she said, "the punching bag."

"Well, she is back together with her ex-lover—you know, the one who slapped her at the party and ran?"

"Yes, I remember, Hilda. Where is this going?"

"They're both here together, standing right over there," Hilda said, pointing toward them.

There was a bunch of women standing outside the club. Dena looked past them and there they were. She remembered Gwenda, but asked Hilda, "Before I approach her, are you sure that's the woman who hit my car the night of your party?"

"Dena, I am positive. Are you going to say something to her?"

"You fucking right, I am." She walked right up to them and just stood there and looked at the woman. Then she said, "Excuse me, Gwenda. Hi, do you remember the night of my cousin's party, when Hilda and I escorted you out of the party, then you slapped Gwenda, hit a parked car, and circled the block a few times before leaving? Well, I'm the owner of the parked car your vehicle hit. You bitch, you know it cost me two hundred and seventy-five dollars to fix my car? Now you are going to live up to your part of the responsibility, or I'm going to whip your ass for sticking me with the fucking bill."

The woman started to stutter, and said, "I'm s-sorry. I didn't know I hit s-someone's—I mean—your car." She reached into her shirt pocket and pulled out her business card. "Here's my telephone number. Call me with your address and I will send you a check for the repairs."

Dena took her telephone number, looked at Gwenda, and said, "Have a nice night."

Hilda had heard everything. "Is that true?" she asked.

"No, my mechanic only charged me fifty bucks to replace the bumper. That was the extent of the damage," Dena said while tearing up the telephone number. "I just wanted her to know you can drive, but you can't hide."

After Kelso got the woman's telephone number, she said she was ready to go. Terry followed them in her sports car. When they arrived on Kelso's block, Dena double-parked her car and told Terry she would be right back. "I'm walking Kelso to her door." Dena waved to Terry after Kelso went into her building and got back into her car. When they arrived at Dena's house, she let Terry have the good parking spot. Terry climbed into Dena's car, and they found a parking space up the block for Dena's car.

Dena made Terry comfortable in the living room. She straightened up her bedroom and put her X-rated tapes away. She was not expecting company, but she always managed to keep her house clean. While heading back to the living room, Dena stopped for a second and looked around the house. She had this funny feeling, like someone had been there. Something was out of place; she just could not put her finger on it. She just knew something was out of order. "Oh well," she thought, "don't have time to figure it out now," and she went into the living room. "Sorry to keep you waiting."

"Quite all right," Terry answered. "Putting away your old girlfriend's pictures?"

She chuckled and asked Terry, "Would you like something to drink, or eat?"

"What are you trying to do, get me drunk so you can take advantage of me? Like I will stop you."

Dena muted the television volume and turned on the stereo. She pulled out the album, *Heatwave*, and played the song,

"Star Of The Story." She told Terry how much she liked the group, Heatwave, and how when she was in high school she would always call the radio station and ask the deejay to play this song. Dena hit the repeat button on the turntable, so she and Terry could make love to her favorite song all night long.

In the morning, Dena woke up pulsating. Terry was already having breakfast: Dena, sunny-side up. Wow. One thing Dena always wondered was, which time of day is the best time to experience an orgasm, or is it all the same any time of day? "Who cares?" she thought, and they made love all morning.

Terry asked Dena, "Do you think you can be exclusive with me?"

She thought about it for a moment, then said, "I like you, Terry. You are very attractive, you're smart, and you make love lovely, but I want to be single."

"Do you think I can change your mind, Dena?"

"Not likely, Terry. I'm hungry. Let's go make breakfast."

The next day, Dena went to work. She was assigned, along with several other officers and captains, to help supervise and assist with the lunches for the inmates. Dena's patience was short that day, and all the inmates were bickering and talking shit about how their food trays were incorrect, how they had requested more meat on their trays, and all the rights they had, which they did—too many for Dena's taste. One inmate wanted his Muslim food tray, and another inmate demanded his kosher food tray. Dena shouted at the inmates, "Get your damn food trays and step away from the fucking window! When your asses were in the street buying crack cocaine, did you specify to the drug dealer that you wanted Muslim crack or kosher crack cocaine? No, so get your damn trays and get out of the line!"

When Dena arrived home, she thought to herself, "What a day. Where is my stash?" She looked for a bottle of cognac and stood in the kitchen and poured herself a drink, then another. She looked down at the kitchen table and saw a brown package. Dena did not recall this package. She quickly opened it. It was a videotape. She looked at the title and it read: The Vargas Family, 1965.

"Only Timo has an 8-mm camera, and only Timo has a spare set of keys to my house," she thought. "The nerve of him, taking it upon himself to enter my house without my permission! I did not give him my keys for that reason. I gave him my keys just in case I locked myself out of my house. I knew someone was in my house." Dena called her dad and asked him if he could come by the next day and bring her keys, and he agreed.

When Timo came by, Dena asked him, "Why are you entering my apartment without my knowledge or permission? Dad, I am home most of the time. If you have something to give to me, call me and then come by when I'm home. I gave you my keys, Daddy, to keep safely in your house, not for you to be walking around with them on your key ring and stopping by and entering anytime you feel like it."

Timo said, "That was the first time I came to your house when you weren't home."

Dena said, "I don't believe you, Dad. I know it's not the first time. Suppose I was home and thought you were a burglar? Or suppose I was home with my company?"

Timo said, "But I am your father."

"What the hell does that mean, Daddy? I know your title. You cannot enter my house just because you're my father. Please, Daddy, let me have my keys."

Timo handed Dena her keys and left without saying goodbye.

Friday afternoon, Dena arrived home from work happy she had a weekend off. She wanted to take it easy that weekend, and planned on going to church Sunday morning. She missed Timo and was still very upset with him because it had been seven months since the key incident, and Timo had not called her. She was always the one to call first and apologize to Timo, but this time she wanted him to act like a man, like her father, and step up to the plate and say he was sorry for once in his life.

Saturday morning, Dena went jogging and came home and washed a load of clothes. After taking a shower, she looked at herself in the mirror and noticed a small patch of premature gray hair. "Where the hell did that come from?" she wondered. She thought it might have come from the stress at work. Then again, Dolores had a full head of gray hair at age forty-five. "Maybe it's hereditary; but damn, I'm only twenty-nine!" She then stepped on her scale. It read, one-twenty-seven. She thought her weight was fine for her height of five-two. Dena always thought she was solid like her dad—not fat, just solid. She always felt she was a strong, solid butch, never a soft butch. "What the heck is a soft butch anyway?" she thought. "A dyke with lipstick and highlights." She laughed to herself. Dena heard the telephone ring, and it was So-So.

"Hi, sweetie," So-So greeted her.

"Hi, So-So, long time no hear from. How are you?"

"I'm okay."

"How is your family doing?"

"Everyone's all right."

"That's good," Dena said.

"Do you have company?" So-So asked.

"Naw, I'm relaxing this weekend, girl. I feel burned out, so I'm going to take it easy today and go to church tomorrow."

"Dena," So-So said, "my girl had to take care of some business in Seattle. She's been gone since Tuesday and she will be home tomorrow. The reason I'm telling you this is because our house was robbed about a month ago, and I was in the house when it happened. The man had on a mask, so I didn't see his face. I froze when he saw me. He just took the jewelry box and left."

"My goodness, So-So, you must have been so scared!"

"I was, and still am. Dena," So-So said, then hesitated.

"Yes, So-So, what is it?"

"Can you please come over? You see, I was working all week, and getting home late from work, and going right to sleep. It didn't bother me that my girl was out of town. Now I've been home all day, and I'm thinking about it, and I'm afraid."

"Okay, So-So, anything for you, baby. Give me your address and directions and I'll see you around seven." Dena hung up the telephone and thought about So-So for a minute, because no one knew she carried a firearm. She had never told anyone. She thought So-So must have just assumed she carried a weapon. Six-twenty p.m. and Dena was looking for her keys when the telephone rang.

"Hi, Dena, this is Terry. How are you?"

"I'm fine, Terry. How are you and your family and your new job? Hitting the six-figure salary yet?" She asked.

"Almost," Terry answered. "What you doing tonight?"

Dena said that she was going over to a friend's house who was not feeling well.

"I want to see you, Dena. Can we make plans for next week?"

"Yes," Dena answered. "I'll call you tomorrow, and we'll set a day, okay? I have to go, Terry."

Dena arrived at So-So's house in Queens. So-So answered the door and invited her in. "So when did you leave beautiful Brooklyn to come to this dull town?"

So-So chuckled and said, "This is my girlfriend's house. She invited me to move in with her so we could be closer."

"That's cool," Dena said. She hugged So-So and said, "I'm sorry, baby. I wish I could have been here to protect you and comfort you."

So-So started to cry in Dena's arms, and Dena held her tight and rubbed her back. So-So invited her to the bedroom and she lay down across the bed. Dena looked around the room, found a chair, made herself comfortable, and listened while So-So talked for hours. Dena guessed she needed someone to talk to besides her lover. "I'm hungry, So-So. Did you cook a splendid meal for me?"

"Err...no. There is a fabulous soul food restaurant up the block from here. Can you please get me some fried chicken, macaroni and cheese, and collard greens? Here's some money," So-So said while reaching into her dresser drawer. "Get whatever you want, baby."

When Dena returned with the takeout, they ate dinner together. "The food is delicious," Dena commented.

"My pleasure," So-So said.

"It's getting late, and you should be exhausted from

talking all night," Dena said. So-So smiled. "Will you be all right?"

"No, Dena, I will not."

"Get an alarm system like I told you and a dog if you have to, to feel safer."

So-So slid over on the bed and held out her hand, making room for Dena to hop in. Dena took off her pants and her shirt and hopped in her bed. She held So-So close, kissed her and caressed her body until she closed her eyes. Dena loved So-So, and would do anything for her. She wondered if So-So knew that. Her body felt so good on hers, soft and warm. Dena tossed and turned until she became comfortable and lay on her back. So-So put her head on Dena's chest and fell asleep.

In the morning, So-So kissed Dena on her lips. "Wake up, baby," she announced. Dena opened her eyes, looked around the room, and was handed a hot cup of coffee. "I'm making breakfast. You have time to take a shower. I'll have breakfast for you when you get out."

"What time are you expecting your wife?"

"She'll call first."

"Okay, let me take a quick shower, and have my breakfast on the table when I get out."

"Yes, dear," So-So happily replied.

After breakfast, So-So walked Dena to the door. She cupped her hands over Dena's ears and held her and kissed her. "Thank you, Dena. You are good people."

Dena went home and was able to attend the eleven o'clock church service. She enjoyed going to church, but it was hard for her to attend when she worked practically every Sunday. On the days she could not attend, she made a small alter in her home and prayed when she felt the need. After church, she put on her pajamas and said, "Today will be communication day." She called her family and checked in on her friends. Then she called a woman she had met some time ago at a party. Dena thought Joni was cute and doable.

"Hi, Joni, I don't know if you remember me. My name is Dena."

"Of course I remember you, the dyke with the green eyes. What's up?"

"Can I take you out to dinner one day?"

"Well, Dena, I work until nine o'clock every night. It would be too late for us to have dinner. Why don't you just come to my house after work?"

"Where do you work?" Dena asked.

"I work at Windows of the World, at the World Trade Center. Have you been there before?"

"No," she replied, "too expensive for me. I can pick you up after work this Friday. Is that cool?"

"Cool."

CHAPTER SEVENTEEN

Dena and Joni dated for a while. Joni's mother was a flight attendant, and she was never at home. They lived in Lower Manhattan. It was just a hop, skip, and a jump from Dena's house. One evening, Joni called Dena and told her she had been given a magnum bottle of champagne. "So bring your ass over here tonight," she ordered.

Dena was looking through some shoeboxes, trying to locate her black wingtip shoes, when she noticed her strap-on dildo. "Man, I've had this thing for so long and never had the chance to use it," she thought. "Well, tonight is the night." She packed an overnight bag and stopped at the twenty-four hour drugstore to pick up some lubricant.

Joni and Dena sat in the living room. They were only able to drink half the bottle of champagne. Drunk or not, Dena liked listening to Joni. She had a sexy voice, and the more she spoke, the more she became aroused. Dena asked Joni if she liked Penny.

"Penny?" Joni replied. "Who the hell is Penny?"

She laughed, and said, "Penetration. Penny is short for penetration. Get it? A strap-on dildo."

"Oh, I see," Joni said, laughing. "I'm not sure, Dena. Maybe if you excite me, I just might let you have your way with me tonight."

"Okay, but before I do anything, let me go to the bathroom. I'll be right back."

Dena was heading toward the bathroom when Joni said, "I'm going to the bedroom to smoke a joint, so give me a chance to air out the room. Meet me back here in the living room. I know about your job and all. I've dated a correction officer before."

"Good," Dena said, "then you're aware of how we get surprise urine tests for drugs and how, if we get caught just once, we're fired, no exceptions.

Dena went into the bathroom to prepare herself. She was having trouble, wondering how the hell do you strap this thing on. Well, ten minutes later she had it on correctly and it was like her own. She took an extra five minutes, looking at her reflection in the mirror—front view, side view. Dildo in hand, she laughed and thought, "I'm excited already."

Back in the living room, she took one look at Joni and said, "Wow-wee! Victoria's Secret!" Then she asked, "Do you have a towel, baby?"

"Look in the small closet in the hallway. And when you come back, turn off the light."

Dena stood in front of Joni and cleared her throat, then said, "Hi, how long has it been...wait, let me rephrase that. How long has it been since someone fucked you right?"

Joni lit a cigarette and sat back on the couch with her legs crossed and made eye contact with her and said, "Go on."

Dena rested her hands on her hips, hoping Joni could see her stiffness. She noticed Joni shift her eyes from her face to her boxer shorts. Joni's breathing became more rapid. It was clear to Dena that she was turned on. "Please, Joni, can I make love to you?" She asked. "I will hold you so tight, and ride you so gently." Joni spread her legs open. Dena took Joni's hand and placed it on the dildo. Joni moaned when she felt her erection.

Dena pulled her boxers down to her knees. "Baby, this is for you. Do you want me? Do you want me inside of you?"

"Yes, Dena, yes. I want you inside of me."

Dena felt Joni shaking and placed her hand on the back of her head and guided her mouth to the dildo, and said, "Now you have to show me how bad you want to come." Joni held the dildo with one hand and placed her mouth on it. She licked every inch of it. Then she used her other hand to find Dena's clitoris. Dena threw her head back in ecstasy, and came hard.

Joni looked up at her and said, "That's how bad I want you."

Dena removed her shorts and laid Joni down on the couch. "Are your bottoms crotchless?"

Joni slid out of her underwear and threw them across the room, saying, "They are now."

Dena climbed on top of her. She was nervous. She lowered her face to kiss Joni—slow kisses. Deep, long kisses. She kissed her breasts until her nipples became hard and Joni was begging her to suck them harder. Dena obeyed, and her fingers found their way to her swollen clitoris. Joni was moaning and grinding her body so readily against Dena's. Dena became aroused, but this was a different kind of arousal. This was the kind of arousal you got before you penetrated a woman. This was how a man felt before he entered a woman, and this was how she was feeling right now. What a fucking stimulating feeling.

Joni was ready for love. Dena reached for the lubricant, squeezed a small amount into her hand, and massaged it on the dildo. Joni watched her applying the lubricant on the dildo, and it made her more excited. Dena lowered her body and let herself in. She rode Joni slow and easy, letting Joni take the speed lead. Dena followed her pace. She could not control her breathing, and neither could Joni. Joni lifted her hips up high to take in every inch of the dildo. "Am I hurting you, baby?" Dena asked.

"No, baby, you feel so damn good. Push harder, baby. I'm getting ready to come."

Dena and Joni started to climax. Joni moaned while Dena shrilled from this powerful feeling. Dena and Joni came together, sounding off in imperfect harmony. "Wow-wee," Dena said, "this is the only way I am going to make love from now on."

Dena liked Joni, but she kept pressuring her to commit to a relationship and to find a job with decent nine-to-five hours. "Look, baby," Dena told her, "you knew I didn't want a commitment from the get go. I'm content being single. I had enough heartbreaks in my life. When I go home at night, I am fine going home to an empty house. I never feel alone or lonely. I have my friends and my family, and, of course, my job has me." She closed her eyes and thought for a moment and searched deep inside her heart to see if she felt anything for Joni or for women in general. She felt nothing, just emptiness. For a second she felt maybe something was wrong with her, but then she realized that it was not about some defect in herself. "This is who I am," she thought, "this is who I've become."

She turned to face Joni. "I have deep feelings for you; I'm just not ready."

"Are you afraid to make a commitment?"

Dena did not answer.

"I know your type. You're the kind of person who's looking for something better to come along. But trust me, Dena, nothing better than me is going to come along. If you don't make a commitment with me tonight, don't come back. There's no second time around bullshit."

"Then I guess this is goodbye," Dena told Joni.

Dena had a date with this female who lived way uptown in Manhattan on 217th Street. Dena never really hung out uptown, but Monroe had begged her all day to come over. She told Dena her sister had gone away for the weekend. "We'll have the apartment all to ourselves."

Dena explained to Monroe that her car was in the shop and she didn't feel like riding the train all the way uptown from Brooklyn. Monroe was much younger than her. Dena had just turned thirty, and Monroe was twenty-two and hot-blooded. She lived with her sister and had a son. She worked in Manhattan. When she received her paycheck every week, she would buy bags of weed, then ask Dena for money—lunch money. Talk about having your priorities all wrong. Whenever Monroe called Dena, she would say things to get her aroused.

Dena thought about it. She knew she would come several times, so she told Monroe okay. "I'll take the train. Expect me around ten p.m."

Dena stopped at the store before boarding the train and picked up two bottles of beer. She looked at her timepiece and said, "Damn, this is a long-ass train ride from Brooklyn, and I have to pee. Freaking beer does it every time. Well, at least I have a buzz." She left the train station and could not make it to the bathroom in Monroe's house. She stopped at a fast-food restaurant and noticed the women's restroom was occupied. Just when she was about to enter the men's room, a lady exited the women's restroom and Dena went in. "What a relief," she thought while peeing. She then headed to Monroe's house, but not before picking up dinner, two packs of Newports, and two quarts of beer. Monroe could have picked these things up a block away from her house.

Before they even started to kiss, Monroe was bitching

about how she did not have carfare to get to work the next week. Dena did not answer her and they began to argue. Dena thought, "I could have stayed home for this bullshit." She told Monroe, "I am going to use the bathroom. Then, I am out of here." Monroe began asking her for money through the bathroom door. Dena explained, "Baby, I don't have any more money. I spent what I had on the way over here." She pulled up her pants and looked for her gun. It was not in the bathroom.

She thought, "Maybe I left it in the living room." She looked there to no avail. Dena panicked. "Where the fuck is my gun?" she thought. She looked under the pillows, all through the house, while Monroe was still asking her for pesos. "Think, Dena, think. Oh my God," Dena thought, "I forgot I stopped at the restaurant! I think I placed it on top of the toilet paper holder! Shit!"

Dena told Monroe, "I have to go," and ran out of the house. She ran about six blocks back to the restaurant, and went directly into the women's restroom. She tore the bathroom upside down. The gun was gone. Dena felt sick. So many things ran through her head: departmental charges, thirty days suspension, someone being hurt or even killed with her firearm, and waiting years before she could apply for another weapon. She was having a panic attack when someone knocked on the half-open door and brought her back to reality.

"Are you finished?" the woman asked.

Dena thought she was fine for a moment and smiled at her as she welcomed her in while she stepped out of the restroom. "Shit, I have more important things to concern myself with right now," she told herself. Dena sat down in one of the booths for a moment to think. "Okay," she thought, "the first thing I have to do is go to the nearest police precinct and file a report. Next, I have to go to my job and file more reports, then turn in my shield and identification card and find out about my suspension." Dena wiped the sweat off her nose. "Oh well, I'm only human. At least I won't lose my job. Next time I will follow my fucking female intuition. I wonder if I still have that power, after turning butch."

She thought she would at least ask the manager if anyone had turned in a fucking loaded gun before she left. "Excuse me," Dena asked him, "what's your name?"

"Miguel."

"Miguel, I left something in the bathroom earlier, about nine o'clock. Did anyone turn in something?"

"Something like what? What did you leave in the bathroom?"

Dena displayed her shield and identification card, then told Miguel, "I accidentally left my gun in the bathroom, and before I file a police report—because it is procedure—I thought I would first ask you if someone had turned it in.

Miguel said that he had just started his shift twenty minutes earlier. "Let me call the evening manager to see if someone turned it in on his shift."

Dena knew it was far-fetched, but she had no choice. She was scared shitless. She began biting her nails, waiting for Miguel to get off the telephone with the evening manager. Two hours later, in Dena's mind anyway, Miguel approached her and said, "The evening manager has your gun. His name is Edwin and he will be here in about thirty minutes. He will call the store from his car and you can meet him outside. He drives a black Nissan Maxima."

She thanked Miguel, and told him, "I'll be right back."

Miguel said, "When you come back, if you're hungry, whatever is on the menu is on the house."

Dena told him, "When I come back, a cup of coffee would be nice. Thank you again."

Dena still felt uncomfortable. She could not relax until her gun was in her hands. She went to look for a cash machine. If she did get her gun back, she would give Edwin a reward. She withdrew the maximum the cash machine would dispense, five hundred dollars. "It's well worth it," she thought. "This guy saved my ass." Dena drank a cup of coffee while she sat in a booth and waited. Forty-seven minutes went by and she was starting to sweat again when Miguel signaled her to go outside.

Dena saw the car double-parked across the street and headed toward it. Edwin instructed her to sit in the passenger seat. They shook hands and Edwin asked to see her identification. After she showed it to him, he handed her the gun and then the bullets. Dena discreetly loaded her gun.

Edwin told her, "This little girl ran out of the bathroom screaming to her mother, 'There's a gun in the bathroom! There's a gun in the bathroom!' I went into the bathroom to retrieve it and told the little girl's mother, 'The gun belongs to me. I carry it for protection because the restaurant has been robbed a couple of times. I went in there to check out something and must have forgotten it. I am very sorry your daughter had to witness this. It will not happen again. Dinner is on the house.'"

Dena shook her head and thought about the little girl handling the gun. Then she thought, "What if I had gone into the men's room like I started to? I would have never seen my gun again." After she had put the gun safely away in the waist of her pants, she handed Edwin the five hundred dollars and thanked him for his honesty. On the train ride home, she thought to herself, "I will never remove the gun from my waist again to use the bathroom. That was a sign to me, no more Monroe."

Dena went home and slept all night and most of the day. She was exhausted. She turned down a trip to Cherry Grove Beach on Fire Island, but was not too tired when she received an invitation from a woman she had been wanting to get with for a while. Belle called her and said that she had broken up with her lover and invited her to see a play called "Sarafina." She asked Dena to pick her up at her beauty salon at five-thirty.

Dena parked her car, went upstairs, and waited for Belle to finish working. She had a nice salon, and she made Dena feel comfortable. Belle turned the high chair toward Dena and said, "Next. Get your deep-penetrating conditioning here." Dena hopped into the chair, and Belle's hands went to work, stimulating her scalp. It was so sensual Dena could not help but become aroused. Dena noticed a futon in the back room. When the last worker left the salon, Belle locked up. She jumped out of the high chair and led Belle into the back room. Dena started to open up the futon as Belle laughed and complained, "Let me wash the conditioner out of your hair, girl. You're dripping."

Dena smirked and said, "I know."

CHAPTER EIGHTEEN

Dolores finally caught up with Dena and asked her if she could make time to bring Nancy home for the weekend. "I will pick her up this Friday if it's all right with you," Dena told her. Dolores agreed. Dolores could not handle Nancy without Dena there. Nancy would beg for money from Dolores and then leave the house at two or three o'clock in the morning.

After work Friday, Dena went straight to the hospital to pick up Nancy. "Hey, girl, how have you been?" She asked.

"I'm okay," Nancy replied. "Do you have any cigarettes for me?"

"Nancy, I've been using filter-tipped cigars to put in my mouth when I have a desire to smoke. I don't light it. I just hold it in my mouth. The woman I date thinks it looks sexy."

Nancy laughed hard and said, "Look, homo sapien, I said, 'Do you have any cigarettes for me?'"

That weekend, Dena noticed a problem with Dolores. She was forgetful and had a hard time choosing her words. She kept saying, "That thing, you know the thing." Dena kept asking her, "What thing, Mommy? What do you mean?" Maybe Nancy was getting to her, she thought. Whenever Nancy came home, she would watch music videos all weekend long. Dena took the girls out to dinner at a diner on Saturday night. Then they went for a long walk after dinner, hoping to tire Nancy out so that after Dena gave her her night medication, she would fall right to sleep.

When they got home, Dena took a shower and wrapped a towel around her body and wondered if she had left a t-shirt there. When she sat down on one of the twin beds, she jumped to the ceiling screaming, "What the fuck?" She looked down and saw a curling iron on the bed with half of her skin attached to it. Dena yelled, "Nancy! Why the hell would you put a freaking curling iron on the bed? You're supposed to do that shit in the bathroom!"

"I'm sorry, Dena," Nancy said.

"By the way, it's eleven o'clock at night. Why the hell are you heating up a curling iron?"

"While you were in the shower, Mommy gave me some money, and I'm going out to see my boyfriend."

"What's your boyfriend's name?"

Nancy just said, "You don't know him."

"Nancy, you are not going out this time of night." Dena had to think fast. "If you go out, we are going to think twice about bringing you home again, and don't you want to come home sometimes?"

"Yes, I do, Dena," Nancy replied, "and you and Mommy are the only two that bring me home."

She added, "And besides, you and Mommy might have to bring me to the hospital," as she took a mirror and looked at the burn on her ass. "Damn, it's at least six inches long!"

On Sunday afternoon, Dolores and Dena took Nancy back to the hospital, escorted her upstairs to the ward, and signed her back in. Dena would always spend an extra night with Dolores after Nancy had spent the weekend. She always noticed how depressed her mother would get after leaving Nancy, and she did not want her to be alone. She would keep her company and they would light a candle and pray for Nancy.

When Dena returned home she found an eight-by-ten photo of this woman taped to the outside of her apartment door. She looked around, then tore it down. It was a gift from this crazy woman she had been avoiding. It read:

Dena,
Had a wonderful time with you. Let's get together.

"Damn," she thought, "this woman rode the train all the way from the Bronx to put this picture on my door. Now it is confirmed: she is crazy."

Dena was starting to believe her girlfriends loved her dildo and not her. Many women she had used it on said it was their first time with one, and not many of Dena's aggressive friends used one. One of her friends had been in a relationship for six years. When Dena took her with her to Toys In Babeland where she was going to purchase a new strap-on belt, she asked Dena, "You use one of those things?"

"You don't?" Dena asked. "And you've been in a relationship for six years? You are buying one today." Two days later her girlfriend thanked her for forcing her friend to purchase the dildo.

Dena needed a change of scenery. She needed to view a different island, one besides Riker's Island, Long Island, and Staten Island. She needed a vacation. She called her friend in Orlando, Florida, and made plans to visit her there in two weeks.

Yes, vacation tomorrow! Dena checked her flight time: 10:00 a.m. Delta Flight 519, leaving from Kennedy Airport.

She decided to park and fly. This way she didn't have to worry about giving her car keys to anyone and burdening them with moving her car to avoid the street cleaners. Dena was restless and excited all day, so she called one of her straight friends, Sydney, and asked her to meet her at a club in Newark, New Jersey, called First Choice. They agreed on eleven o'clock, and Dena started getting ready. She shined her shoes and left the house.

Dena walked in the club and saw her friend. Sydney had already ordered her a beer. She handed it to Dena and asked her, "What time is your flight tomorrow morning?"

"Ten a.m.," she answered.

"Then we better get started. Finish your beer and let's go."

"Let's go where?" Dena asked.

"To my house," Sydney said.

Dena looked around the dance floor and noticed strippers dancing everywhere throughout the club, and asked, "Are you sure you want to leave all this?" She also noticed this woman she liked and was always trying to rap to, but who was always with someone. The one time it seemed like she was alone, Dena had to leave.

"Dena, would you finish your beer and come on?" Sydney insisted.

Dena hollered, "What are you talking about? I came out here to party," when Sydney grabbed her by the hand and dragged her out of the club.

Sydney pulled up in front of a small townhouse and opened the front door. They walked up a flight of stairs. Once inside, she handed Dena another beer, and they sat in the living room and started to talk, when Dena asked, "We left the club for this? To talk? We could have talked in the damn club, woman!"

Sydney lit a cigarette and exhaled, then explained to Dena, "I'm ready to come out, and from the first time I saw you, I wanted you to be my first lover. I want to make love with you, Dena, and I want to make love to you tonight."

Dena became nervous. "Why didn't I see this coming?" she thought. "Maybe because I was so excited about going to Florida tomorrow. Or maybe it's because when a woman tells me she's straight, I don't give the woman a second thought sexually." "Sydney," she said aloud, "this is your first time, and this is my first time with a virgin. Are you sure about this?"

"Yes, Dena."

"Are you nervous, Sydney?"

"Yes, Dena, but more excited than nervous."

Dena and Sydney talked about women making love. They even discussed the subject of strapping on. Dena asked for another beer. While walking to the kitchen, she told herself, "After this beer I will make my move. It's getting late." She undressed Sydney and asked, "Why did you choose me to be first?" to calm her down.

"Well, I liked you. Then after I got to know you better, I thought you were jaunty and crazy, and I really fancied you." Then Sydney asked the same question.

Dena replied, "Because you are fine as hell, and you look like a model. How tall are you?"

"Five-eight, and you?"

She smiled and said, "About six inches shorter."

Dena and Sydney were panting and gasping for air. Sydney was breathless when she said, "It was everything I thought it would be and more...lovely." She kissed Dena and asked her, "Did you bring your strap-on?"

Dena's eyes lit up and she hollered, "You fucking A, I never leave home without it! Do you want me to go get it? It's in my car."

"Yes," Sydney replied.

Dena hurried to put on her clothes and went to the car to retrieve it. She came back and went to wash up in the bathroom. Then she came out of the bathroom. "I got the strap-on and the lubricant," and started to suit up.

Sydney asked, "Can I strap it on and make love to you with it?"

"Whoa, hey, I'm the butch here. What is wrong with you? Your testosterone level high tonight?"

Sydney smiled and asked, "So this dildo thing is only one-sided, huh? Only the butch can strap on?"

"Look, Sydney, I'm your first female lover. You'll have plenty of chances to strap-on with someone besides me. That is what femmes are for. Look, there are some aggressive women that are so butch, they refuse to have a woman go down on them, ever, and there are some feminine women who refuse to go downtown on their lover. That's just the way it is."

"What category do you fall under, Dena?"

"A woman, Sydney, a gay woman…okay, a strong butch, dyke, truck driver, lesbo, gay woman," Dena laughed out loud, "not the kind of woman who gets fucked with a strap-on."

Sydney grabbed the strap-on and asked, "How do I put this thing on?"

"You don't," Dena answered while wiping the sweat from her face. "You're not giving up, are you?"

"No," Sydney answered, "I'm not." And she got up off the bed and said, "You're not leaving until I fuck you with it. Look, you don't have to throw your legs up in the air and hold them with your hands, unless you want to," she laughed. "Just lie on the bed and let me get on top of you and ride you slowly. I'll be gentle."

Dena became a tad excited and said, "All right, just know it's been a long time since I've been with a man. So take it easy. Please don't tell anyone about this ever. Oh, and one more thing, do yourself a favor and when you get excited, please don't say, 'Oh God.' That bothers me."

Dena left the next day around seven-thirty in the morning and headed straight for Kennedy Airport. She checked the trunk of her car to make sure her suitcase was still there. She was glad she had put her suitcase in her car the night before, just in case. She opened up the car window for some fresh New Jersey air and thought to herself, "If I had known I was going to be leaving from New Jersey, I would have booked my flight from Newark Airport. It's just five minutes away. Now I have to drive like a pipe head to Kennedy Airport, hoping I have enough time, with rush hour traffic and all." Dena smiled when she thought about Sydney strapping on. She hadn't thought it was possible, but she came lovely.

Dena's friend, Cora, was hours late picking her up at the airport. Dena went into her bag and pulled out a book and read while she waited. She was supposed to spend two nights at Cora's grandmother's house, then two days at a Holiday Inn. Cora believed she could save Dena a couple of dollars this way. Dena had felt uncomfortable, but she eventually agreed. Sitting in the airport, she thought, "If, for some reason Cora doesn't show up, I'll take a taxicab to the hotel and make reservations for two more days."

"Hey, handsome," Dena heard someone say. She looked up and it was Cora. Dena stood up and smiled and lifted Cora in the air. She was happy to see her.

On the drive to Cora's house, she noticed Cora driving the stick shift and quickly became excited. She distracted herself by asking her, "How do you like living in Florida?" Cora had lived in New York, then New Jersey, and could not nail a decent job. So she had decided to try something new and give Florida a try. She stayed with her grandmother after her grandfather died. Her grandmother loved her company and her help.

"Are you hungry?" Cora asked.

"No," she replied, "I grabbed a bite at the airport."

"Do you want to go out tonight, or are you tired? Do you want to relax and watch a movie? Have you seen 'Fried Green Tomatoes' yet?"

Dena said, "Never heard of it. Is it Julia Child's autobiography?"

Cora laughed and said, "No, silly, it's like a gay movie, but not a gay movie." In a short time, they arrived at Cora's house.

"Relax, take a shower, everything you need is in the bathroom," Cora told her. "I'll start the movie when you return." Dena came out of the bathroom and went into Cora's room, Cora said, "I went to see if my grandmother was awake, and she wants to meet you. Come on."

"But I'm in my pajamas."

"Come on, scadie-cat," Cora insisted.

Dena walked to what seemed like the other side of the world. Cora knocked on the door to her grandmother's bedroom, and her grandmother told her to come in. She introduced them and told her granny she would be home tonight watching television and to call her if she needed anything.

Dena told Cora, "Man, you can have a party in your room and she wouldn't even know on account of your room is so far away from hers."

The next day, Cora had made appointments for the girls to get full body massages. Dena was ecstatic. She could not wait. She swallowed her breakfast in one spoonful and said, "I'm ready."

The girls lay side by side in the same massage room. Dena told Cora, "Stop yapping and be quiet so I can concentrate on my massage, please."

But Cora continued to talk, saying, "How do you know when you've received a great massage?"

"I don't know," Dena replied.

"One is, if you fall asleep before it's done, and the second is, when you feel so totally relaxed that you have to move your bowels."

"Come again?" Dena said.

"Okay," Cora said, "you know how when people die, their bodies are so relaxed that soon after they die, they move their bowels and urinate? You work in a jail. Did you ever notice how they put on a diaper on a prisoner before he or she is executed?"

"I've never seen a prisoner put to death before, and I thought the diaper was for the fear of dying." Cora was still talking when Dena fell asleep.

When Cora awakened Dena, she was already dressed. "You fell asleep, baby. The massage was good."

"How long have I been asleep?"

"After the massage was over, about twenty minutes or so. It's okay, though. They usually let you sleep for a couple of minutes before they wheel your ass out." Dena nervously lifted the towel off of her butt and gave a sign of relief.

"What are you looking for," Cora asked, "your wallet?"

"No," Dena answered, "I was so relaxed, I wanted to make sure I didn't do ca-cky."

Dena stayed home and helped Cora's grandmother around the house, watched television, and slept all day while Cora went to work. Cora called the house and told Dena, "We are going to the club tonight, so have an outfit ready. I managed to get the next couple of days off." Cora arrived home around eight o'clock and looked at Dena.

Dena said, "I know, I know, the club closes at midnight, so we don't have much time."

Cora looked at her and said, "No, at two o'clock in the morning, and how did you know that?"

Dena asked, "What's for dinner?"

"Well, what are you in the mood for?" she asked.

Dena said, "I can go for some pizza."

"Well, wait until you go back to New York for that, because the pizza here doesn't taste as good as in the city."

"Why? Because of the water?" She asked. "I would like a burger then."

After dinner, Cora began getting dressed and Dena decided to call her mother to see if she and Nancy were okay. They were both fine, except Dolores mentioned that she and Timo were thinking about getting back together. She thought that was impossible, since they had been divorced for years and he was still happily married to his second wife. Dena told Dolores, "Mom, we will talk more about this when I get home, okay? Love you." She hung up the telephone and wondered for a minute about Dolores, then asked Cora, "Are we there yet?"

"Where is the club?" Dena asked, as Cora drove.

"Right over there," Cora answered, and pointed to what looked like a wooden shack.

"That's the club?"

Cora yelled out, "I am sorry, baby, it's better once you get inside. It's no Networks or Garbo's, dear."

"Wow, it's nice in here," Dena said once they were inside. The club had mirrors on the ceiling, a large sunken dance floor, and dancers everywhere.

"Where's the bar?"

"This way, baby. They make some really good Long Island Iced Tea. Would you like to try one?"

"I really don't like mixed drinks."

"Try it this one time, for me," Cora prodded Dena.

"Okay, okay, order me one." Dena took one look at the drink and said, "What the...this drink is in a lemonade pitcher, and this is one drink?"

"Yes, Dena, all you need is one of these drinks and you're good for the entire night."

"I get change back too? You kidding me. This pitcher is only three dollars? Please give the bartender the change, Cora."

After a couple of dances, Dena was thirsty again. "I shouldn't mix the iced tea with a beer. I'll get sick," she thought. "I'll just order another Long Island Iced Tea and only drink half of it." Well, Dena could not stop at half and drank the whole pitcher. She was drunk, and Cora had to take her home early.

"Wake up, Dena, we have to get ready to go," Cora's cheerful voice announced.

Dena looked at the clock and said, "You must be kidding me. It's four-thirty in the morning."

"I know. I have something nice planned for you today."

"Take off your clothes and hop in the bed. That would be nice."

Cora dragged her out of the bed and said, "Get ready now. There's a bottle of Advil in the bathroom cabinet."

Driving down International Drive, Dena begged Cora to stop for coffee. "Please, please, please, why can't we stop for coffee?"

"Because we are already running late."

Dena said, "The next coffee shop you drive past, I am jumping out of this car."

Cora stopped for coffee, and said, "I hope we don't miss them. If we do, it's all your fault."

"Miss who? Where are we going?"

"Just finish your coffee and let's go."

Cora pulled into an empty parking lot. There was a van parked there and a couple of cars. Two men were standing outside the van, waiting and looking at their timepieces. They were upset when they announced, "You girls are late. The other riders already left. We might be able to catch up with them if we leave now."

Dena and Cora jumped into the van. Dena asked the two men, "Where are we going?"

One of the men looked at Cora and said, "You didn't tell her? We're going hot air ballooning."

"You must be kidding me," Dena said, suddenly feeling wide awake.

"That is why you're up so early," one of the men told her. "We have to get the balloons up in the air before traffic begins."

Cora smiled at her and said, "Surprise!" Dena smiled back.

The van came to a full stop at what Dena thought was a football field. "Okay, everyone out of the van."

Dena hollered, "Go, Go, Go, Go!" like in the military.

Cora said, "You are so silly."

The girls talked while the men set up the balloon. They laid the balloon down on the field and attached the basket to it and turned on the roaring flames. When the balloon was almost full and ready for takeoff, the pilot of the balloon said, "Okay, ladies, one at a time, jump into the moving basket."

Dena jumped in first, then Cora, and the balloon started to rise. Dena asked, "What about Jimmy? Isn't he riding with us too?"

"No," Hal said. "He's the driver of the van and has to set a clear path for us. I will be talking to him by means of radio contact."

"So Jimmy is in the van showing you the way to go?"

"Yes, Dena," Hal answered.

Jimmy's voice was transmitted through the radio, "Check one, check two."

Hal answered, "I read you loud and clear, good buddy."

"Hal, the basket is only up to my knees," Dena protested. "If we hit a strong wind, I could easily be tossed out of the balloon."

"Then I suggest you hold on tight to the rope, because we're about to go up to at least seven hundred feet."

"Shit," Dena said to Cora, "what the hell am I doing up here?"

After Dena had relaxed a bit, she was starting to enjoy the beautiful scenery, when Jimmy said on the radio, "Hal, watch out for the telephone wires. You're coming too close to the wires. Pull up, man, pull up!"

"Where, where are the wires?" Hal asked, then looked at the girls. "We do that to all of our customers."

Cora chuckled nervously, when Dena said, "Give me the radio. Jimmy, are you there?" She heard Jimmy laughing. "Jimmy, expect to get your ass kicked when I get down from here, man."

When Dena finished packing, she looked at Cora and said, "I guess I'm ready." They were already missing each other.

While driving to the airport, she thanked Cora for a splendid time. After they arrived, she was told her flight would be delayed. Three hours later, Dena told Cora, "I booked this flight for four p.m. so I wouldn't have to fly at night. I hate flying at night, and it's almost seven-thirty. Damn." She hugged Cora and said, "Darling, my flight hasn't arrived yet. You look tired. There's no need to wait here with me. I'll call you when I get home."

Cora asked, "Are you sure? You promise?"

"To the best of my ability," Dena answered.

Cora started to walk to her car when she turned around and said, "Don't forget, I want to come to New York soon."

Dena replied, "I can't wait. Just give me at least two weeks' notice so I can make reservations to take you bungee jumping off the Empire State Building."

CHAPTER NINETEEN

The flight was over four hours late taking off, and Dena had about ten beers at the airport bar before boarding. It was a long, tiring flight. "It feels good to be home," she thought as she opened her front door and turned on the light. She dropped everything and headed for the shower. Then she sat down in the living room and scanned her mail and threw it on the coffee table. She glanced over at her telephone answering machine. It displayed eleven messages. Dena leaned over and pressed play. "Baby, where are you?" she heard a voice on the first message say. "Call me ASAP. You know who this is. Bye."

Message two was from Timo's wife. "Dena, your father had a heart attack this morning. He's being admitted to Long Island College Hospital."

"Oh my God, when did she leave this message?" Dena said to herself. "It was two days ago. Damn!" She quickly dressed and ran out the door. Thank goodness the hospital was only a few blocks away. In her rush, she entered through the wrong side of the hospital building. "Shit," Dena cursed to herself, "I get so confused in this hospital. I just cannot get used to this building. It's not like Bellevue."

She finally found the Intensive Care Unit, and she spotted Timo's wife, Gloria. Dena embraced her, and Gloria started to cry as she demanded, "Where have you been?"

"How is he doing?" Dena interrupted.

Gloria started crying uncontrollably when she said, "The doctor pronounced him dead at eleven-twelve p.m.!"

Dena looked at her timepiece. It read eleven forty-seven. "My God, I missed seeing my father alive by a matter of minutes," she thought. "Where is he?" She asked.

"Where the hell were you? Where were you when your father was asking for you? You couldn't even stop hanging out for one second to visit your father in the fucking hospital? He loved you so much…"

Dena froze, thinking to herself, "How can this be? My father is only sixty-one years old." At that moment, she noticed the medical transporter enter Timo's room and wheel his body out on a stretcher and down the corridor toward the patients' elevator. She rushed to catch up with him. Dena recognized the transport worker and told him, "That's my father and I am coming with you to the morgue. I need five minutes alone with him." She displayed her shield, which hung on a silver beaded chain around her neck, to the hospital police and the hospital staff workers. She knew most of them from working at the hospital from time to time, taking sick prisoners there. Long Island College Hospital had good staff, who respected all city workers. Dena was granted time alone with her father.

Timo was in a line in the hallway waiting to be placed in the fridge. Dena nervously pulled the sheet down and stopped it at his chest. "Hi, Daddy," she said, then took her hat off and added, "I know, I know, I'm supposed to take off my hat indoors. I remember when I was younger, and Mike's friends would come to our house and walk in wearing their Beaver hats and Apple Jack hats. You would say, 'That's a nice hat you have on, son. Looks great on you, but respect my house and take off your hat. No exceptions.'" Dena laughed and took a deep breath because she was trembling now. "I'm sorry, Daddy.

You and I never had the chance to become best friends. I guess I'm too much like you—stubborn." She smiled and wiped the tears from her eyes. "No matter what we've been through and what you might think, I love you dearly and respect you to the highest level. I will miss you, Daddy, very much, and I will see you again, and we will have a lot to talk about then. Oh, and don't worry about Nancy. I will always look after her." Dena kissed her hand, then placed it on Timo's heart and left.

After Timo's service, Dena pulled Mike to the side and asked him if he had lost his job. Mike said, "No, why would you ask me a question like that?"

"Because Mommy said that you lost your job and were staying with some friends."

"Dena, I've been working at this job for sixteen years. Where am I going? And if I were staying with some friends, you would be the first to know, because I might need your sofa bed again." They laughed, and Mike added, "I think Mommy is losing her mind."

On the drive home, Dena asked Nancy if she wanted to spend the night at their mom's house, and Nancy agreed. She thought, "Dolores and Nancy should not be alone tonight."

She made the girls a pot of tea, and they all sat around the kitchen table and chatted for a while. Dolores continued telling Dena about Mike losing his job. Dena cut her off and said, "Mom, I just spoke to Mike tonight, and he said he did not lose his job."

Now Dolores cut Dena off and said, "He is losing his job. They are moving out of state, and he has to find another job."

"Mommy, it's not true—"

"You don't know shit, Dena," Dolores sternly told her. "You think I'm stupid."

"Whoa," Dena thought. Even though Nancy was on medication, she was still wise enough to know that her mother needed help. "I'm tired, you guys. I'm going to bed," she said, and kissed Dolores and Nancy goodnight. Dena thought to herself, "I have to keep a close eye on Dolores."

The next morning, Dena woke up and Dolores was gone. She grabbed her jacket and ran downstairs in her pajamas and found Dolores standing in front of the building. "Oh God, what is going on here? Mom, what's up? What are you doing out here? Who are you waiting for?"

Dolores stated, "I'm waiting for Mike. He's supposed to pick me up here, and I am going to stay with him for a couple of days."

"Are you sure?" Dena asked. "Let me call Mike on my mobile phone and see what's going on here." Dena explained what she could to Mike with Dolores standing there. Mike said that he had never made plans to pick up Dolores. "Okay, Mike, I'll call you later and explain," she said. "Mom, Mike said he didn't have plans with you today. You must be mistaken."

"Don't tell me that," Dolores yelled, and repeated over and over, while talking over Dena, "Oh, yes, he did. Oh, yes, he did. Oh, yes, he did…" Dena gave up and just kept quiet. While riding the elevator back upstairs, Dena smiled at Dolores and thought, "Damn, she's only been retired a little over two years and this is occurring. Shit! I have to get her help."

Monday morning, Dena started her car and prepared for her journey back to work, after taking some time off. It was a chilly morning, and she was moving in slow motion. She decided to drive down Atlantic Avenue to take the Interboro Parkway, AKA the snake road because of all the twists and turns. It was a shortcut. She liked to take the parkway because she had a choice at the end of the road to connect either with the Grand Central Parkway or the Van Wyck Expressway, whichever had minimal traffic. Dena was waving to a station wagon to go ahead in front of her, when this vehicle coming from the opposite direction jumped the divider, which was only about two feet high, and became airborne. It flew right over the station wagon that she had waved on ahead of her. Dena had to hit her brakes to avert hitting the station wagon.

Dena quickly looked up at the car and said, "Oh my God!" The station wagon was now a convertible. She pulled her car over to the side of the road to see if she could help. She saw other motorists getting out of their cars and chasing the driver of the other car that had jumped the divider and pinning him down to the ground, where they waited for the police to arrive. Everyone was yelling for someone to call 9-1-1. Dena looked at the roof of the station wagon on the side of the road and wondered about the passengers of that car. Where were they? She walked over to the station wagon and looked in. She placed her hand over her mouth to prevent herself from throwing up. "My God," she uttered. The driver and the woman in the passenger seat were decapitated. Both of their seats were reclined, due to the force of the other car on top of theirs.

Dena was throwing up when she heard a child crying. She looked in the back seat, and there were two little boys there. Both were alive. One of them was upside-down. She thought about grabbing him, when she heard a siren. The ambulance had arrived. A woman screamed, "There are two kids in that car who need medical attention!" Dena slowly walked back to her car, got in, started the engine, and for the first time in her driving life, put on her seatbelt.

While driving to work, she thought, "If I hadn't let that station wagon go first, that would have been me." Dena made the sign of the cross and blessed the two passengers' souls, then thanked God that it had not been her turn. "Dolores always said I have an angel watching over me."

When she arrived at work, she told her coworkers what had happened. One of the officers said he had been in the military and had never seen someone decapitated. The next day she bought the newspaper, which had a small article about the accident. It read: A drunken driver jumped the divider and killed the parents of two young boys, ages six and three.

Dena began spending a lot more time with her mother. She made an appointment for Dolores to see her medical doctor, and Doctor Polar referred Dolores to a neurologist in four weeks. "Doctor, is there any way we can make an appointment for her sooner?" Dena asked.

Doctor Polar said, "The neurologist is only here on Fridays, and he's booked until then. That's the earliest appointment available."

Dolores and Dena were blessed with a loving neighbor who cared for and looked out for Dolores. When Dena went to work, Molly would wake up in the morning and knock on their door for Dolores to come over for coffee. They both would remind each other to take their medication while they had their coffee. It became a ritual at "Molly's Coffeehouse." Molly would also invite Dolores and Dena over for some good home cooking. Dena thought Molly should have had her own cooking show. She always looked out for Molly every chance she had, but she also knew she could not burden Molly with her problem.

CHAPTER TWENTY

Thursday morning, Dena went to work. She always tried to clear her head before she arrived. She never brought her home life to work or her work life home. At Riker's Island, you always had to be alert and prepared for anything. She said a prayer, signed herself in at 13:00 hours, and waited for roll call.

She was assigned to a corridor patrol post and assisting with the inmates' dinner feeding. She arrived on post and made a security check of the doors, windows, locks, and screens. "No holes in the walls today," she thought to herself and went to work. After she had lunch, it was dinnertime for the inmates, so she hurried because she did not want to be late. The dinner feeding went well—no assault on the staff, no inmate fight, no stabbing. Dena looked at her timepiece and it showed seven-thirty p.m. "Damn, two more hours to go till quitting time."

Dena made her second security check and found one corridor door that led to the outside world unlocked. "Oh shit," she thought to herself, "I wonder if the main control room alarm rang when I opened the corridor door like it's supposed to?" She waited a minute to see if she got a radio transmission about the door being ajar. Nothing. If the alarm had not sounded when she had opened it, how many inmates could have already escaped through that door? "This is some serious shit here," Dena thought. She called for the D House captain to come to her post ASAP.

Captain Kleen arrived at the location, as did the warden, the deputy warden, and the assisting deputy warden. They ordered a complete lockdown of the entire facility, no inmate movement, and a head count of all the prisoners. About two hours later, the head count was completed. All the inmates were accounted for. No escapees. The jail was blessed that night, and the security captain informed Dena that she would receive a medal of commendation. After writing reports all night, she was finally able to leave work after midnight.

Two days later when Dena arrived at work, she was informed that she was being brought up on departmental charges for not doing her job. She could not believe her ears. They wanted her to sign some papers, and she refused. She told them she would wait for her hearing. Dena was outraged. "I knew that motherfucker was not going to give me a commendation," she thought, "because I am gay, female, and minority." She went home that night and reread her rules and regulations manual, and it stated that an officer working a corridor post had to conduct two security checks in an eight-hour tour. It did not mention any particular times to conduct the checks, but just that you had to make two checks and that you had to make notations in a logbook and in your personal memo book. Dena had covered her ass by doing both. "So why am I being brought up on departmental charges?" she wondered.

The day of Dena's hearing, she sat on the bench waiting to be called. She was fifth in line. "Damn, is this an everyday thing?" she asked another officer.

"Well, this is my fourth time in here this month," was her reply. Dena laughed.

Another officer stated, "Did you people read the *Correction Newsletter*? They lowered our life expectancy after retirement from five years to three years. So that means after we retire, we only have three years to live, according to this survey."

"Damn," Dena remarked, "three years. I guess it's because of the stress level the job carries, especially on account of unnecessary bullshit like this."

One bench space at a time, she inched her way closer to the hearing office. Some officers came out mad as hell and shaking their heads. Others come out smiling, knowing they had beaten their charges.

"Officer Dena Vargas," the captain's voice called out from his office. She did not know what her defense was going to be.

"Officer Vargas here," she said and remained silent.

"Were you offered a union representative?" the captain asked.

"Yes," Dena answered.

"And you refused?"

"Yes."

"These are some serious charges here. Are you sure you don't want to reconsider?"

"Yes," she answered. Dena had always been told to give one-word answers during hearings and court proceedings. "What am I being charged with?" She asked. Because she had not signed the papers, she had not been given a chance to see what she was being charged with.

"One: Failing to secure your post."

"How is that?" Dena asked. "If it wasn't for me, we would have had an escape on our hands."

"Two: Failing to make a security check during the course of your tour."

"Are you kidding me?" She yelled at the top of her lungs, adding, "You must be crazy! It states in the rules and regulations manual, two security checks per eight-hour tour. What the hell do you think I did? I conducted the first one at 13:15 hours at the beginning of my tour and the second one at 19:30 hours at which time I found the damn door unlocked!"

The captain stated, "Sign here, Officer Vargas."

"I am not signing a damn thing! Let me tell you something: if I go down, everybody is going down, from the security captain to the warden, and I am bringing everyone up on charges for discrimination!"

At that moment, Deputy Warden McGill entered the office because of the disturbance Dena was making. "What's going on in here?" he asked.

Dena responded, "Deputy Warden McGill, you were there the night I found that corridor door unlocked. Well, they're bringing me up on departmental charges because of it."

"WHAT?" he blasted. "Where's the paperwork with her charges, Captain?" The captain reluctantly handed Deputy Warden McGill the paperwork, which he ripped up right over his desk. Then he ordered the captain, "In the future, do not waste my time with bullshit like this. You can go, Officer Vargas. All of the charges have been dropped."

She thanked the Deputy Warden, then looked at the captain and said, "I am still writing everyone up for discrimination," and walked out of the office.

The next day, Dena arrived at work with a different attitude. She had really cared about her job before all this had happened, and had always tried to do the right thing. But now she realized she was just a shield number to this department and nothing more.

She entered the prison and approached the control room window to hand in her firearm. Officers were not allowed to carry firearms in the jail, just in case they were ever in a situation where they were overpowered by the inmates. The control room captain said, "Bitch, I'm going to miss you."

"What do you mean by that?" Dena asked. "You have me going out on a hospital run."

"No," the captain replied, "you've been transferred to Bellevue Hospital Prison Ward. I don't know how, because you jumped a lot of officers on the transfer list with more time on the job than you."

Dena thought, "It must be because I threatened to write up discrimination charges. Whatever the reason, I'm out of here." Then it settled into her brain. She threw her hands up in the air, did the moonwalk, and said, "Yes! Thank you, God!" "I will drop the discrimination charges," she thought, "because being transferred to Bellevue is like going to the head of the class!"

Dena arrived at Bellevue Hospital Prison Ward and loved it. She had never realized how large it was. They had merged the old Bellevue building with the new Bellevue building. "Oh my goodness! So many beautiful nurses and female employees working here," she thought to herself. "But I still have my rule: never mix business with pleasure."

Dena and six other newly transferred officers sat in a conference room for orientation, new locker assignments, and such. While waiting, the officers introduced themselves to one another and talked. They were all thankful to be there.

One officer asked, "How many inmates are housed here?"

Another answered, "Only about fifty or so."

"Damn, what a difference from the jail I came from, which held about eighteen hundred inmates," the first officer remarked.

A third officer challenged the rest, "See if you guys can beat my story. I saw an inmate spit two razor blades out of his mouth and into his hands without cutting himself."

The next said, "Well, I seen a jailhouse shank large enough to enter your stomach and come out of your back."

"Damn," someone exclaimed, "when I started the job, the jail used to sell ten-packs of razors at the inmate commissary."

Dena's turn came and she said, "One day I was escorting an inmate back from court, and this mate must have thought he was going to be 'court no return,' and be released to New York. But he wasn't. So when I escorted him back to his housing area, the other inmates were doing house gang—cleaning up, sweeping, mopping. When I handed him over to the housing area officer, along with his floor locator identification card, another inmate grabbed the metal mop wringer—which is now plastic, probably because of this incident—and cracked it over his head, right alongside of me. His blood splattered all over me and my uniform. Then the inmate stood over him and said, "Steal my cigarettes again, motherfucker."

The last officer looked nauseated as he was about to tell his story. He said, "One day I was assisting with the lunch feeding, and this inmate was in line waiting to pick up his lunch tray, when another inmate came up behind him with a razor blade in each hand and proceeded to cut both sides of the inmate's face, starting with his mouth and ending when he reached his ears." The officer exhaled, then continued. "The inmate's jaw dropped to his chest, because the other inmate had sliced both sides of his cheeks, so he had no control to hold his mouth closed shut."

"Oh my goodness! Gross! You win, Officer, you win!"

CHAPTER TWENTY-ONE

Dena found a one-bedroom apartment with a backyard in the Clinton Hills section of Brooklyn. Hilda and Kelso had been trying to get her to move to that area for years. They called Clinton Hills a mini Greenwich Village, because a lot of gay women resided there. She liked the fact that her apartment was located on Lafayette Avenue on the corner of South Oxford Street, one block away from the C train, just in case she did not want to drive to work.

She cleaned up the apartment and felt like having company that evening. She decided to call Terry to see what she was up to. Dena missed Terry and had been thinking about her a lot lately. She was regretting that she had not made a commitment with her.

"Hello, may I speak to Terry?"

"Dena," the voice on the other end answered, "how have you been, girl?"

"All right." Dena heard the sound of a baby crying in the background and asked, "Are you babysitting, baby?"

"No, sweetie, I'm married now, and I have a three-month-old son."

"Wow-wee! Congratulations!"

"Dena, I have to go. Take care of yourself," Terry said and hung up the telephone.

Dena opened a bottle of merlot, lit a candle, and called it a night. She lay on her bed and let her mind drift. She thought,

"I am going to be thirty-three years old in a couple of months. I want to settle down and be in love. I need structure in my life. For the first time in her life, she felt lonely. She thought about all the good women who had been in her life and regretted not making a commitment. "Now they're all gone. I feel wiser now. I'm going to love with my heart from now on. This is going to be my new mission. I don't want to play anymore."

The next day Dena stopped at the neighborhood gas station to purchase some gas and get a cold drink. When she entered the store, a female worker approached her and asked her if she needed any help. Dena smiled and said, "No, thank you."

"I like older women," the cashier said.

"I'm flattered. How old are you?" Dena asked.

"Twenty."

"Damn, girl, I'm old enough to be your father!"

The cashier laughed and said, "It's all good, though."

Dena whispered in her ear, "See you in ten years."

Kelso called Dena and said she was in the neighborhood and was it all right for her to come by. "I have to go to work soon, but come up for a little while," Dena told her. Kelso and Dena talked and Kelso invited her to a party on Saturday.

"The lovely ladies of Purple Diamonds are giving it. I'm meeting a woman friend I recently met at a party there," Kelso told Dena excitedly.

"Why would you bring her to a party?" She asked. "To me, that's like bringing her to an orgy—so many woman distractions. But then again, Kelso, you're so loving, you would treat her like she was the only woman at the party. Okay, write the address down for me and I'll see you there. Let's get out of here, baby. I don't want to be late for roll call."

Saturday night came and Dena had a hard time finding a parking space. "Damn, this party must be jumping, or there's another party going on around here." She waited patiently for someone to pull out of a parking space. Almost an hour later, she locked up her car and went to the club. She spotted Kelso right away and walked toward her.

"What's up, bro?" Dena greeted her. They hugged each other, and Kelso introduced her girlfriend.

"Brandy, this my brother, Dena. Dena, this is Brandy."

"Nice to meet you," Dena replied.

"Honey, I'm going to get a drink. Would you like one?" Kelso asked Brandy.

"A white wine, thank you."

"I'll be right back. Dena, walk with me to the bar." Kelso was cheesing from ear to ear when she told Dena, "So-So is here."

But Dena barely cracked a smile. She just said, "Your girl-friend is a hottie."

Kelso blushed and said, "Did you hear what the fuck I just said?"

"I'll say hello to her later. How much for all three drinks?" Dena asked.

"Fifteen dollars," the person behind the bar answered.

Dena reached into her pocket and handed the bartender a twenty-dollar bill and said, "Keep the change." Dena laughed and told Kelso, "The party is nice, but the open bar means open up your fucking wallets, dykes."

Kelso said, "Thank you for the drinks, but I don't want to leave my girl alone for too long."

Dena yelled at Kelso as she walked away, "Come by and say goodnight before you leave, bro." Then she went to look for So-So.

So-So saw Dena approaching her and put her drink down to receive her hug. So-So was always so warm and loving, and she always made Dena feel special. She introduced Dena to her hang-out buddies, and she smiled and said hello. Dena looked around and asked So-So, "Where's your girlfriend?"

"We broke up," she answered.

"Sorry to hear that. I'm going to get me a drink. Would you like one, baby?"

"No, Dena, thank you."

"If you need anything, let me know." Dena turned around to walk to the bar, when So-So put her hand on her shoulder and stopped her.

"There is something I need from you, a ride home, if you don't mind."

"Okay, So-So, let me know when you're ready to go. I won't leave without you. Can I go get my drink now, woman?"

So-So smiled and let Dena's shoulder loose.

Dena danced and mingled and found herself liking this woman named Kayla. As they were talking, another woman approached them and asked to speak with Kayla. Kayla told her, "I'm busy right now." Then she turned to Dena and said, "The woman likes me, but I don't like her that way. Kayla grabbed a napkin off the bar and wrote something down. "Here's my telephone number. Call me."

After she got Kayla's telephone number, she was ready to leave. She found So-So and told her she was leaving. "Where did you park your car?" So-So asked. After Dena told her, So-So said, "I'll meet you at the car in ten minutes."

Dena looked for Kelso to say goodnight, and she was gone. She laughed and thought, "Didn't I tell that bitch to say her goodnights before she left? Typical dyke." Dena left the party and waited for So-So in the car. "She's the only one I would do this kind of shit for," she thought.

"Sorry, baby," So-So said as she got in. "Thank you for waiting."

"Not a problem," Dena told her, and drove five or six blocks before pulling over to the side of the road. "So-So, I am driving you to Queens. But if you broke up with your girlfriend, you probably don't stay in Queens anymore. Where to, dear?"

"Keep going straight, baby."

"Now, So-So, you know I cannot go straight."

So-So laughed and said, "Okay, forward." She leaned toward Dena and placed her hand on her thigh and whispered, "I want to go home with you, Dena."

"What? Are you sure?"

"Yes, Dena, I am sure. I told you I never break a promise."

While driving home, Dena felt like it was her wedding night. She was so nervous, and for good reason. She had wanted to make love to So-So for years, and now So-So had finally given in to her. She held So-So close to her while walking to her building. They entered the apartment and Dena led So-So into the living room. She lit a candle and turned on the radio to WBLS.

Dena paced back and forth for a couple of minutes, then asked, "Do you need anything?"

So-So replied, "Just you, and something to drink."

Dena blushed and said, "I have brandy, white wine, beer, water, and whiskey. What's your pleasure?"

"White wine, please," So-So smiled.

"Okay, coming right up." She poured the wine and had herself a shot of whiskey while thinking, "Damn, she is so fine with her clothes on, can you imagine how her body looks and feels naked? Wow-wee!" She handed So-So the wine and sat on the edge of the coffee table. While they talked and warmed up to each other, Dena's mind was racing.

"Are you surprised I'm here, Dena?"

"Oh my gosh, So-So, yes. What made you change your mind?"

"It wasn't a matter of changing my mind. It was a matter of timing. I always wanted you, sexually. I think you are so butch yet so sweet and mysterious. How are you feeling, Dena?"

"I can die a happy dyke now."

So-So finished her wine and took Dena by the hand and led her into the bedroom. Dena started to sweat, and thought, "I haven't felt this nervous since my first lover." She placed her arms around So-So's waist and moved her body closer to hers. Their bodies touched. "Now I can comprehend what a lamp feels like after being plugged in...electrifying." Dena started to shake, and she noticed So-So breathing heavier. "So-So, I'm so happy you're here with me. I love you." So-So put her finger on Dena's lips, but Dena could not shut up. She was so happy for this moment, having So-So in her arms and in her life. She now realized she was in love with So-So.

Dena inhaled her every breath, and listened very carefully for her excitement. They kissed and caressed each other's bodies for what seemed like an eternity. They undressed slowly, never taking their eyes off each other, wanting this moment—this night—to last forever. After So-So removed her outerwear, she stopped and waited for Dena to remove her underwear. Dena took a moment to absorb all of her beauty. She looked so beautiful. Dena reached behind So-So to remove her bra, when So-So noticed Dena shaking. She held Dena's face and kissed her lips, then whispered in her ear, "Relax, baby."

Dena smiled and said, "Easier said than done," as she removed her panties. So-So pushed Dena down on the bed and slid on top of her. She lowered her face onto Dena's. Her soft, moist tongue was welcomed by Dena's lips, and their tongues caressed. Dena became so aroused, she almost came. Dena gently laid So-So down on her stomach and climbed on top of her. She glided her hands all over So-So's body, at the same time licking and sucking her so she would not fall asleep from the massage. She was excited and relaxed. She rubbed her arms, deeply penetrating her muscles while sucking her fingers. So-So shook with excitement. After Dena finished with her arms, she worked So-So's back with her thumbs and palms. She reached her lower back and squeezed and bit her ass. So-So elevated her body to let Dena know she was enjoying her.

Dena was ready to have her, but she thought to herself, "Have patience." She continued down to her thighs and legs, and when she arrived at her feet, she asked So-So to turn around. Dena pulled up a chair to the edge of the bed and put some oil on her hands and massaged So-So's feet. Women love having their feet massaged. Dena remained in the chair and slid So-So down to the edge of the bed so she could taste her. She spread open her legs and enjoyed the view for a moment. She lowered her face and inhaled her sweet aroma. She separated her lips with her fingers and found So-So's priceless gem.

Dena drew her clitoris into her mouth and held it there tightly while sucking her. So-So moved her body directly into a climax, but Dena did not let go of her clitoris. So-So tried to push her head away, knowing how sensitive her clitoris was after an orgasm. Dena continued gently clinging onto her clitoris, and in a matter of minutes she became aroused and the sensitivity went away and she started to grind Dena's mouth till she went into another orgasm.

"Damn, who are you?" So-So said, and laughed.

Dena went to the kitchen to get a bottle of water and to take a moment to catch her breath. About thirty minutes went by, and she was ready. She lay on top of So-So and kissed her.

Dena opened her legs with her knees while searching for the right position to grind her, then she interlocked their bodies together. Three seconds later, Dena was moaning and sounding off a climax. So-So and Dena laughed, and Dena said, "I pre-ejaculated, baby. Sorry." Dena did not need a moment before she came again. She still did not want to stop. She continued to make love to So-So, while kissing her. So-So pulled her lips away to look into Dena's eyes, and whispered, "I want to come with you, Dena"

Dena held her closer, tighter, and tried to move with her rhythm, So-So wrapped her arms around Dena, pressing her body firmly against hers, when Dena confessed, "I am coming now, baby." Dena's breathing became more rapid, she trembled in So-So's arms and they came together. Dena and So-So were glowing. It was the best night of Dena's life.

After they caught their breath, she announced to So-So, "I love you."

So-So lovingly answered, "I love you too, Dena."

"No, So-So, I am in love with you. I fell in love with you the first time I met you at the Gay Parade. How long have you and your ex-lover been apart?"

"About two months," So-So answered.

"I love everything about you. I would love to have you in my life."

So-So placed her hand on Dena's face. Dena noticed tears rolling down her face when she said, "I love you and think I have always been in love with you, and we have good everything: chemistry, great times, and now the greatest sex. Our timing has always been lousy. I cannot marry you, Dena. I am still in love with my ex-lover."

Dena was hurt and started to cry, saying, "Your ex-lover is a blessed woman. I wish you the best at getting her back." She kissed So-So and thanked her for their special night together, adding, "If you ever need me for anything, So-So, I will always be here for you." She waited for a response from So-So, but she had fallen asleep. Dena smiled and kissed her, then drifted off to sleep.

CHAPTER TWENTY-TWO

Dolores' neighbor, Molly, told Dena that Dolores was routinely packing an overnight bag and waiting outside the building for either Timo or Mike to pick her up. "I went downstairs and brought her back upstairs a couple of times. I tried to talk some sense into her," Molly said. "I told her she must have had a dream, because Timo is gone. She told me, 'You're right, Molly, you're right. It must have been a dream.' But the next day, your mother was right back in the lobby doing the same thing all over again. Dena, your mother needs help, and she needs help now. I witnessed the same illness with my mother."

She told Molly, "We have an appointment with the neurologist this Friday."

Dena could not believe this was happening. She was hurt and dismayed. She did not think her mother deserved this, and neither did she after enduring Nancy's admittance to a mental institution.

Dena checked Dolores' appointment card. Six-forty-five p.m. Dolores kept asking her, "Where are we going? Who makes a doctor's appointment this time of night?"

They entered the doctor's office and the doctor started the examination. "What year are we in?"

"I don't remember." Dolores answered.

"What month is this?"

"I don't remember," Dolores again answered.

"What day is today?"

"I don't know."

"Who is the president?"

"You know ... what is his name? You know ... that asshole," she answered.

Dena smirked and said to herself, "Well, she got that question right."

Dolores was diagnosed with a moderate stage of Alzheimer's, at sixty-six.

The neurologist wrote Dolores two prescriptions, telling Dena, "These work well together. Give them to her once in the morning and once at night."

Dena thought, "Who is going to be there to give her the medicine at night? I have to stay with her until I get a home attendant, because she will surely forget to take her medicine at night."

Dena hired a home attendant, but Dolores would not let her in the house. Shortly afterwards, Dena had to fire her because Dolores claimed she had hit her. She didn't know if it was true or not, but she was not taking any chances. So Dena stayed with her mother as much as she could. But she still had to work, and that meant she had to be gone at least ten hours a day. When Dolores started a small fire, Dena called her brother, Mike. For Dolores' safety, they had no choice but to place her in a nursing home. She felt so bad when Dolores grabbed her arm and said, "Please don't leave me here. I'm okay. I want to go home."

Dena cried and said to Mike, "How many times must history repeat itself?"

Dena put in her eight hours at work and occasionally some overtime when it was necessary. One day at work, she wanted to use her whistle to notify the staff that some inmates were fighting. When she removed the whistle from her utility belt, she realized her whistle was filthy. She thought to herself, "The department has a leather case for everything on our workbelt except for the whistle. There is a case for our flashlights, a leather case for our handcuffs, even a damn case for our latex gloves. But our whistles are just hanging from a metal loop with no case to protect them and keep them sanitary. When I get home, I will do a patent search to see if there's a similar product patent pending. If not, I'll design a leather whistle case."

Dena became excited when she found out there was no such product on the market. She hired a patent attorney and started developing her invention. She called the product exactly what it was: a Whistle Case. As soon as she found out her invention was patent pending, she began to advertise her product by writing to uniform companies and sending out e-mails and samples. On her days off, she would go to police precincts and traffic academies, security sites, and even building door attendents who used whistles to hail taxicabs for the tenants, and she would give them free samples.

When Dena went to work, for the first time, her mind was elsewhere. She was getting older and her patience with prisoners was getting shorter. "Wow, what a long day," she said one night as she was walking to her car. She noticed someone had written something on her dirty car windows. It read: I wish my wife was this dirty. Dena laughed and said, "I needed that."

On Dena's next day off, she went to pick up Nancy and took her to visit Dolores at the nursing home. She gave them some time alone, because she had already visited her mother two days earlier. After an hour or so, Dena joined them.

"Mom," she said, "you know, I'm sorry I never gave you any grandkids."

"That's okay, Dena. I am blessed with Mike's four beautiful sons. Dena, I want to go home to my house and watch 'All My Children.'"

"Mom, I will put the television on channel seven. You see? Your soap operas are on this television too. Group hug," she announced. "Mommy, I have to bring Nancy back to the hospital by a certain time, so we have to leave now. I love you, and I will bring you the items on the list that you gave me when I come back on Monday."

Dena dropped Nancy off, then went home. She contemplated going out to the club and having a drink or two. She dressed, undressed, then dressed again, looked at the time—midnight—and decided to go out.

The club was crowded. She walked around and said hello to friends, lovers, and coworkers. One of her coworkers, Vicky, said she was leaving and asked Dena to walk her downstairs. They were having a good time catching up on things, and Vicky stayed an extra hour, talking. Dena noticed this beautiful woman sitting across the bar. Dena could not take her eyes off of her. Vicky was forced to wave her hand in Dena's face, saying, "Hello? Are you listening to me, girl?"

Dena tilted her head and continued to scope out the woman while answering, "Yeah, yeah, yeah." Dena saw this butch sitting next to the woman and realized she could be her lover. No one this fine was ever alone.

The aggressive woman started to approach Dena and Vicky, and said, "Hi, my name is Jules. How you guys doing tonight? You want some popcorn?" Dena declined on the popcorn, but Vicky grabbed a handful and thanked her, and Jules walked back to the cutie-pie.

"I wonder if she thinks I was flirting with her. Was that a nice way of saying, 'Stop looking at my girl?'" Dena wondered. Vicky finally kissed her goodnight and left. Dena was taking one last, long look at the woman before going upstairs when Jules waved for Dena to come to her, and she complied.

"I told you I don't want any popcorn," Dena said as she approached her.

"Say what?" Jules replied.

"Just kidding, man," Dena said and laughed.

"What's your name?" Jules asked.

"Dena."

"Dena, this is Collette. Collette, this is Dena."

Collette extended her hand and Dena touched it and said, "Nice to meet you."

Jules walked away to let the girls have some privacy. Dena realized they were not lovers. Collette explained how she was going to get her hair done that night, but she found out the hairdresser had cancelled her appointment when she arrived at the salon. So, being that she was already in the city, she had decided to stop in at the club on the way home from the salon and say hello to her friend, Jules, who worked there.

Dena thought, "We were meant to meet each other tonight. Thank you, God." They exchanged telephone numbers before Collette went home.

Dena and Collette first got to know each other by means of the telephone. They talked for hours and hours. Collette would sing to her, and they laughed a lot and started to like each other. Only thing, Collette was never at home. She was always on the go—work, gym, hanging with her friends, traveling. Dena knew she was popular and had many friends. She knew she had to work a little harder to win her love. Dena and Collette dated for months without a single kiss.

On New Year's Eve, Dena purchased a bottle of champagne and had it delivered to Collette's house, along with a card that read: If you don't have any plans for tonight, would you like to bring in the New Year together?

Collette called her, and they finally got together. They fell in love, and Dena was happy and wanted their love to flourish. She was deeply in love with Collette. Only thing, sex was not important to Collette. She could take it or leave it. But to Dena, on a scale from one to ten, sex was one, two, three, four, and five.

Collette wanted Dena to move in with her, and she did. She was happy that Collette resided in Brooklyn; and for a year, things went well. But then Dena started working steady evening hours from four p.m. to midnight, and Collette was always out with her friends. They never saw each other. Dena would sleep all day on one of her two days off. It was her way of relieving the stress from work. Collette did not like that one bit. She felt Dena had no motivation. "Go to school," she would tell her, "sell your patent, but do something more with your life."

Collette worked for a large publishing company, and she went to New York University part-time. Dena argued, "Would you leave me alone? At least I have a job, woman."

Saturday morning and Dena woke up wanting Collette. "Damn," she thought, "I never thought making love to my girlfriend would be such a challenge." She found Collette lying on the sofa in her robe, talking on the telephone. Dena sat on the sofa and contemplated her move. She lay on top of Collette and kissed her lips, and Collette turned away to continue talking on the phone. Dena kissed her neck and breast and Collette pushed her away, saying, "Don't you see me on the phone, dyke?"

Dena laughed and did not pay her any mind and opened Collette's robe and proceeded to enter her. Collette took a deep breath and said to the person on the other end of the phone, "Yes, I'm okay. Let me call you right back," and hung up the telephone and gave in to her. Afterwards, Collette said, "I'm calling the police."

"For what?" Dena asked.

"For making love to me against my will."

"Oh hush, Collette...and you coming will be your evidence."

"No, your strap-on will." They laughed.

Dena said, "Wouldn't that be some shit? The first case in history: Female arrested for strapping on and fucking her girlfriend against her will...tonight on the 'Ten O'Clock News.' They would arrest me and say, 'Get the evidence,' and put my dildo in a Ziploc bag. 'Exhibit A: A chocolate-colored dildo.' I would yell out, 'Objection! A vibrating, chocolate-colored, strap-on dildo.'"

They laughed, and then Collette said, "Let's go into the bedroom."

Dena answered, "Oh, now you want me? I don't know, Collette. My prostate's been acting up lately."

"Then forget it, then," Collette snapped.

Dena starting walking toward the bedroom and said, "We're right behind you."

It was Collette's idea for them and two of her friends to go on a seven-day cruise from New York to Bermuda. The girls had the time of their lives. They went jet skiing, sang karaoke, gambled, rented motor scooters, and ate until their buffet pants exploded. On the way home from their trip, Collette told Dena that things were going to have to change between them. "Let's buy a house together, or a duplex condominium, and try to change your schedule to the day tour, because your four-to-midnight tour is killing our relationship."

Dena thought, "Easier said than done for my work hours." "It's very hard to get a day tour," she explained, "and I'm spending all my money on my patent. It takes money to make money." Collette's words had gone in one of Dena's ears and out the other. "Look, Colette, I can't do that right now."

Two weeks later, Collette asked Dena if she wanted to go out with her that Friday. She informed Collette that on Saturday she had an appointment to see the salesperson of a major uniform equipment company about her invention. "The company might be interested."

Collette told her, "The appointment is not until one p.m."

"I know, I know," Dena answered, "but I don't want to be hung over or get up late, so I'll pass and catch the next event."

Collette whispered something and walked out the front door to go to work.

Friday evening and Dena was sitting in the living room, getting her paperwork ready for her big day when Collette walked in the house from work, showered, got dressed, and told Dena she was borrowing the car. She went to kiss Collette on her lips and tell her to be careful and have a nice time, when Collette turned her face. So instead of kissing her lips, Dena had to kiss her cheek. Dena placed her hand on the front door to prevent Collette from leaving the house, and said, "That's a nice blouse you have on. I've never seen it before."

Collette answered, "What's your point?"

Dena said, "My fucking point is, you are showing a lot of cleavage—too much for your woman's taste. Where are you going again?"

"Out with some friends." Collette pulled the door open and said, "You were invited, remember? But you chose not to go. I'll call you later," and walked out the door. Dena sat down on the couch and put a pen in her mouth, trying to think about her presentation for her interview the next day, but all she could think about was Collette's breasts, and the feeling of trust.

Dena went to sleep around eleven o'clock and woke up around two-thirty to use the bathroom. After using the toilet, she went to the living room to see if Collette had left a telephone message. Just some of her friends wanting to know where Collette was...said they would try her mobile telephone. "Whatever," she thought. She went back into the bedroom and looked at her mobile phone—no message. Dena set her mobile phone to message reminder, so that it would beep every five minutes to remind her that she had missed a call. She sat in the bed and thought about how it was not like Collette not to call her and tell her who she was with, and that she was all right. But no call, so she decided to call Collette on her mobile phone.

It went right to her voicemail. Dena left a message, and continued leaving messages until four in the morning. She called some of Collette's friends, and they informed her that before she called the hospitals, she should first call Collette's friends. She called most of Collette's friends she could think of, and retrieved more numbers from the answering machine's caller identification feature. No one had seen her or heard from her that day. Dena lay awake in bed until Collette finally called around ten a.m.

She first asked, "Are you all right, baby?"

"Yes, I'm at a friend's house." It was a friend Dena did not like or care for.

"Why didn't you call me? I was worried sick about you. I called all of your friends and was about to call all the hospitals." Collette seemed shady and distant. Dena asked again, "Why didn't you call me?"

Collette replied, "Because I didn't feel like it."

She said, "You know what, Collette? I have a meeting at one o'clock. Have my car here by noon," and hung up the telephone. Dena was furious, and thought out loud, "Damn! I was trying to be with her for forever! I never cheated on her! She never had to worry about that! And I had plenty of opportunities, but turned them down because I love Collette so much. I was just trying to make things better for us. If she slept with someone, that means she doesn't love me and it's over between us."

Collette came home around eleven-forty—not much time for them to talk. Dena looked at her to see if there were any signs she could read without Collette opening her mouth. "Did you have the bitch in my car before you took her home and fucked her?"

Collette became cocky. "How else were we going to get to her house?"

Dena went off on Collette, yelling and screaming, and Collette ignored her. When she finally calmed down, she asked Collette, "Is this what you want? I'll pack my things and leave if this is what you want." Collette did not say a word, but just looked at her. Dena said, "I will get my things when I come back from my meeting."

When Dena arrived in Queens, she was a wreck. She was completely distracted because of Collette. She kept trying to remember her pitch. She went into the office and shook hands with the saleswoman.

"So, what is your product, Miss Vargas?"

Dena pulled out three of her best prototypes and handed her one, and laid the other two on her desk. She explained, "There are thousands of correction officers, police officers, and traffic officers in New York City and all over the country with the same problem: not being able to use their whistles because they are unsanitary. Here is a uniform utility belt." She placed her own utility belt upon her desk. "Every item on this belt is mandatory equipment that we must carry, even the whistle. As you can see, there is a leather case for every piece of equipment on this belt except for the whistle. There's a case for our flash-light and a case for our handcuffs, but notice how the whistle is just hanging on a key chain, dirty and unprotected. The only item on the belt that an officer puts in his or her mouth has no protection. There are so many germs and airborne diseases. My product, the Whistle Case, will house and keep the whistle clean and sanitary.

"Imagine, this sample cost me less than a dollar to make. You could sell this product in stores for eight to ten dollars. It has a metal loop, so you can hang it on your key chain. The only difference is, now it is protected."

"Wow," the saleswoman said, "I think it's a good idea. I want to show the product to my boss. May I keep a sample?"

"Yes, you may." Dena handed her a business card. "Nice doing business with you. Hope to hear from you soon."

"You know what, Dena? May I call you Dena? I think you might hear from us real soon."

It took Dena a couple of days and a couple of trips to get all of her belongings out of Collette's house. Collette never discussed with Dena the events of that night, nor did she ever apologize. In Dena's mind, no explanation and no apology in her relationship was unacceptable. When Dena had gathered her last bag, she looked at Collette and said, "Here are your keys. I made an appointment for you for this Saturday with the ADT security company. The appointment is between twelve and three p.m. I know this neighborhood is up and coming, but until then, I just want you to be safe."

"Thank you," Collette whispered, and Dena left. She was still very much in love with Collette.

CHAPTER TWENTY-THREE

Mike came by Dena's house after work to help her out with a few things in her new apartment. After he installed her door lock, they had a couple of beers and reminisced for a while before Mike had to go. Dena walked him to the door and said goodnight. She thought, "There is no reason why these last two beers should go in the refrigerator." So she opened them and drank them both. Then she dozed off on the sofa, when she vaguely heard the telephone ring. She picked up the receiver before it clicked over to the answering machine. "Hello?"

"Hi, may I speak with Dena Vargas?"

"This is she."

"Hi, Dena, this is Barbara Cole from the uniform company. How are you doing?"

"A lot better since you called, Barbara."

"The president of the company is interested in your product, the Whistle Case. He wants to put a small production of your product on the market to see how it sells. Is that all right with you?"

Dena was about to say, "Hell yeah," but caught herself and answered, "Yes, it's fine with me."

"Can you come to my office this Thursday, so we can discuss a possible trial royalty contract? Say, two o'clock?"

"Okay, Barbara, I'll see you then."

When Dena hung up the telephone, she could not believe what had just occurred. She was ecstatic. She jumped up and down and said, "Yes! Thank you, God!"

Dena called all of her coworkers and handed out flyers at Riker's Island, all the city department training academies, went to the uniform stores, and encouraged people to purchase the Whistle Case. The few that did not sell, Dena purchased herself. She e-mailed, faxed, and called the uniform company and constantly asked them for more of the product, stating she had gone to the uniform store and they were sold out. She had her male friends do the same so they would not think it was her calling every day. Five months later, she received a telephone call from the president himself, saying how well her product was selling, and he was sold on her product and wanted the exclusive rights to her patent. He informed Dena that she should hire a patent attorney and that he would cover the lawyer's fee. Dena's patent attorney drew up a contract stipulating that she would collect royalties on every sale. The Whistle Case was a success, and Dena continued to help advertise and promote her product as often as possible.

After a year of brisk sales of her Whistle Case, Dena was doing well financially. She began looking for a house. She was still in love with Brooklyn, and she was not ready for the country life—watching tumbleweeds roll by and listening to the crickets nightly. She also loved Asbury Park in New Jersey. It was just something about the area that made Dena feel right at home. It was like she had lived there in a previous life. It was an hour away from New York City, just in case she wanted to see a show or just hang out. It was also an hour away from the casinos in Atlantic City. That was nice because she enjoyed playing craps every now and again. She signed the paperwork and closed on a large two-family house with four bedrooms and three bathrooms and a finished basement, all the while knowing she would be the only occupant. Once this was set, Dena thought about retiring early. She had exhausted all of her patience at the Department of Correction, and she did not want to risk doing anything foolish and losing her pension after all those years of working. She retired at age thirty-five with a little over ten years under her belt.

She cleansed her new home with a bottle of holy water. She placed a couple of drops in every corner of the house and said a prayer. She then walked around the house, sat on the living room sofa, went to the kitchen, and said to herself, "I think this house needs a pet around here." She had always promised herself that when she retired and had the time, she would get a dog. She went to the nearest animal adoption center and adopted a puppy. Dena held up her new puppy and said, "I'm going to call you Zoey." Dena and Zoey went everywhere together. He became Dena's sidekick.

Saturday morning, Dena was sitting on her porch having a cup of coffee with Zoey. She sat back in her chair and thanked God that she had been able to retire early and that her invention had been successful, but there was something missing. She felt empty and incomplete. She thought back to when Timo was alive, when Dolores was well before she developed Alzheimer's, and when she and Nancy were children, before she became schizophrenic. She missed having a girlfriend in her life.

Dena went downstairs to her basement. She turned on the light and sized up the room. She thought about Nancy. "Out of all her years of being ill, Nancy has never been assaultive. Dolores, yes," she chuckled, "but Nancy, no. So maybe she can live here with me. All Nancy needs is a television set, so she can watch her music videos, and a recliner and a bed, and she is set. There will be no smoking in the house. All she has to do is walk a couple of steps and she is in the backyard. She can smoke outside. I have to see if I can get her to become an outpatient, and she must be willing to take her medication and not leave the house late at night, or else I'll let Zoey get her. And she must attend programs and meetings during the week to keep her busy. Sounds good, and I promised Timo I would take care of her."

A few weeks later, she went to Pilgrim State Mental Institution in Long Island to pick up Nancy. This was Dena's third visit to the hospital. She had to fill out paperwork and show proof that she was Nancy's legal guardian and of her residency. Now it was time for Nancy to be discharged after so many years. Dena thought, "Maybe we will be like the lovely Delany Sisters from Mount Vernon when we get older." Nancy was so happy. She had spent most of her adult life in the hospital. This was the third hospital since her first admittance to Kings County Hospital some twenty years ago. Dena parked her car right in front of the hospital and walked toward the building.

She heard Nancy yelling out the window, "Hi, Dena! You made it! I'm ready, Dena!"

Dena stopped for a minute and wiped a tear from her eye, knowing how Nancy's happiness depended on her and how glad she was that she was able to set her free and bring her home. Dena knew it was going to take hard work to get Nancy to do her chores and follow the rules. "If she can cooperate in the hospital, she can cooperate at home. God will help us," she thought.

Dena thought about Dolores. "I remember I made a promise to Dolores when I was younger. I said, 'Mom, I would never leave you,' and I did. Let me get Nancy settled in the house first, then I will go get Dolores discharged."

Three months later, Nancy was settled in just fine. She was happy. She was at home in her own room. She went to her programs, took her medicine when Dena reminded her it was time, cleaned her room, and even helped out around the house.

Dena was free to work on furnishing Dolores' bedroom. She completed all the paperwork and hired a bilingual live-in home attendant who was experienced with senior citizens with Alzheimer's disease. Dolores did not have a clue she was coming home. Dena thought to herself, "Nancy has the basement, Dolores and her home attendant have their own rooms on the main floor, and I have the top floor. Zoey and his new female friend, Zola, have access to the entire house."

Monday morning, Nancy and Dena drove to Cabrini Hospital in Manhattan. Nancy and Dena were so excited they could not wait for their mother to come home. They had missed her dearly. Dena reminded Nancy about her condition, and Nancy said, "I will have patience with her and help her out." They arrived at Dolores' room and Nancy said, "Surprise!"

Dolores' eyes lit up when she saw her children. "Dena, I cannot get a clear channel on this thing."

Dena handed her mother some clothes and said, "Mom, you don't have to worry about that problem anymore. How about watching your soap operas on a clear, big-screen television set?"

"How's that?" Dolores asked.

"Mommy, here are your clothes. Nancy and I are bringing you home today to stay."

Dolores stood up from her bed and said, "I am going home with you girls today to stay?"

"Yes, Mommy."

"I don't have to die in here, Dena?"

"Mommy, you are not dying. Nancy, tell Mommy the other two surprises, okay?"

"Okay. One, I also live at home with Dena, and two, we know how much you love animals, and we have two dogs named Zoey and Zola."

Dolores hugged Nancy and started to cry and asked, "What about Mike? Is he going to live with us too? I heard he lost his job."

"Mommy," Dena said, "I spoke to him yesterday and he said he found a better job, paying more money."

"Oh, I am so happy for him!" Dolores said, hardly able to contain her joy.

"Now get dressed, Mom," she told Dolores, "so we can go home."

Things were going well in the Vargas household. During breakfast, Dena asked Dolores, "Mom, what do you want for Christmas?"

"I want to go to church."

"Yes, Mom, we're all going to church. What do you want for Christmas?"

"I want a nice warm robe, Dena. You know I'm always cold. And get some warm pajamas for the dogs. They always look cold too."

"Okay, Mom, you got it. Nancy, what would you like for Christmas?"

"I would like a Walkman, please, and some clothes too."

Dena smiled at the home attendant and said, "I'm going to miss you when you go on vacation—a whole week, huh? What am I going to do without you?" Dena said, laughing.

"You will manage," she replied.

"I appreciate you very much. You do take good care of my family. Thank you." Dena handed her an envelope with one thousand dollars in it, her Christmas bonus. Then she hugged her and said, "Have a great time in Puerto Rico, and we'll see you when you get back, God willing. And do not hesitate to call me if you need a ride to or from the airport."

"Merry Christmas, Mommy. Merry Christmas, Nancy. Merry Christmas, Zola and Zoey."

"How come you are always the last one to get out of bed, Dena?" Dolores asked.

"Because she needs the most beauty sleep, Mom," Nancy answered.

"Did anyone press the little red button on the coffee pot? You know, the thing in the kitchen that says Mr. Coffee?"

"Yes, Dena, I turned it on for you, knowing how much you want a cup of coffee when you wake up."

"Thank you, Nancy, but how come I don't smell the aroma?" She looked in the kitchen and noticed the pot was unplugged.

"Thank you for my Walkman, Dena," Nancy said.

"You're welcome, sweetie."

Then Dolores said, "The dogs liked their sweaters, but where are their pajamas, damn it?"

"Here, Dena, Merry Christmas," Nancy said, handing her a present. "This is from Mommy and me."

"Oh, girls, you didn't have to. What is it? What is it?"

"Open it and find out," Nancy told her excitedly.

Dena ripped open the wrapping paper and smiled. "Thank you, Nancy and Mommy. I love it." It was a candle snowman that would burn in Dena's heart forever. Dena cried and said,

"Group hug. Now I know why God spared my life so many times." Then she went to the kitchen to make some coffee. She told the girls that Mike called and said he might stop by the house later.

Dena went to the stereo to put on the Salsoul Orchestra Christmas Jollies, when Nancy asked, "What are you getting ready to play? Play some Donna Summer, Dena."

"Does Donna Summer have a Christmas version of 'Love To Love You Baby'?" Dena asked.

"No," Nancy replied.

"Okay, when she comes out with one, we'll play it on Christmas Day. Now get out of here."

Nancy laughed and said, "Thank goodness I have my own room."

Dolores asked, "Can someone find the Christmas Parade on television for me, please?"

Dena had never understood her brother Mike. Dolores had never had a chance to get to know her youngest grandson. Mike would come by the house and stay for about an hour, and Dolores would not see him again for another three to four months. "Well, Mike never showed up," Dena informed Dolores and Nancy. "Maybe he'll visit for New Year's Eve, maybe not."

Dolores' home attendant returned from her vacation, and Dena decided to go to the city to have a drink and get out of the house for a while. The girls were in good hands. Dena went to get dressed. She grabbed her car keys and her mobile telephone and headed for Brooklyn. She stopped at the flower shop and picked up Collette's favorite flowers, white orchids. She wanted to surprise Collette, so she waited outside her apartment building until someone exited the building so she could let herself in. Dena stood in front of Collette's apartment door. She patted her hair and pulled down her shirt, took a deep breath, and knocked on the door, and continued to knock on her door.

"If Collette isn't expecting any visitors, she will not be the least bit curious to check through the peephole to see who is knocking," Dena thought. She just leaned her head back against the wall while deciding what she should do. "Should I call her on the telephone, or should I go home?" Dena placed the flowers on Collette's doormat and left.

Dena sat in her car for a moment and decided to go have a drink at her and Collette's favorite happy bar in Brooklyn. It was called Friends. She opened up the glove compartment and pulled out the first compact disc her hand touched. It was The Moments. She pressed track number eight and played a song called "Girls." She rolled up her windows so she wouldn't disturb other drivers and cranked up the volume to ten, and bopped her head all the way to the bar. Dena entered the bar and sat down at a table. She ordered a shot of whiskey and a beer. She thought to herself, "Damn, I should have known Collette would have been spoken for, especially after waiting over a year to make a move. Oh well, what did I expect?"

Dena focused her sights on the front of the bar. She observed the entrance door open and Collette walking in, holding the flowers. Collette's eyes searched the bar for Dena. Dena stood up from the chair. Collette saw Dena and smiled.

THE END

855865

Made in the USA